ONE NIGHT AT KEDASI

Ashton Macaulay

Shadow Dragon Press

ISBN: 978-1-963832-34-1 (paperback)
ISBN: 978-1-963832-48-8 (ebook)
LCCN: 2025941022

Printed in the United States of America

This book was handcrafted by skilled artisans. No AI was used in the writing or cover design for this book.

Names, characters and incidents depicted in this book are products of the author's imagination or are used fictitiously. Any resemblance to actual events, locales, organizations, or persons, living or dead, is entirely coincidental and beyond the intent of the author or the publisher.

Shadow Dragon Press
9 Mockingbird Hill Rd
Tijeras, New Mexico 87059
www.shadowdragonpress.com
info@shadowdragonpress.com

For everyone who read and gave feedback on this story along the way. Garrett Moran for slicing and dicing Act 1, Kendyl Daniels for trying to teach me how to use commas, and John Ceccarelli for being my first and constant beta reader for the last 9 years.

And to my dad, for taking me to the theme parks that inspired this wild adventure.

Prologue

Asset Reclamation

Dillon swept his rifle-mounted flashlight across the decaying ruins of what should have been the galaxy's largest amusement park. Towering scaffolds of iron-supported roller-coaster tracks were silhouetted against three glittering moons that made up Kedasi's night sky. The commercialized former asteroid was sandwiched perfectly in the habitable range thanks to the nearby gas giant's convenient atmospheric properties—and billions of terraforming credits. Despite the eerie twilight that made up Kedasi's night cycle, the air remained perfectly comfortable.

Dillon wove his way down an unfinished area themed after a midway. His boots clicked on the polished promenade built for thousands of guests, echoing as a hollow reminder that there were none. There was no wind, no weather, only a practiced hush—and a lot of unpowered animatronic clowns.

Dillon hadn't previously put thought into how many clowns were too many, but the brains behind Kedasi's theme park had found the number. Their dead eyes stared at him. He sighted one with his rifle. "I've got my eye on you, asshole."

His itchy trigger finger was interrupted by a voice over his comms. "Dillon, check in. Got anything?"

Dillon made an exaggerated sweep across a series of abandoned carnival games. "I don't know, Kane, any interest in a bunch of plastic clowns?"

"Dillon, at least try and take this seriously."

Dillon found it hard to take much seriously when staring at a strength test machine filled with stuffed tigers. "Same as orbit. Whatever gas leak got them off world, it's not here anymore."

"I don't like it. Rendezvous at point Alchemist, stay sharp."

The price of crystal-clear comms was that Dillon could hear every waver in Kane's voice.

Neither of them knew why mercenaries were required for a simple extraction, but both knew that no one paid an expensive team for a walk in the park.

"Roger, on my way. If you're lucky, I'll bring you a prize."

Dillon lifted his arm and brought up a holographic projected map of the park on his wrist terminal. Seeing it all in one image was staggering. If construction had finished, the full park would have taken weeks to experience.

The mission brief said work had been halted when excavators uncovered a gas pocket in the asteroid. Dillon checked his oxygen monitor for the hundredth time. It still read green, no toxins, no particles, just clean air. Of course, he couldn't smell anything beyond the funk of a sealed vacuum suit with a sweaty merc in it, but the air read clear.

Why in the hell would they hire mercenaries for a gas leak anyway? It didn't add up. He hoped the Manchester Family, their benefactors, were just a combination of rich, lazy, and dumb. Wouldn't be the first time.

Dillon returned his attention to the map. Their objective was near the transport station leading to the hospitality sector. Future plans showed fifty hotels, each with a different theme. Currently, there was only one, a gaudy ghost tower standing alone, abandoned, and surrounded by grey rock. Point Alchemist was two kilometers away, back toward the park's central hub.

Dillon took a deep breath and tried to focus. You don't die when you're paying attention. At least, that's what Kane always said.

He left the midway and entered a street done in the style of Old Earth. Dillon had never seen Earth—most people hadn't. The Earth he knew was a wasteland of radiation, apex predators, and a planet desperately trying to reclaim its surface from the remnants of a hostile civilization. Humans hadn't lived there for hundreds of years. Looking down the street at the facades, intricate latticed wooden buildings, and cheery shops, Dillon understood why they might have. The buildings were less than three stories and made of brightly painted wood. Their short stature left unobstructed views of the sky. It was freeing.

A large, unlit sign read: *Journey to Old Earth*. Beneath it were turnstiles and a cavernous entrance leading to an attraction housed in a large show building. Dillon looked into the tunnel feeling both a sense of longing and unease. He had grown up visiting Manchester Family amusement parks; most of the people in the galaxy had. A part of him wanted to see what such an attraction could entail.

Then he heard the creak.

A single, solitary creak. It came from somewhere down the street toward the center of the park. Dillon moved sharp and swift, pointing his rifle at the noise and sighting the building. He opened his comms. "Got a creak over here."

"A what?"

"A creak, man." Dillon tried to keep his voice steady. He felt his hands shaking.

"Probably one of those clowns."

Dillon swept his rifle back and forth. "I'm telling you, man, I heard something."

Kane sighed. "Relax, it's probably just the wood settling."

"Settling?"

"Yeah, all this wood is new, sometimes it creaks as it settles. It's not like the fancy habs you grew up in, but it's nothing to worry about."

"Right."

"Take it easy, man, your vitals are high. Deep breaths."

Dillon inhaled through his nose and let it out through his mouth. "OK, OK, one click out."

"Get a move on."

Dillon looked up and down the street once more then chuckled to himself. "God damned clowns."

A cold sensation closed around his neck followed by a brief, but sharp sting. Pain faded quickly to dizziness as the world turned like a sickening washing machine. He heard a hollow thunk as his head hit the ground. A faint noise came from his comms, but none of it made any sense.

Dillon stared at his own feet. Blood pooled around them. *Is that my blood?* A shadow overtook him, huge and unending. His eyes blinked, more automatic than anything. Not a shadow.

Part 1 – A Legitimate Job

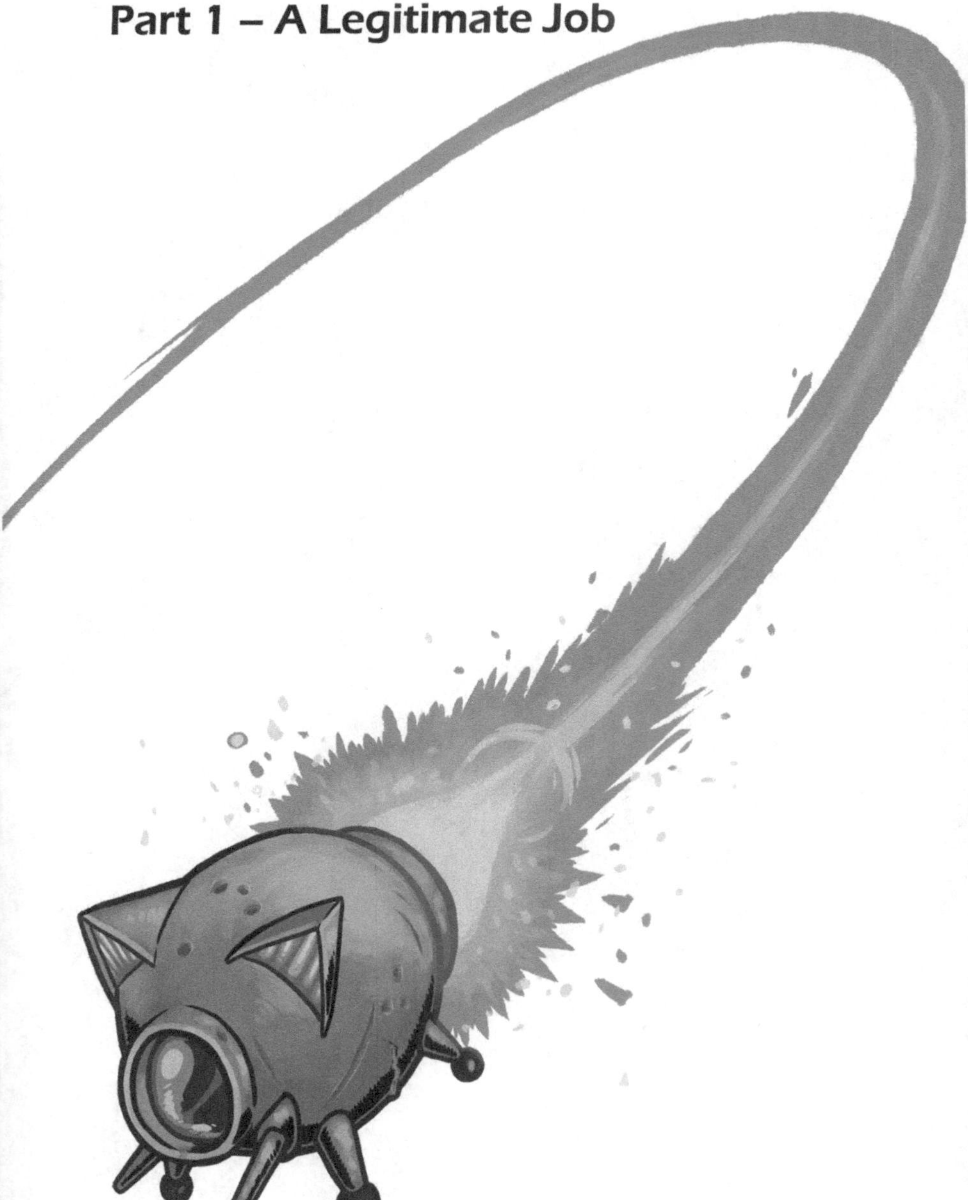

1

Drinking in Cheap Bars

Zip Turbine sat in a corner booth nursing the dregs of a mediocre glass of whisky. It would be the last for a while unless she decided to sell her ship. Docking fees were getting more expensive by the day, and her settlement from the botched government job on Crustacea was running out. Every month, supply and demand made finding a berth just a little harder. More rich pricks being born with spaceship keys in their mouths meant less room for upstarts. Sooner or later, she'd face the choice of contracting on someone else's ship. The thought alone was enough to make her wish she could pay for a whole bottle.

Tom, a five-foot tall bipedal shrimp, also a remnant of the job on Crustacea, slid into the seat across from her. There was a part of Zip that would never get used to him. "How are you feeling, Captain?" Tom's voice was hollow and mechanical, coming through a primitive translator he held between two of his many appendages. Despite offers for more advanced translators, Tom refused. Even when the homemade device zapped him with rogue electrical currents, he cradled it his last piece of home.

"I've been better." Zip took another tentative sip from her glass, just enough liquid to feel the burn, not enough for it to do anything worthwhile. "I'm almost out of money. We haven't had a decent job in a month, and *The Hog* is just sitting there racking up fees." Zip was unreasonably proud of her custom-made cargo hauler, shaped like a flying swine. It's blend of comfort and capability for violence always put her at ease. And it was all hers.

Tom pondered Zip's statement for a moment—or, at least what Zip had come to know as pondering. His antennae twitched back and forth, and he cleaned his eyes a little more than usual. "Perhaps if we took an official job with the—"

"I don't know how many times I have to tell you: The Union is a sucker's game."

"Union jobs pay out at a rate of—"

"Five to one compared to freelancing. Yes, Tom, I've read the signs." Every docking bay, transit stop, errant alley, dive bar, and bathroom stall was coated in them. Bright colors, big promises, and a friendly face on the doom of freelancers. "What those adverts don't say is that Union gigs are binding contracts, and if you get sent down to some miserable bug planet on the whim of a politician, you're shit out of luck."

"Like Crustacea?"

"Where else, Tom? Look, I found you down there, but that was a close one. I try not to get so near to death when I can help it." Freelancing carried risks, but at least Zip could blame herself when things went to shit. "I plan to keep on living as long as possible and keep this glass full while I do it." She shook the whisky and finished it in a quick gulp. There was the real fire. It spread down her throat like an ancient reminder of what it felt like to be financially stable.

Tom nodded. "I—"

"What's that bug doing in our bar?!"

Zip's breathing slowed reflexively. No one made violence like angry freelancers between jobs. Marvin's had cheap drinks and palatable food, but that meant everyone down on their luck knew it existed. She lifted her head. *Of course it's a Cheri.*

Cheri were an odd species, and that was true even on a melting-pot planet like Prota. They were one of the first civilizations to make contact after humanity established a toehold beyond Earth. Cheri might have looked bizarre and almost cute from a distance, but they were far from friendly—minds big enough to make words, but small enough to have legendary short tempers. Cheri stood around six feet, had four arms, brightly colored fur, and faces where their stomachs should have been. Their wide mouths nearly split them in two, and big, bulging black eyes took up the upper half of their torso. The one standing before Zip had bright blue fur and looked pissed.

That's a lot of face to punch. Zip had never fought a Cheri, but the whiskey told her she could.

"Zip, it's OK, we can leave," said Tom, his translator box incapable of a decent whisper.

"Let a bug leave?" asked the Cheri, its voice deep, its fur bristling.

Zip smiled. "See? Tom, it doesn't want you to leave." All the rage she felt against the Union bubbled to the surface, and she was happy there was a large face to take it out on.

The Cheri flexed its arms. "You with this bug?"

Zip continued to smile. Some would have called it a shit-eating grin, she called it a friendly threat. "No, I'm sitting next to a bipedal shrimp by accident. Walk away, and don't call my friend a bug. It's rude."

The Cheri snorted. "That's nice. Boys?"

Zip realized the depth of her miscalculation. Three Cheri stood up from a dark corner of the bar—well, darker than the rest of Marvin's. Despite their multicolored, fuzzy appearance, they were more fight than she could manage. Twenty arms were a lot more than two, and she wasn't sure how many shots she'd get off before the smashing would set in. *Screw it.* Zip stood, putting herself at eye level with the first Cheri. "I'd hate to mess up my favorite bar." She let a hand casually drop to her hip holster.

The implication wasn't missed. "You're a dead woman."

"You wouldn't be the first to try."

The Cheri let out something between a roar and a gurgling burp.

Zip winced at the smell but pulled her pistol all the same. Her finger was curling around the trigger when a piercing warble cut through the air. She dropped to her knees and clamped both hands around her ears. The pistol clattered to the floor. *And that's it, I'm dead.* Zip braced for blunt force trauma. It never came.

The warble cut off as suddenly as it had started.

Zip raised her head and saw that she wasn't the only one on the floor. The four Cheri were hunkered low, grimaces exaggerated by the sheer size of their faces. *No time like the present.* Zip reached for her gun, ready to restart the fight, but a polished shoe blocked her way.

"Might we postpone the bloodshed for a moment?" The voice was elegant and false; the kind that only came from money.

Zip looked up at a set of tailored slacks, a shiny metal-lined blazer, and yet another punchable face. *Corporate goon, nice pants, bad bar; he's about to offer us a job.*

"Stay out of it, square," growled the Cheri.

The man tutted his tongue. "So rude to a man that's about to offer you employment."

Knew it. "You look like the type used to working with the Union. Maybe you missed the memo, but this is a non-Union bar." Zip pushed herself to her feet and sized the man up. He was skinny, but with the expensive attire, and confidence, he was likely packing some kind of personal defense.

"Yes, I had a feeling you might say that. That's why we're willing to pay up front, just for your *valuable* time. A portion of course, but a sizable one." He waved a gold-plated card through the air. "This is enough credits to transport you to our corporate facility, and to get you blind drunk in a better bar than this. All you have to do is listen."

Zip shook her head. "You really shouldn't flash cash like that in a place like this."

The Cheri was off the ground in a split second, fur bristling, eyes twitching, and charging at the goon. Its furry palms barely touched the man's jacket before a sizzling pop and an excessive jolt of electricity sent it flying backward. The Cheri collided with a corner booth, snapping the table clean in half. The impact rattled every glass in the bar.

The corporate man brushed singed fur off his jacket. "Please, don't try that again." He flicked a card toward the bar, sending it sailing through the air. "We'll pay for the damages, of course. Now, is anyone interested in something other than electric shock?"

Zip was preparing to make a violent mistake when Tom piped up, loud and proud as ever. "We're interested!" Tom bobbed his head up and down, noticeably avoiding Zip's murderous gaze. "We would be happy to listen to your proposal." Tom reached out a claw and plucked the gold card delicately from the man's fingers. "And my captain would be happy to get blind drunk on this money."

Zip's mouth hung open. *What are you doing?* Something about the shine of the gold card in his claw stopped the words from coming out.

"Splendid. Tomorrow, noon, ask for Roman, don't be late."

2

Wealth and the Word 'No'

Tom was nervous. He had been on Prota with Zip for almost a year but couldn't get used to the speed of automatic drivers. Even in a luxury car, outfitted with the finest synthetic leather, calming music, and a general aroma of relaxation, he still felt like he was on the edge of death. Every slight rise or gentle bank reminded him that he had no control.

Zip sat across from him, alternating between glares and exasperated sighs. Between them was an empty table that would have no doubt been laden for more prominent guests.

For the first part of the journey, they rode in silence. Tom passed the time wondering about fiery deaths at the hands of automated transport, and Zip stewed in silent anger. When Tom began fiddling with various compartments around the transport cabin, a cheery, but admonishing voice played on the overhead speaker. "Please do not attempt to open any compartments. If you are looking for something, maybe you should try asking."

Tom still wasn't fully versed in human tone, but he was certain there was low-level aggression present in the automated driver's voice. "We were told there would be free drinks." Strictly speaking, Tom didn't drink much, but a deal was a deal.

"One moment." Calming music played while the AI thought the request over. "Fantastic news. You are each cleared for one standard drink. Please, enjoy."

The center table split open and a platform with two glasses of brown liquid rose from inside. Tom reached out and pushed his to Zip's edge of the tray as a peace offering.

She glared at the drink, then back at him, and eventually let out a long breath. "It's a start." She picked the tumbler up, took an experimental sip, and drained it in a single gulp. "Not bad."

"Zip, I—"

"Why would you take a job without asking me first?" There was heat in her words, but Tom hoped the drink was working at cooling it.

Tom ducked his head and fiddled with the knobs on his hydration suit. It never leaked and kept him perfectly moist, but fiddling kept his many limbs occupied. "We need the money, and we don't have to take the contract to get it." In Tom's mind, the calculation was simple. "If we don't want the job, we still get free drinks."

Zip picked up the second glass and sat back in her chair. "Sometimes, I forget this is your first experience with humans."

"Technically my second."

"I don't think your ancestors getting picked out of a tank and dropped from orbit counts."

"It counts."

"If it counts, you should have learned a lesson."

Tom tried to think of a retort, but comebacks were not a strong suit. The fact was, nearly all of his interactions with humans had been unfortunate. Zip was right, he should have learned a lesson or two. Even still, he expected the best out of any situation; that was his nature. Instead of expressing his disappointment, Tom goggled at Zip in what he hoped approximated anger. Humans were very particular about expressing the right emotion at the right time, and it seemed like he and Zip were in a fight.

Zip snorted a laugh and visibly eased. "Good anger face. Look, there's no such thing as 'free' on Prota; you'll learn that eventually. We don't have to take this job, but turning it down isn't going to be easy. Next time have a little faith that I know what I'm doing."

Tom bobbed his head in assent. "If we don't take this job, can we talk about looking for a Union contract?"

Zip crossed her arms. "Really pushing me today."

"If you lose *The Hog*, you can move on and join another ship. If I lose *The Hog*, I either barter passage home, or die on the street."

There weren't many things Tom felt strongly about, but losing his captain was one of them. Zip was a decent human on a planet full of much worse. His chitinous appearance made him a pariah and led to the oft-used slur: bug. Bugs were for squashing, or so the citizens of Prota thought.

"Tom." Zip leaned forward, looking straight through him.

She had a habit of doing that when she was being serious. "I will never leave you to die on the streets. When I plucked you off Crustacea, I took you on as my responsibility."

"Thank you, Zip."

"Look, I think we both thought the ambassadorship with the UCP was going to have a little more stability."

"An understatement."

Despite many communications and negotiations from Crustacea, the killing of a United Commission of Planets ambassador by a rogue lobster faction was not an easy slight to overcome. Despite Zip's report detailing the many attempts she and Tom had made to save the ambassador, the UCP refused all negotiations until the lobsters were dealt with. Given an accelerated breeding rate of deep-water creatures and a general lack of Crustacean desire to commit genocide, this was easier said than done. It quickly became apparent that an ambassador was not necessary when neither party was willing to budge on their position. Tom was furloughed and told to either return to Crustacea or find a job to maintain his visa status.

"Their loss, my gain. You're a good co-pilot." Zip leaned her head against the window, looking out at the city skyline blurring past.

Tom did the same, trying to quell his nagging sense of fear. Prota was a beautiful place. Beyond the prime city, huge swaths of untamed wilderness spread out in a vast web. Ordinary vehicles traveled low, between the city's skyscrapers, away from true sunlight. At street level, the only brightness was artificial or from hollow reflections in glass. Luxury cars had luxury permits. Their vehicle skimmed the tops of the tallest buildings, affording Tom his first real view of the horizon that hadn't come off a tablet or video feed. It was breathtaking.

"What do you think this corporate goon wants, anyway?" asked Zip.

Tom had thought it over several times in the last twelve hours. "He must have been desperate to come to Marvin's, no offense to us."

"None taken. You're right. Whatever this is, he wants it done off the books, and he's not worried about precision."

"Never a good thing."

Zip nodded. "Never a good thing. Worse, I think he was there for us specifically."

Tom twitched. "Us?"

"Us and the Cheri. He dropped two cards, didn't talk to anyone else in the bar and left. He wasn't recruiting randomly."

Tom tapped his limbs against the faux leather seats. "That

is also not good."

"You're starting to get it."

"But why us?"

Zip shrugged. "Maybe it's my good looks and feminine charm." Zip ran a hand through her bright pink hair, dramatically tossing it over the side of her face.

"Maybe he likes shrimp," offered Tom, twitching in an approximation of the gesture Zip had made.

Zip doubled over with laughter.

Tom swelled with pride. "I made a joke!"

Zip wiped a tear from her eye. "You sure did, pal."

The car decelerated and banked toward a gilded skyscraper.

"Well, that's subtle," said Zip.

The vehicle approached a landing pad with a shining inlay that would have blinded any non-artificial pilot. The edges were encrusted in jewels the size of boulders, refracting the setting sun in dazzling rainbow light. Past the landing pad was a wooden pagoda. None of the trees on Prota were suitable for timbering, meaning it was either synthetic or imported from off world. The taxes alone would have bankrupted several families in the streets below.

"That is quite something." Tom shielded his eyes, the beams of light causing sharp splinters of pain—a downside of seeing one too many spectrums of light.

"Well, at least the drinks will be nice."

"Starting to come around to my idea?"

Zip shook her head. "If we refuse a job from people like this, we're dead by tomorrow."

"Why do you say that?"

"People who build expensive rooftop structures aren't used to hearing the word 'no'. An assassin wouldn't even register as a footnote on their budget."

The transport set down on the landing pad with a gentle thunk as magnets in the surface locked it in place. Tom's heart pounded in his head with the weight of his own mistake.

"Hey, Tom." Zip reached out and put a hand on his carapace, a gesture they had both deemed as reassuring.

"Yes?" The translator skipped as his hands fumbled faster than usual.

"If we survive this, never mention the Union again."

3

An 'Agreement'

Zip recognized several figures sitting at the oblong table. Most notably, a Cheri with singed blue fur and a grudge. Others were noted mercenaries. Zip hoped to hell she hadn't ripped any of them off. Tension buzzed in the dim room like carrion flies. The head of the table was unoccupied, but a large screen at one end paid endless tribute to the Manchester Family by scrolling images of their successes and labeling them 'Titans of Industry'. Above, a vaulted ceiling spiraled into inky blackness punctuated by fake stars meant to look like deep space. It was a halfway decent attempt but clearly crafted by someone who had never seen space outside of a television screen. A lack of color gave the galaxies a muted, monochromatic tone that was far from their true beauty.

The sound of heavy boots on polished tile brought Zip to attention. Her spine stiffened and she sat up a little straighter. It had been five years since she left the military, but it seemed the military still hadn't left her.

The man walking in wore a wide-brimmed hat that belonged on a dusty ranch that no longer existed. A long-healed scar on his cheek added an edge of menace to his easy grin. His black coat was a mess of torn stitching where security had likely removed hidden weapons and ammunition. The face bore new lines, but the sight of it was enough to set a hot flush of anger and something else familiar up Zip's neck. "No."

"Afternoon, Zip. Fancy seeing you here." His voice was calm, soothing almost, polite, but overlaying practiced violence.

"Seems they take all kinds for this job, Jack."

"Indeed, they do." Jack sat across the table, his eyes never leaving hers.

The prolonged eye contact was enough to create several warring feelings from various parts of Zip's body. "Screw it, this isn't worth—"

At that moment, their host walked in. "Apologies for my lateness!"

Zip recognized Roman from the bar. The dark boardroom suited him more than the dank booths of Marvin's.

He moved to the front of the room, making sure to give Jack a wide berth. "My name is Roman, and I'm here to make a proposal that's going to change your fortunes forever."

Cynical mutters rumbled around the room.

Roman, unfazed, took his seat at the head of the table and stopped the slideshow of Manchester triumph. In its place, pictures of every person sitting around the table popped up with a laundry list of illegal acts next to them. Some of the names were familiar to Zip, but others were new. Techni, half woman half circuit board, was known in every hacking circle as someone who should never be let near a ship control board or a bank account. Lars Ulren was a middle-aged war hero turned mechanic who had a bad habit of turning to bloodshed when he got annoyed. Jack was Jack. The Cheri had a death sentence on twelve systems but had bribed the right UCP officers. Finally, there were Tiny and Big, with no description other than *Work in a pair, highly dangerous, most wanted.*

Zip grinned at the length of the list next to her name. Assaulting a UCP probation officer; moving illegal cargo; disturbing the peace; and her personal favorite, impersonating a member of the Royal Galactic Church. The photo wasn't half bad either. Something about a pink mohawk against a prison backdrop brought out her eyes. Tom's profile was simply a photocopy of his UCP ambassador badge with one line: *Visa set to expire.*

"My visa is going to expire?"

"If these people want it to, it will," replied Zip.

"Apologies for the bluntness of my approach, but I believe this puts us on better footing." Roman looked up at the photographs with a mix of bemusement and pity.

Big looked down at the screen in consternation, scratching his bald head. "This says I kill twenty people. That is not true."

"Big, you've definitely killed twenty people," hissed Tiny.

"No! I kill more. At least thirty."

Roman pulled out a data pad and tapped at it. "Not a problem, we'll adjust."

The figure changed from 20 to 30.

"This is better." Big smiled, revealing a mouth resembling

a bleached lumber pile.

"What the hell is this?" grumbled the Cheri. "That says I was arrested for starting a bar fight." He turned his big, bulging eyes to Zip and Tom. "I didn't figure you for snitches." He stood, flexing and bristling. "I'm going to deep fry that shrimp."

Zip drummed her fingers on the table, watching as two enforcers made their way out of the shadows and one put a rifle to the back of the Cheri's neck. "I'd have thought you learned a lesson the last time you tried to pick a fight with my friend. A single click from an ordinary shrimp's claws can produce a sonic boom. What do you think a giant shrimp can do?"

"That's mantis shrimp, Z—" started Tom, but Roman cleared his throat, interrupting him.

"Let's take the temperature down, shall we? None of these charges have been filed yet, and if you can put aside old rivalries and unsettled scores, they might never be. That's the beauty of this arrangement. You get to walk away rich... If you do what you're told." Roman beamed.

Zip pressed her fingers into the palm of her hand, willing them to not throttle the man. "Like I said, Tom, nothing on Prota is free."

"Quite so," answered Roman.

Jack leaned forward. "Skip to the point, fancy pants. The longer we sit here, the better chance one of us snaps and kills the others, maybe you in the process."

Roman folded his hands. "I have faith in my security. Are you sure you don't want additional time to review your charges, Jack?"

Jack waved a hand. "I'm sure you've got something on there that would put me away for a good long while. So, I figure we just get to it and cut the shit." He grinned, showing a shiny diamond in a front tooth.

Roman smiled his plastic smile, revealing his understanding that money could buy death faster than a bullet. "Of course. The rest of you, if you want time to review your 'applications', I suggest you do it quickly. In the meantime, here's a tidy nondisclosure agreement, standard practice."

On cue, the shiny black table illuminated as white legal documents appeared on its surface. Zip looked at the writing, saw its length, and realized it was pointless to read the whole thing. The time for having a choice in matters had passed. If they rejected the Manchester offer, there was a good chance they'd be dead before they left the building. Zip skipped to the bottom. It read: *To acknowledge this statement, simply state "I agree."* Zip turned to Tom who was scanning through the document and twitching all the while.

Eventually, he stopped and looked at her. "Do we have a choice?"

"No, we don't." Zip turned back to the document. "I agree." A white flash lit up the table, capturing a picture of her face. The table returned to its blank, black surface.

"I agree." Tom winced at the flash.

Rapid flashes around the table signaled unanimous assent. Mercenaries were fast thinkers. Sometimes those thoughts weren't the smartest, but they did come quickly.

Roman clapped his hands together. "Wonderful. I think you'll find that despite your initial reluctance, this is a career-making opportunity."

"Funny way to talk about forced service," said Lars from the end of the table.

"Think of it like a contract."

"I'll think of it how I like."

Zip grinned.

Roman hid a grimace and tapped at the table in front of him. The surface lit up once more, now showing a tactical map of an asteroid. Lines of metal crisscrossed the surface and clusters of buildings hung together at odd intervals.

Zip recognized the layout immediately. "This is a theme park."

"Not just any theme park," replied Roman. "This is the Manchester Family's greatest achievement: an entire asteroid, over 1,600 kilometers in diameter, dedicated to amusement, relaxation, and adventure."

Zip recognized they were the first genuine words the man had said all day. Whatever else, Roman was a true sycophant of the ultra-wealthy.

Zip scrolled through pages upon pages of thrill ride specifications, hotel theming, and just about everything else that was unhelpful for anyone who wasn't planning a vacation. "I'm guessing mercenaries aren't your target demographic, so what happened to the place?" She had a sinking feeling she wasn't going to like the answer.

A mutter of agreement rose from around the table.

Roman stiffened, but only a little. "Fine, the short version." He tapped at the table and the map zoomed in on an ornate tower just outside the park's main attractions. It was suspended above a wide chasm, surrounded by metal supports and walkways. "This was meant to be the jewel of the park, literally and figuratively. The Opus was our accommodation for only the most premium customers. The spire on the bottom is where our high-value guests would have stayed." The map zoomed in, showing a spiraling patchwork of metal and glass. "This chasm is crusted with gemstones. I'm told that anywhere in The Opus offered a breathtaking view during the asteroid's night cycle."

Examining the building, Zip thought it looked like an accident waiting to happen. The views might have been nice but at the cost of low railings, glass that likely wasn't impact resistant, and other cut corners. All it would take was one wealthy couple with a penchant for child neglect and there would be a lawsuit. "Why not just strip mine it?"

"Mining was deemed too dangerous. The asteroid is porous toward the middle and extracting the gems could have caused the whole project to collapse. The Manchester Family values its workers."

Zip knew the Manchester Family valued profit. If a few workers died, it didn't matter, so long as the bottom line was upheld. "Alright, so solve a problem by building a theme park."

"That's putting it simply, but—"

Tom piped up. "Earlier you said 'literally' when referring to The Opus as a crown jewel. Were you using it in the correct fashion, or merely as a colloquialism?"

Roman tapped the table again, a little too hard this time. "A diamond, nearly three feet tall, was to serve as the hotel's centerpiece. Its unique properties would allow it to reflect spectrums of light rarely seen to the human eye." An artist rendering of a dining room set beneath glittering beams of light filled the screen.

Zip had to admit, it did look pretty.

"A diamond that size would weigh nearly three thousand pounds," said Tom.

Roman nodded. "A normal diamond, yes. This gemstone is not a diamond as we have come to know it. The structure is lighter and yet somehow still durable. It will be heavy, but not overly so."

"So, you want your pretty rock back," said Jack.

"That is over-simplifying again—"

"Why not just go to the planet yourself?"

"Asteroid," corrected Roman. "Legally, we can't call it a planet. And I'm getting there." The images shifted, this time showing a medieval thoroughfare. "The Manchesters wanted cutting-edge attractions, which meant terraforming significant portions of the asteroid's surface to match specific themes."

It always comes back to the terraforming. Plenty of planets looked good from the outside, but it was what was under the crust that mattered. "Let me guess, hollow asteroid, digging too deep, you found a bug nest?"

Roman grimaced. "No, nothing so dangerous as that. Whatever created the gems left behind pockets of gas just beneath the surface. Of course, we had already created an atmosphere, and now the gas is trapped there."

Zip sat back in her chair, privately relieved. "That's it? Gas? Any space jockey with a proper filtration suit can handle gas."

"Yes, *that's* it. Just a deadly neurotoxin that has rendered all work on the theme park moot and completely shut down a multi-trillion credit project." Roman's dismay was plain. Whatever else, he felt affection for money. "*Your* services are required because they will be discretionary on pain of imprisonment. It's the cheapest way to buy silence."

"Honesty, that's a new one. That fancy gem is the Manchesters trying to recoup their investment?"

"Recoup would be too generous. It is a paltry sum compare—"

Zip sighed, loud and long, cutting Roman off. "What do you think, Tom, want to go to a theme park?" They would be going either way, the heavily-armed enforcers in the shadows made that point very clear.

"Sounds... fun."

That made Roman smile. "Well, two out of eight, how about the rest of you?"

There was a mix of assent and curse words that strained Roman's patience, but generally confirmed assent.

"Splendid. Our documents indicate that two of you have ships. Zip, Jack, I'll need to speak with you privately."

Zip's shoulders tensed. "And why is that exactly?"

Roman's face was plastic menace. "Because we're going to be sending two teams."

4
Misery Loves Company

Tensions were high. Tom stood pressed against the wall of a waiting area cramped with the other mercenaries. On the far side of the room was a set of oak-paneled double doors that were doing little to dampen the sound of animated arguments on the other side. Zip and Jack were trading insults that stretched the boundaries of the common language while Roman presumably attempted to mediate the situation.

To avoid the growing panic creeping in at the edges of his mind, Tom studied his potential future crewmates. He had read the crimes, put faces to names, and was filled to the brim with terror. It didn't help that the Cheri wouldn't stop staring at him, and that a murderous glare was all the more threatening when a creature's face made up half its body.

"THAT'S BULLSHIT!" roared Zip's voice from behind the door.

Tom's body contracted involuntarily. In water, he could have curled into a tight ball and jetted away from danger. At the surface, it only made him look small and uncomfortable—at least that's what Zip had told him.

The Cheri glanced at the door and then turned its attention back to Tom. "I'm going to kill the bug." Matter of fact, to the point—Tom almost appreciated the honesty and brevity.

Lars, who had been brooding silently in the corner, lifted his head. "You want to start a fight in a room this small?"

The Cheri advanced. "Won't be much of a fight. More like squishing a fly."

Tom scanned the room looking for a means of escape. The walls were smooth, paneled wood and the golden vents inlaid in the ceiling were too small to crawl through. At the far end of the room were the double doors. The incessant shouting between the two captains on the other side meant they were not a suitable exit. *No way out.*

"I'd like to point out that there are two security cameras," said Techni, busy working at a circuit board in her arm.

The Cheri looked up at the cameras with a degree of uncertainty.

Tiny slithered away from the wall, made a throaty gurgling noise behind its hood, and spat black goop up toward the ceiling. Twice. Its spit stuck to the cameras with a wet smack. "Well, would you look at that? No cameras."

"Why would you do that?" Lars stood with a groan and twisted back and forth, popping his back. The man was getting older, but his arms bore lean muscle. He stared at Tiny with dull, grey intensity.

Tiny shrugged. "I like having big friends."

The Cheri grinned. "Good."

Techni touched the circuit board on her arm, and it receded. A skin-colored panel slid closed, hiding it. "Well, shit."

Without a moment's hesitation, the Cheri lumbered across the tiled floor, shaking the ground with each step. A huge furry fist swung from the side and this time there was no one there to block it. Tom felt the sudden impact and the world flashed white as he was knocked sideways. There was a second thud as he hit a wall, but he barely felt it. The fact that he had been punched registered long before the faintest glimmer of pain came into Tom's awareness. Everything was muted, fuzzy, and unfocused.

Tom fussed with his eyes, limbs clumsy, trying to refocus the world. How had it gone so bad so quickly? The world stuttered back into clarity. Techni was in front of the Cheri dodging another swing while Lars lifted a wooden chair over his head and brought it down with brutal force. The wood splintered and cracked but brought the Cheri to its knees. There was a moment when the fight seemed like it might be over, but then Big ran behind Lars and wrapped a thick arm around his neck.

Tom sat huddled in the corner, afraid to move, unsure of what to do.

"Fight!" shouted Techni.

Only then did Tom realize she was staring at him. "I'm sorry?"

The Cheri was returning to its feet and advancing on her once again. "We're defending you, asshole, now get up and help us before we change our mind!" She ducked low as the Cheri swung again. The creature was powerful but slow.

Tom stood, legs wobbly, still feeling the throbbing impact

of the Cheri's fist. Water leaked from his suit at several puncture points. There would be time to fix it later. Whoever these mercenaries were, they were on his side, and that made them friends. Tom protected his friends. His claws weren't effective against an opponent of that size, but they would still hurt. He scuttled forward, ready to attack the Cheri's backside and buy Techni some time.

A wet slap around his midsection stopped Tom mid-charge. He looked down and saw a slimy appendage wrapping around his waist. Without thinking, he snapped with the larger of his two claws. Ordinarily, it wasn't good for much, being smaller than a lobster's or a crab's, but Tom's claw ripped through the soft meat of Tiny's body like tissue, nearly severing the limb. Black blood spurted from the wound, coating the no doubt expensive upholstery of the waiting room's furniture.

Tom recoiled, horrified at what he had just done. "Oh dear, I am so so—"

Tiny shrieked, the sound halfway between a hiss and a howl. "MY ARM! HE TOOK MY ARM!"

Big let go of Lars and kicked him in the back, sending him sprawling into a wall. "Tiny?" he asked, looking toward the creature with a surprising softness.

Tiny didn't respond with anything other than howls of pain. It cradled its nearly severed appendage with two others.

"You hurt Tiny." Big crossed the room in three confident strides. "Now I hurt you."

Tom raised several appendages in hopes he would seem threatening. He looked to Techni for help, but she was still occupied—trying to fend off the Cheri in what was quickly becoming a losing battle.

Big took no notice and reached out toward Tom.

Lars jumped on Big's back. "I thought we made it clear. You don't hurt the shrimp." He wailed at Big with his free fist, barely making an impact, but it was enough to distract him from Tom.

Big turned and flung Lars off his back. This time he landed hard, head smacking against the tile.

Tom found what little bravery remained and charged at Big's back. He slammed into it with all his might. It was like hitting a brick wall. He bounced off and crumpled on the floor.

"First I kill old man, then you," said Big, advancing on the stunned Lars.

The Cheri had a fist around Techni's midsection, and her face was growing pale.

The double doors at the far end of the room snapped open. "WHAT THE HELL IS GOING ON IN HERE?!" shouted Zip.

The combatants turned to look at the door, momentarily ceasing their fights while they considered whether to continue.

Roman stepped forward past Zip and clucked his tongue. "My, my. Mother always said mercenaries make poor dinner guests."

The Cheri kept its stranglehold on Techni who struggled, gasping for air.

Tiny was whimpering and cradling its arm.

Big had Lars pinned under one boot. "I still kill him."

Roman sighed, reached into his pocket, and produced a small rectangular brick with two metal prongs at the end. A quick button press and they crackled to life with electricity. "No, you need to listen to your captains now. Kill each other on the way to Kedasi if you like, just make sure I'm not cleaning up your mess."

The Cheri looked at the taser and dropped Techni with an unceremonious thud.

Big stepped back, giving Lars room to get to his feet.

"Is anyone going to help me with this?" whined Tiny.

Jack stepped into the room. "Don't worry Tiny, you're with me. More than enough medical supplies on the ship to get that fixed up. Big, you too. And… I'll call you Fluffy." He pointed at the Cheri.

The Cheri grimaced. "My name is—"

"Yeah, sure, but I can say Fluffy, so it's Fluffy for now."

The Cheri thought it over, fists flexing, obviously thinking about another fight. "Yes, Captain."

"Good. I like that. Now, let's get the hell out of here. I've spent too long without my guns." He turned on his heel to walk out the door but paused. "Be seeing you, Zip." He flashed her a grin and left.

The other mercenaries followed.

The second they were out, Zip walked over to Tom and offered him a hand. "You alright?"

Tom grasped Zip's hand with several appendages, a gesture she had initially disliked but had come to tolerate. "My head hurts, and my vacuum suit needs repairs, but I will be alright."

Zip nodded. "See you made some new friends. Techni, Lars, I've got good news for you. As you can see, you're with me, which means you're going to live."

"We're going to live, what a joy." Lars stood and spat blood onto the floor.

"Each of those tiles was handcrafted in the outer worlds," hissed Roman.

Lars grinned through bloody teeth. "I was hoping so."

"Where is your ship?" asked Techni.

Zip eyed her with deep suspicion. "Docking Bay 94. *Nana's Hog*. Don't even think about hacking my systems."

"Wouldn't dream of it, Captain." Techni gave a curt nod and left.

"Well, she seems like a bundle of fun," said Lars.

"Will you please get the hell out here?" asked Roman, the last of his patience evaporating.

"Not a problem, champ." Zip clapped him hard enough on the shoulder to make him stumble.

"Thank you for the opportunity," said Tom.

5
Nana's Hog

Zip listened to the familiar hum of the freight elevator as she examined her new crew. None of them seemed particularly comfortable, but they didn't have to be, so long as they weren't at each other's throats. In that respect, it appeared she had dodged a bullet. There weren't many mercenaries on Prota that would have stood up for Tom. In any other waiting room, she would have likely walked in to find him no more than shrimp paste. Whatever else Lars and Techni might be, they were also temporary friends.

Zip focused her attention on their gear, looking for any hint at what she might be dealing with. Neither carried much. Lars was limited to a rifle and a single long duffel slung across his back. The bag still bore the faded logo of his military unit. Techni had a series of small interlocking boxes made of polished metal. None of them knew exactly what they were getting into, so packing light seemed to be the best option.

Hundreds of hexagonal grey berths flashed past as the elevator rattled along its aging track. Docking Bay 94 wasn't the newest or the nicest, but it did come with a certain level of discretion Zip needed for her activities. The Private Cay Docking Corporation didn't care what docked so long as it had the proper paperwork, forged or otherwise. Zip hoped that whatever bogus flight manifest the Manchesters had given them would clear the bureaucracy and get them a quick launch authorization.

A muted chime sounded, and the elevator doors slid open, revealing *Nana's Hog* in all its glory. The ship looked like a dull metal piggy bank, still bearing a series of battle scars from their last job. The cockpit sat unlit, an oblong viewport where the creature's snout would have been. Immediately below it were two tusks hiding antimatter guns that were both effective and highly illegal.

"That's it?" asked Techni.

"Well, she was supposed to get a polish..." Zip paused and crept up to the edge of the elevator, hand dropping to her side. "But it looks like the maintenance crews took off early."

"That normal?" asked Lars.

"Not especially. Maybe Jack paid them to take the day off, slow us down." Stacks of supplies and munitions orders sat in the hangar just outside *The Hog's* closed cargo bay doors. The hangar, normally buzzing with activity and various colorful curse words, was silent. Zip took a few tentative steps outside the elevator.

Lars unslung his rifle.

Techni eyed him.

"What?"

"Paranoid much?"

Zip unholstered her pistol, just to be safe.

Techni rolled her eyes, the motion uncomfortably consistent and mechanical. "I scanned the hangar, no life forms aside from us." She tapped a finger to the side of her head.

Zip sighed and put the pistol back in her holster. "Any other fun tricks I should know about?"

Techni narrowed her eyes. "I have taken the less useful pieces of my corporeal form and turned them into something functional. I have a hundred 'little tricks', but I keep them to myself until they're needed."

Zip fought back the urge to press. "Alright, your business. This still feels too quiet." She took another look around the hangar. It looked as though the workers had stopped mid-shift.

"Let's get you all aboard and see if we can expedite our passage off this rock." She moved toward *The Hog* and motioned for them to follow. Unease had settled around her like a cold shroud. She wanted to be on her ship and in the vacuum of space.

Stepping into *The Hog's* shadow brought a modicum of relief. Her ship was many things, but it was also home. Its cold metal body and bulbous portside windows looked almost cozy.

Zip punched in a keycode on her wrist terminal and transmitted it to the rest of the crew. "This will be your guest entry code, good from now until we're safely back from Kedasi." She tapped another keycode and a section of *The Hog's* body detached and folded down into a ramp, revealing the packed cargo hold.

Lars whistled. "Lot of inventory. It's legal, I'm assuming."

"Don't poke any of it too hard or you'll find out."

Zip was used to running *The Hog* with a crew of one. Tom had been with her for over a year and even that was cramped. Now there were suddenly two strangers on her ship—two lives that she was presumed responsible for. She walked into the cargo hold and turned to face the new team. "Before you set your stuff down, I've got a few rules. There aren't many on this ship, but the ones I have are there for a reason. The first two are the most important: no scrapping and no screwing. I find the second tends to lead to the first."

Lars let his gun drop to his side, sized up Techni, turned to Zip, and then even took a brief look at Tom. "Yeah, I think I'll manage."

Zip scowled but smoothed it over. What did she care?

"No one gives me problems, I won't give them any," said Techni.

"I am not built for scrapping, or..." Tom trailed off. "I will follow the rules."

Zip smiled. "I appreciate the sentiment. The ship has six rooms on the main deck; anything that opens is yours, anything that doesn't isn't." She didn't like being a hard ass, but she didn't like people touching her shit either.

"Warm and fuzzy," confirmed Lars.

"OK, get your stuff down, and let's get to work. Tom, you're in the cockpit, get us prepped and ready. Give the dockmaster a call and see what the soonest launch time we can get is. Lars, meet me out front, we need to pick up the slack with the cargo those techs missed. Techni..."

Techni stared at her, eyes whirring with far too many mechanical bits for what was supposed to be organic matter. "Yes, Captain?"

Zip regretted the words even as they came out of her mouth. "Just this once, I would like you to review *The Hog's* security protocols."

Techni's eyes lit up, literally and figuratively.

"But don't make any major changes without telling me first."

"Of course."

"Why don't I trust that?"

Techni was already walking away, a holographic projection of *The Hog's* interior schematics glowing on her wrist.

Lars dropped his bag in the cargo bay but kept the rifle on his back. "Letting a world-famous hacker into your ship security. Ballsy."

"She was going to get in there one way or another. At least

now she thinks I allowed her to do it."

Lars raised an eyebrow. "Smart."

"I'm aware." She held Lars's gaze for a few seconds, feeling a hot flush at the edge of her neck. There was something about grizzled middle-aged marines she would never fully get out of her system. She broke the eye contact before she decided to break one of her own rules. "Let's get to work."

Tom, who had been bobbing slightly in awkward silence, said, "I will go to the cockpit."

"Thank you, Tom. Keep an eye on the hacker."

Tom vibrated with excitement. "Yes, Captain."

Zip watched him walk away and ran a hand through her hair, feeling the grease of a few days without a shower. Planetary leave was supposed to be the easy part.

6

New Friends

TOM SAT IN THE cockpit listening to the jubilant 'hold' music of the Private Cay Docking Corporation. A screen on the console before him read: *Your departure has been delayed. An estimate will be provided shortly*. He was used to delays. If there were any issues in the launch tunnels, Private Cay would prioritize by highest paying berth. *The Hog* was somewhere near the bottom of that priority list. Tom wasn't sure exactly where Zip's money went, but it certainly wasn't to lodging for her prized flying swine.

He turned on a display of the cargo bay security feed. Lars and Zip were almost done loading the crates. Zip was smiling. It wasn't often that Zip appeared to enjoy life and usually there was mortal danger involved. She was always happy to get back to *The Hog,* but this had a tinge of something different. Perhaps it was because they were both ex-military. Zip would not talk about her service much with him, and he didn't press. In either case, if Zip was happy, Tom was happy. He leaned back in his chair, staring out at the grey berth beyond, feeling content.

"Spying?" came a voice from behind him.

Tom spun so fast that he slipped off his chair, crashing to the cockpit floor. His limbs flailed indignantly, scrabbling for purchase until he was finally able to right himself.

Techni stood in the cockpit doorway, smirking. "High tension. You know they make pills for that."

"Captain says you're not supposed to be in here."

"Relax." Techni lowered herself into one of the jump seats behind the captain's chair.

Tom followed her movements closely, remembering Zip's directive to "keep an eye on the hacker." He asked, "How are our security systems?"

Techni twitched. “Full of holes. Some can be patched quickly; others will require a full system overhaul.”

“Zip said—”

“Not to touch her ship. Yeah, I heard her, and I haven’t. Besides, I’ve got more pressing matters.”

“More pressing than ship security?” Tom could not read Techni. Well, he couldn’t read most people, but Techni above all was inscrutable. Everything about her movements down to even the slightest flinch was mechanical.

“Making sure my crewmates can keep me alive.”

Tom fussed with his eyes, still not quite understanding.

“Right, I’ll spell it out. Can you fire a gun?”

“I—” Tom had tried to fire a gun only once and it had not ended well. “Not efficiently, no.”

Techni nodded. “I thought not. May I take some measurements?” She held out a small rectangular box with glowing infrared light coming out of one end.

“For what?”

“Your… Our boss has a veritable hoard of weapons in the hold. I’m sure there’s something we can modify to fit your particular needs.”

“Zip isn’t going to like that.”

“I’ll talk to her. Nothing without permission, right?” Techni held up the box and shook it back and forth. “Will only take a second.”

“Alright.” He stood. “Just, make sure you ask Zip before you go rooting through her crates. She’s very sen—” His translator box picked that moment to arc and zap him with a burst of electricity. He shook it off, embarrassed.

Techni approached and looked at the device with interest. “I could also take a look at that if you want.”

“Just the measurements, thank you.” Tom knew the translator box was suboptimal, but it was one of the last things he had from home, and he would not be giving it up so easily.

“Alright, just the measurements.” Techni moved around Tom, methodically placing the scanner near pieces of his torso. Each time, it let out a small chime, and she would move on. Eventually, after what felt like a hundred scans, she backed away and put the rectangular device in her pocket. “There, that wasn’t so bad, was it?”

“It’s the weapon that scares me.”

“Weapons should scare you.”

Tom bobbed his head.

“Look, you might not trust me, and I certainly don’t trust you, but we’re going to have to figure something out if we’re going to survive."

Tom thought the words over. "You are right. Thank you for helping me, Techni."

She flipped a hand at him. "Don't get all mushy, I'm helping myself. I'll see what I can make." With that, she walked out of the room and the cockpit door shut behind her.

What an odd person. Coming from Tom, odd meant a lot. He returned his attention to the cargo hold camera. Zip was holding up Old Faithful, another in a long line of highly illegal weapons, and showing it to Lars. The gun was capable of transmuting any matter in the surrounding area into ammunition. While effective, in its first human trials the gun had occasionally deemed the wielder to be suitable ammunition material and deconstructed them. Zip swore she had patched that 'minor issue', but all the same, Tom would never want to be near the rifle in a fight. He was relieved to see her put the weapon back in its triple-secured box and back in the hold.

A pleasant chime played over the control board's speakers. Tom looked to the other screen. It now read: *Your scheduled departure is in twenty minutes. Please begin pre-flight checks and submit your flight plan*. That at least gave Tom something to do other than mental spiraling about weapons. He tapped at the controls, beginning *The Hog's* simple pre-flight check system. Meanwhile, he took the data card they had received from the Manchesters and uploaded what was no doubt a bogus flight plan to air traffic control.

Then, he opened the channel to the cargo hold again—and froze. Standing on the edge of the platform were several black-robed figures in shining silver masks.

7

Guns for Hire

Zip was loading one of the last crates when she realized something was wrong. Lars, who had been cracking jokes and she suspected flirting—at least a little—had gone silent. She peered around the edge of the loading vehicle and saw him crouched behind the remaining crates, quietly unslinging the rifle from his back. Zip had a few seconds to process what that meant before she caught sight of three hooded figures in billowing black cloaks and silver masks. They stood in a line at the edge of the cargo bay, trained, poised, and ready for violence.

"Ah, shit." Zip dove off the loader, aiming for cover behind crates that she hoped to hell weren't munitions. Gunfire raked her cover's surface, spraying sparks and slivers of metal above her head. She pressed herself low against the concrete surface of the dock. The crate's lid gave way and bullets tore apart whatever was inside. Among the acrid smell of gun smoke and melted metal, Zip caught the distinct aroma of fish flakes. *Sorry, Tom.*

She waited for a gap in the assailants' fire. The seconds dragged long as bullets hit *The Hog's* underbelly, ricocheting all over the hangar. None hit their mark, but with dumb luck, it was only a matter of time.

The assassins were well-trained. They reloaded in a staggered pattern, leaving little room for return fire. Zip heard a slight ebb in gunfire, pulled her pistol, and popped her head above cover. Bullets whizzed past her head, making her ears ring. She kept her breath measured and sighted the middle assassin. Her pistol barked twice, striking once in the chest and once in the head. The cloaked figure crumpled, leaving a cloud of red mist hanging in the air.

The assassins were distracted, but only for a second. Zip

seized the opportunity and continued firing as she moved to a better position. At the same time, Lars leaned over his crate and provided cover. He fired with military precision, only shooting in short bursts, and never flinching. His expression was that of grim determination.

The remaining assassins fell in quick succession, and the rattling of Lars's rifle ceased. Zip slid into cover next to him as he ejected a magazine and rammed another in its place. "Any idea who those assholes might have been?"

"Parting gift from Jack if I had to guess." Zip replaced her pistol mag. "Trained assassins, and here I was hoping for flowers."

The days of Jack sending Zip flowers were gone and hadn't lasted long to begin with. "Judging by the masks, they're Herukas. At least he didn't cheap out." Zip kept her eyes on the elevators leading into the hangar bays.

"Herukas?"

"Assassins that believe they're the direct descendants of an Old Earth cult. Crazy as all hell, and expensive to match."

"Oh, goodie. At least I can feel special before I die."

A small chime echoed across the hangar as both service elevators arrived at the same time. Hooded figures poured out of them. Zip tried to get a quick count, but between the billowing cloaks and the sudden appearance of their rifles, she decided it didn't matter. "Our odds just got a lot worse."

"Yes, they did."

The Hog's landing lights blared to full brightness, blinding the attackers.

Zip ducked as the attackers began to fire.

Lars followed suit. "That Tom?"

Zip smirked. "I wish. Probably Techni."

"I'm assuming your ship has guns?"

"None I want her using indoors."

Bullets ripped through the hangar. Lars pressed against the crate. "I understand not trusting her, I don't trust her either, but—"

"Everyone stay down if you want to remain in one piece," came Techni's voice over *The Hog's* loudspeaker.

Zip heard the familiar hum of weaponry warming up beneath *The Hog's* tusks. "Not those guns!" she shouted.

It was too late. The thundering of the attackers' rifles was drowned out by the furious hum of antimatter guns. Zip crawled to the edge of cover, getting a sliver of a glance at the chaos. The hooded figures barely had time to process their mistake before they met the same fate as everything does when it meets an antimatter round: disassembly. The cloth of their cloaks, the metal of their rifles, and the meat of their bodies suddenly and violently ripped into their component parts. Chunks of matter exploded outward, becoming smaller and smaller until it was nothing but fine particles of dust.

The controlled firing of antimatter guns was a true art, and unfortunately, one Techni had not had time to master. While she quickly dispatched the attackers, her line of fire extended for a few seconds too long. Several holes opened in the metal of the dock's elevator carriages, ripping through support structures and the concrete behind them. Techni stopped her fire, but as the sound of the guns died, a new one rose to take its place. Metal creaked and groaned as the service elevators tried to stay upright. Oil spurted from somewhere deep inside the machine's gearbox, and then in an instant, the whole thing fell away.

Screeching groans and booms echoed from the elevator shaft as the debris hit the many platforms below. Docking Bay 94 was so named because it was on the 94th level. Zip wasn't sure how much damage a hunk of metal falling through a hundred floors would do, but she didn't want to stick around to find out. Self-defense against assassins was an argument that only worked if you hadn't dispatched said assassins with highly illegal weaponry.

Lars whistled. "And here I thought antimatter guns were banned after the war."

Zip grimaced. "War never really ended."

Lars nodded. "Same shit, different planet. Still, those are going to get us in some serious trouble."

Zip stood. "You're not wrong. I think the Gatling would have done just fine."

Lars ran a hand through his greasy hair and looked around the hangar. "Yes, in hindsight, this does feel a bit like overkill. But we're not dead."

Zip felt her heartbeat slowing. "We might be soon."

Lars shrugged. "Not because of this. Knowing the Private Cay Corporation, it will take them a long time to figure out what the hell caused that mess."

Zip opened a comms channel to the cockpit. "Tom, please tell me we have a departure time."

"Pending," came Tom's monotonous voice.

"I could fix that," said Techni.

Zip let her head fall. "Why would you use *those* guns, Techni?"

"Who puts the antimatter trigger next to the Gatling?!"

Zip shook her head. "You're reading the manual when we get off this rock."

Across the hangar, a gout of flame erupted from the elevator bay.

"I'm starting to think we're in a hurry," said Lars.

Zip nodded. "Techni, get us priority launch access, but if we get caught, you're taking the fall."

"We won't."

Zip could practically hear the smirk in Techni's voice. "She's going to be a problem."

"Hackers often are."

"I need a drink."

"Your ship, you're buying." Lars grinned at her.

Zip smiled back. "Fair enough. Let's make it a quick one."

8

An Interlude with Air Traffic Control

Paul took pride in his work for the Private Cay Docking Corporation. A fifteen-year plaque commemorating that pride and service sat polished on the edge of his desk. In those fifteen years, he had never once seen a mess like the readout currently in front of him. Almost a hundred red alerts flashed, representing the crushing wake of a faulty elevator. The thought of it made him sick. If people didn't trust the elevators, then they wouldn't trust the docking company. Private Cay's reputation was everything, and if it suffered, Paul suffered. Specifically, his income would suffer. With six kids, child support payments for each, and legal fees from the divorces, income was important.

Sweat beaded on his brow, and he mopped it with a company-issued towel he kept in his side drawer. "Cristina, get me a status update!"

The frazzled woman swirled around the various monitors in her station, desperately looking for something that might have changed. Nothing had. The maintenance techs were still doing their best to piece through the charred wreckage and see if any poor souls had been aboard when the elevator crashed. Cristina tapped at her screens, switching between technical readouts and news feeds with furious abandon. "Nothing, sir. Would you like me to get on hold with customer support again?"

Paul chewed the inside of his lip. It would be the second time that day, but elevator malfunction was not to be toyed with. "Patch them through to my desk. In the meantime, get the dockyard moving again, but keep traffic to a single launch tunnel. We can't afford any more mistakes." Yes, that was good, no mistakes. A single launch tunnel would snare the queue, but it would ensure that everyone got out of the docking bay safely.

He took a deep breath, searching for the confidence that calling customer support required, and motioned to Cristina.

There was only a brief trill over the intercom before a pleasant man's voice, clearly synthetic, came over his speakers. "Hello and thank you for calling Ventnertech. You ask for the future, and we deliver."

"Ventnertech," he grumbled. A mad scientist had one good idea, and suddenly they were letting him innovate all forms of major infrastructure. Paul made peace with his god every time he stepped into an automated vehicle run by the bastards.

"Yes, Ventnertech!" answered the cheery voice, with a complete lack of understanding for Paul's displeasure. "How may I be of assistance?"

Paul paused. What *did* they need? "Uh—" he faltered. "Well, one of your elevators seems to have come off the rails and caused some serious damage to my docking bay."

There was a trill to indicate processing. "I'm sorry to hear that, sir. Would you mind telling me the make and model number of your elevator?"

"Make and model?"

"Yes, that's right."

Paul tapped through the elevator protocols, searching the long list of data. Of course, the make and model were nowhere to be found.

"Are you still there, sir?"

"Yes, dammit, I'm still here. Just give me a moment." A message chimed from Cristina on his screen with the full schematic readout for the elevator in question. He mouthed a silent, *Thank you*. "Alright, I've got the numbers right here."

"I'm hearing that you have the make and model number. Is that correct?"

"Yes," ground out Paul, resisting the urge to swear at the synthetic again.

"Fantastic, what are they?"

"It's the Hollywood Tower make, model M-7-8-9-4-2." Paul had been to New Hollywood on vacation once and hadn't seen anything remotely resembling one of his docking elevators. *Bunch of pinheads with their clever names.*

"OK, I am seeing your model. How can I help you today? You can say: help me with my elevator service, when is my next service date, or where can I purchase a similar model?"

It took all of Paul's effort not to smash his head into the screen in front of him. Warp-speed travel happened in moments, and yet customer service was stuck hundreds of years in the past. It had to be deliberate. "Help me with my elevator service, I guess."

"One moment." There was a pause, filled again with the low-level processing trill that must have been specially designed to get on one's nerves. "I'm seeing your elevator isn't scheduled for service for another nine months. Is there anything else I can help you with?"

"The elevator doesn't need servicing; it's fallen straight off the damned rails. People might be dead!" He immediately regretted using such language, but there were occasions when it slipped out. You could take the boy out of The Undercity, but you couldn't take The Undercity out of... *Oh to hell with it.*

Processing trill. "Let me connect you to a live customer service representative. One moment." Without waiting for a response, the line switched over to hold music so old, it might have been one of the original artifacts carried over from Earth.

Paul let out an aggravated sigh and pressed the mute button. "Status, Cristina! Where are we?"

Cristina pulled up a screen showing the bottom of the elevator shaft. Ordinarily, it was a wide expanse with multiple doors leading off from a shining central concourse. Currently, it was filled with acrid black smoke and a group of men and women in orange hazmat jumpsuits. They were all staring and pointing at one of the doors that was shooting a consistent gout of blue flame. "Uhm... That, sir. That's the status."

"Sass me again and it's going in your permanent—"

"Hi sir, I'm sorry, I didn't intend to offend you," came the voice of the sudden and inconveniently available customer service representative.

Paul cursed the mute button and whatever god had sought fit to throw the dice for him. "Hi, yes, I'm sorry, that was for my subordinate. We've got a little bit of a situation down here at the Private Cay Docking Corporation."

"Yes, I heard that from our synthetic assistant. It said that you're in need of scheduling maintenance?"

If Paul's blood could have literally boiled, well, he would have been dead—but the metaphor would have been quite apt. "No," he ground out, trying not to shatter his teeth. "One of your elevators has fallen off the rails and caused catastrophic damage to our docking system."

There was a pause on the other end of the line. "Are you sure it was one of our elevators?"

Paul tapped his fingers on his desk, one, two, three. The man was testing him, but he would not fail. "Yes, quite sure. The model number is—"

"I'm sorry, for catastrophic failures, I'm going to need to

transfer you to a manager."

Before Paul had a chance to argue, the hold music was back. He rubbed at his temples. No amount of pay was worth staying on the line with customer service for more than a half hour.

On a big screen in the center of the room, green ship identifiers were slowly moving from their berths into designated launch tubes. Good, at least traffic was running, even if it was running slowly. Every second the dock was closed was incalculable—at least for Paul—sums of money that vanished into thin air.

"Pull up a view of the launch tunnel, please," he directed to Cristina. It didn't hurt to be polite. Wasn't that always what his therapist said? There was something about anger, resistance, and heart attacks in there as well, but Paul couldn't be bothered.

"Yes, sir."

The traffic screen disappeared, replaced with a real-time feed of an octagonal launch tunnel. Cargo docks, while important, weren't aesthetically pleasing, so they had to be built far below the higher reaches of the city. As such, several long launch tunnels ran out from subterranean berths, spitting spaceships out just beyond the city limits. It wasn't efficient, but it kept the status elite happy. So long as those in the gilded towers got their overnight interstellar goods on time and didn't have to see pesky spaceships, they were happy.

A bulky, swine-shaped ship slid into the launch tunnel. Red-hot exhaust vents in the makeshift ears made it look like a hog straight out of Hell. "I swear, the designs get more bizarre each year." No two ships were alike, and the pilots seemed keen on reminding Paul of that. Sure, there had been days when uniform function-favoring models got the job done, but as warp technology got cheaper to install, pilots had to find another place to throw their money. Whether it be sleek vessels that looked equipped for murder, or cartoon hogs, every ship left a mark. Never mind that they all did the same thing: travel in space.

"Hi there, sir, my name is Margaret, and I'm one of our senior account managers here at Ventnertech. It sounds like you've had a catastrophic failure with your elevator unit."

"Yes, that's correct." Paul winced, anticipating the next question.

"Are you sure it's one of ours?"

"Yes, I have the model—"

"No need, we can pull that off the synthetic transcript. Let me find the emergency camera from that unit and see what happened."

If you had the cameras, then you knew it was your goddamned elevator.

"Oh my. You might want to look at this. May I have your permission to use this line to transfer security footage?"

Paul's eyebrow raised. "Yes, of course."

The Ventnertech logo, an hourglass with ever-changing sand, popped up on his screen and was quickly replaced by a camera feed from inside the elevator. Paul's heart froze. He was looking out at the very same swine that had just entered the launch tunnel. The ship was unmistakable. In the video, a large group of hooded figures approached and fired on the docking bay. Then out of nowhere, flashes of light thundered out of the ship's tusks, spraying neat cubes of matter all over the docking bay. The lights only lasted a few seconds, but a gout of oil from off-screen was enough to let him know that they had hit the elevator unit.

"Sir, I don't think this is going to be covered under your standard use warranty. Might I suggest contacting your insurance?"

If Paul had been angry before, he was volcanic now. No one used illegal guns in his docks, no one. "Cristina, stop that ship!!"

9

Hit and Run

Zip watched the grey walls blur past as *The Hog* rocketed out of Private Cay's two mile launch tunnel. Her collection of antique bobble heads adhered to the flight console shuddered and nodded in uniform agreement that spaceflight was indeed radical. Somewhere above, the citizens of Prota were going about their daily lives, completely unaware of the ships coming and going right beneath their feet. Ahead, Zip watched a small square of light steadily expand, until suddenly, they were flying through the open air, leaving the city behind. A vast tangle of greenery spread out below, expanding ever outwards, representing the clear boundary of human civilization. Long shadows from the skyscrapers stretched out like teeth in the afternoon light.

Prota's main city was situated on top of a vast rocky plateau, pockmarked with lakes of fresh water pushed up by geothermal pressure. Below, it was surrounded by an impenetrable forest, lush and taunting. The original plan for Prota's settlement was to build bases on the planet's many plateaus and expand to the forest beyond. In a few hundred years, not a single survey team went into the jungle without returning mute or not returning at all.

Zip watched the treetops passing below, quickly blurring to a uniform green. Each time she left Prota, she wondered what lay in the depths. Scientists said it was toxic pollen that caused extreme disorientation, but Zip had her money on something with a lot more teeth. What little life they had seen on Prota was well adapted to its surroundings, and humanity was nothing but a guest on the surface.

A red light flashed on the console followed shortly by a blaring alarm. Zip tensed and punched in a scan for pursuing ships or other potential hazards. *The Hog's* systems check returned all clear, no damage, no malfunction, which only meant one thing.

"Incoming call request," said Tom.

"Of course there is." *We're not doing anything illegal.* For once, she was sure the mantra was true. Whatever was on Kedasi might not be legitimate, but they weren't on Kedasi yet. Suddenly seven pings appeared on the proximity scanner—pursuing ships, and they were closing fast. "Shit. Put it on the main screen."

A portion of the cockpit canopy converted into a large display, showcasing a red-faced man in high definition. Sweat clung to his jowls and dripped to the collar of his shabby grey uniform. Whoever he was, he was not having a good day. "This is Captain Paul Veers of the Private Cay Docking Corporation."

A captain, Zip mouthed to Tom. "Afternoon, Captain, how can a lowly cargo vessel such—"

"Return to berth immediately!" Spittle flew from the man's mouth with each spiteful syllable.

Zip remained calm and pulled up their launch authorization form. "There must be a mistake, Captain. We had permission to launch, and we're burning time as is."

Captain Veers's neck muscles twitched on the edge of a massive stroke. "You have violated UCP arms code 24172-B, possession, and use of illegal antimatter—"

Zip pushed a button and killed the connection.

"That was rude," said Tom.

Zip shrugged. "I never heard the charges they were filing. Must have been a glitch with our communications relay."

Tom leaned back, unfurling in a pensive gesture. "You think they will believe you?"

"I'm banking on them having other problems between now and when we get back from Kedasi." Zip liked the Private Cay docks, but there were plenty of other berths on Prota. If the Manchester money came good, they'd be able to park wherever the hell they wanted. "For now, let's just focus on the danger at hand. How are we looking?"

Tom's nimble appendages moved over the controls, spiderlike and precise. "Warp drive is calculating a route to Kedasi, vents are ready for atmospheric breach, and I have my anti-anxiety mechanism." Tom squeezed a small rubber alien whose eyes popped out slightly from the pressure. Despite being new, the edges were already worn from overuse.

"Then I'd say we're sitting pretty." Zip turned on the ship-wide comms. "This is your captain speaking. We're breaching atmosphere in one minute, at which point I will turn off the fasten—"

A red light blinked on the console in front of Zip followed by a persistent low tone.

"Is that a missile lock?" asked Techni, her voice tinny through the speakers.

"Shit," hissed Zip. "Might want to hold off on unbuckling. Tom, tell me about those ships."

He spun to the side, examining several screens worth of data at once. "Seven ships, all with official government designations, all with missiles currently trained on our position. Also—"

"Let me guess, we have another incoming call."

Tom turned and nodded.

"Patch it through."

This time, a calm woman in a pressed blue uniform appeared on the screen. A blinking red light in the corner of her screen notified Zip that the conversation was being recorded, and a badge number in the bottom left was supposed to make her feel safe.

Somehow, Zip still felt like she was one bad twitch away from becoming a very bloody vapor trail. "Afternoon, Officer." Zip tried to sound unassuming while also checking their distance to vacuum. A warp jump had never been attempted from atmosphere, and she didn't want to be the one that boiled humanity's largest settlement by trying. Heat sensors along *The Hog's* edge indicated they were getting close, but not close enough.

"*Nana's... Hog,* you are hereby ordered to return to dock for immediate boarding and search. Our records indicate the use of illegal antimatter weaponry by your ship. You will follow the flight plan being transmitted to your navigation systems, or you will be shot down. By standard UCP regulation, you have one minute to comply."

Zip's mind raced through the various countermeasures available to her. Most involved use of deadly force, and killing a police officer was not as easily forgotten as destruction of property. "One minute isn't enough time. This is an old ship. If we power down our engines that quickly, we—"

The police officer let out an audible sigh and a countdown appeared on Zip's screen showing forty-five seconds. "*Nana's Hog*, I've heard it all before. Please, power down your engines. Lethal force against your ship means a lot of paperwork for me, and I'd rather just go home."

Behind Zip, the cockpit door hissed open as Techni strode

in. "I knew that was missile lock."

Zip muted her communications. "Gold star for you. We're in trouble."

Techni took the chair immediately behind Zip and pulled out a hand terminal. "I can get us out of trouble."

"We kill an officer, we're never coming back to Prota."

"*Nana's Hog,* you have twenty seconds to comply," came the voice of the officer.

"I have an idea, but you need to buy me some time." Techni tapped at her terminal, the sound somehow audible over the constant droning missile lock alert.

"Seven ships with missile lock, four missile bays a piece. I put our odds of avoiding fifty-six missiles very—"

"Never tell me the odds. Everyone strap in, we're about to have engine failure."

"What?"

Zip waited until she heard the gentle click of Techni's belt and hoped to hell Lars was still listening below. Then, she unmuted. "Officer, this is Captain Turbine, powering down now, but again, this is an old ship, so you never—" Zip cut *The Hog's* engines, sending it into an immediate and unceremonious free fall. Gas hissed on all sides as automatic stabilizers stopped the ship from going into a spin. Anything in the cockpit that wasn't weighed down floated, bouncing off the walls.

"Zip!" shouted Tom.

"I did tell you to buckle up. Get me a reading on our pursuers, Tom. Techni, we've got about a minute before we're going to run into serious problems."

"Just need a few more—"

"Captain Turbine!" roared the officer. "When I said I had seen every trick in the book, I meant it. You have exercised your last warning!"

"Missiles have been fired." Tom squeezed his stress alien so hard that the rubber finally gave way, spilling sand into the floating cockpit.

"Yeah, I was afraid of that." Zip flipped several switches on *The Hog's* main controls and the engines roared to life all at once. "See what you can do about those missiles."

Tom pulled up a screen displaying *The Hog's* weapons systems.

"And try not to hit the officers while you're at it." Zip pushed the throttle forward. Everything that had been floating in free fall came down at once, clattering to the floor. Most of the debris was just misplaced knickknacks, but the sound of shattering glass followed by an unforgettable scent told Zip she had forgotten to secure her stash of puffin rum. *God damned pigs.*

The ship vibrated as Tom started working the defensive cannons. Muted booms rang out as missiles were destroyed before they could make impact. "Two down, only twelve to go."

Zip gritted her teeth and angled *The Hog* back towards the sky. The chances of them outrunning missiles to atmospheric breach were slim, but with nothing but open air around them, she wasn't going to outmaneuver their guidance systems. "Techni, how's our cure-all coming?"

"Patience is a virtue."

The Hog shuddered and pitched hard to the left as Tom hit a missile that nearly made contact.

"Not right now it isn't!" Zip quickly scanned down a list of *The Hog's* critical systems. Some were blinking yellow, but nothing had gone to red yet. That meant all compartments still had pressure and she wasn't going to accidentally kill Lars by flying into vacuum.

"One more chance, *Nana's Hog*. I've got a lot more missiles where that came from, and you're on my last nerve," said the officer over *The Hog's* speakers.

"Can't we shut her off?" asked Zip.

"I need a video file," said Techni, still calm as ever.

"What do you need a video file for?!" Zip pushed *The Hog's* engines to their absolute limit. The hull vibrated with strain as the ship buffeted against the limits of atmosphere.

"Fine, I'll get it myself."

Zip watched in horror as one of the screens in front of her blinked and was suddenly under Techni's control. Hundreds of files popped up at once. "Some of that is private!"

"Calm down, I just need a file. Ah, there we are." Techni's cursor settled on a video titled: *Crustacea, A Watery Place*. She clicked it, and the video filled the screen.

The officer blew out a breath, patience running out. "Alright, have it your way. Pilots, the use of excessive force is authorized, go get them." She gave a sad look at the camera and killed the connection.

"All missiles have been fired," said Tom. "I can't stop them all."

"Techni?"

"Crustacea is a place unlike any other," began the documentary narrator.

Techni quickly muted it and set her hand terminal down. "Three."

"What?"

"Two."

"We don't have time for games."

"One."

The drone of missile lock and the alerts of incoming projectiles stopped.

"All frequencies are now jammed." Techni folded her arms and leaned back in her chair.

Zip looked at her screens. Sure enough, every single pursuer was gone. No more missiles, no more calls from angry police officers. "And the documentary?"

"I imagine it will annoy them."

"We almost died!"

Techni scoffed. "No, we didn't. I had it under control."

Zip was halfway to fighting but focused on her breath. Eventually, through gritted teeth, she managed, "Dismissed."

"Fine by me. I have some projects to work on anyway." Techni unbuckled and walked out of the cockpit.

"Don't touch my ship!"

The door shut with a snap-hiss. She keyed the cargo bay comms. "Lars, you alive down there?"

"You're lucky I added extra security on the cargo, or this would be a very different story," he panted.

"Any holes in my ship?"

"Oh, is that my job now?"

Zip smiled and turned off the comms. It was going to be a fun trip to Kedasi. "Tom, how about you?"

Tom looked around at the mess in the cockpit from the sudden freefall. "I will need to do some cleaning, but I am alright. We will also require more double-sided tape," he said as he picked up the remnants of his plastic alien and placed them next to the console in front of him. "For securing valuables. I will also require a new stress device."

"When the Manchester money comes through, we can get you more than one."

"One for each appendage?"

"Was that a joke?"

"Ha. Ha."

"You're getting better at that."

"Thank you." A red light blinked on Tom's console. He flicked a switch, and it turned solid. "Ready for atmospheric breach, Captain."

Zip pushed a series of buttons, giving the engines a final kick. The less time they spent on the edge of atmosphere, the less hull cleaning was needed later. She sat back in her chair and watched as flames licked the edge of the cockpit, forming a burning ring of fire. *The Hog* rumbled and shook, pressing with all due force at Prota's atmosphere, and then suddenly went still.

Outside, the chaos and fire gave way to inky blackness filled with billions of multicolored stars. The sheer size of space always gave Zip pause, no matter how many times she traveled through it.

"Wow," said Tom, same as he always did.

"Wow is right," she agreed, same as *she* always did.

Their reverie, while short-lived, was a calm spot in the storm of life. It was broken by the silent green blinking light, indicating the warp drive was ready, and a distant memory of pursuing ships.

"You want to do the honors?" asked Zip.

Tom's appendage was already halfway to the blinking green button labeled 'WARP'. "Next stop, Kedasi." He pushed the button, and reality tore itself apart, giving way to the multicolored mind-bender that was warp speed.

Part 2 – Kedasi

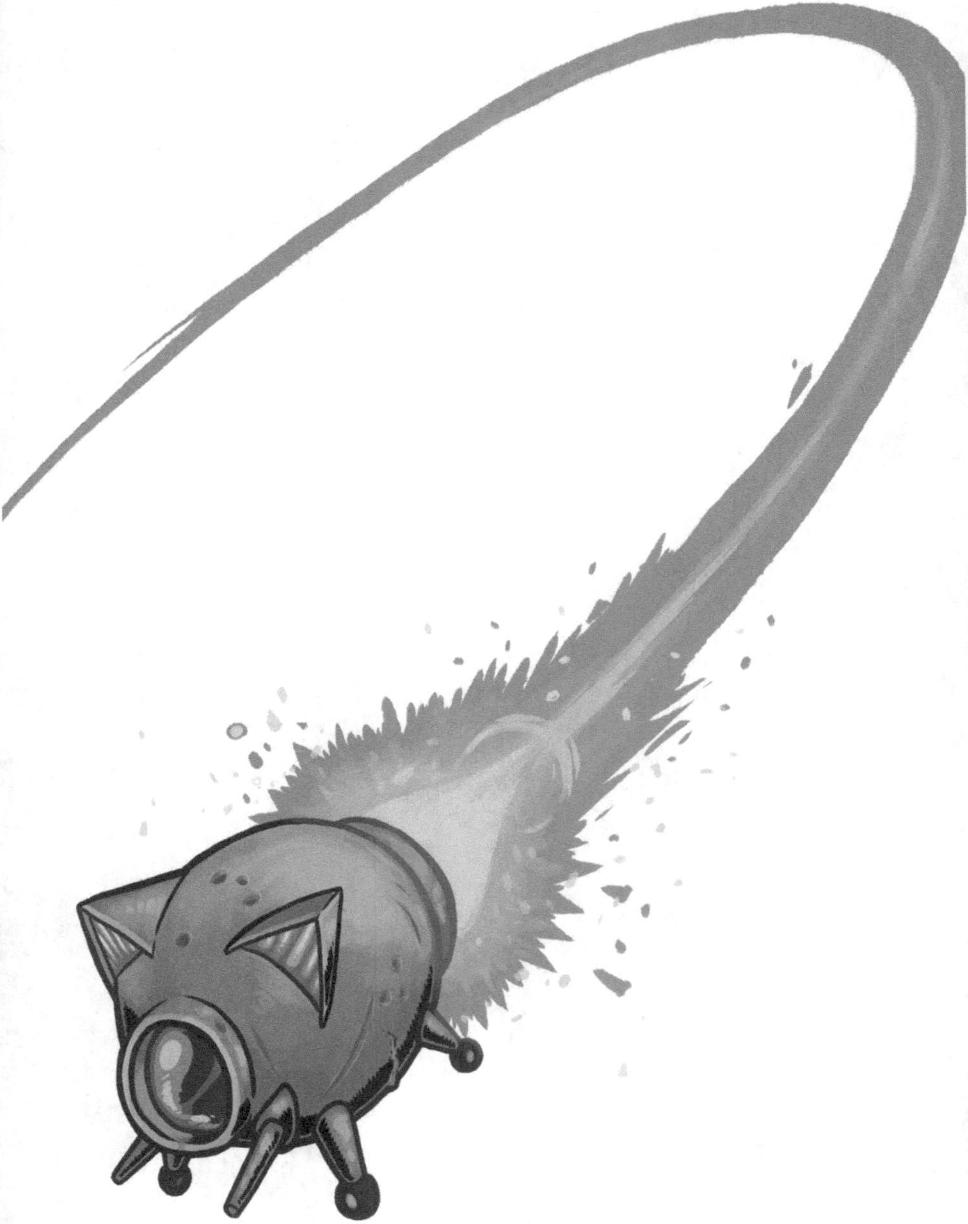

1

Warp Speed, It Just Works

Tom had been through ten launches in the last year but never felt fully prepared for the terrifying mess that was warp speed. Despite repeated reassurance that it was safe, he tapped repeatedly on the red, laminated, single-page manual for comfort. The page displayed a stenciled image of a prototypical early spaceship that looked like a children's cartoon. Beneath it, in big, yellow letters were the words: *Warp speed, it just works*. In an effort at additional comfort, the signatures of the original scientists behind the technology—long dead of course—were scrawled along the bottom of the page. While most of society was content to leave their interstellar travel in the hands of 'eggheads', Tom was unnerved.

On Crustacea, he had taken pleasure in the control that came from working on simple machines to achieve complex goals. His entire career had been built on understanding the unknown. Unfortunately, as with most technological advances on Crustacea, he was limited to what could be salvaged from the bottom of the ocean. Coming to Prota had been like drinking scientific progress through several fire hoses. The most ubiquitous discoveries were the most complex, and by the choice of the simple majority, unexplained.

He stared out the cockpit window, hoping to avoid the headache that came from thinking too hard about society's comfortable ignorance. Loops of bizarre colors splattered against the glass like spaghetti of varying density. Each noodle dissipated before it truly made contact, but it still felt like traveling through a space giant's lunch. There were no space giants, of course, but the metaphor was the only way in which Tom could begin to understand what he was seeing. Colors bent and blurred while reality folded in on itself. Processing that observation along with the practical applications of warp travel in the same instant was impossible.

"You thinking about leviathans again?" asked Zip, her voice taking on a slight slur that might have been drunkenness, exhaustion, or both.

Tom contracted his body at the mere idea. "I am now." Space giants might not have been real, but leviathans were. No one could be sure what they were, how they were, or even why they were, but they were sure that they *were*. Evidence for the creatures was slim to none and primarily consisted of a single disturbed radio call that had managed to punch through several layers of physics for two sentences: "Dear god, what is that? It's a leviathan!" The pilot's screaming tone might have indicated a psychotic break, but the message coupled with the occasional ship going missing at warp led to a myth that most pilots took as fact.

"We're not going to get eaten by a leviathan."

"I know the statistics." The chances were low—so low that it was almost more dangerous to be outside of warp. Space, as it turned out, was perilous. There were a million good reasons to stay planetside, but Tom kept it to a comfortable list to manage his panic: shrapnel from past battles, debris from cosmic explosions, garden-variety micrometeorites, and the fact that it all existed in a perfect vacuum. That wasn't even accounting for the human elements of error and piracy. Warp avoided all those dangers by stepping out of reality's traditional plane and into one that no one quite understood. Whatever warp was, it was mostly harmless. Even still, Tom found himself dwelling on the slim chance of encountering a ship-devouring beast hiding somewhere in the cosmic spaghetti.

"Hey, Tom." Zip snapped her fingers, making up for clumsy drunken dexterity with sheer force. It was a miracle her finger bones stayed intact. "Why don't you switch to a different nightmare for a while? Why don't you read through some of my old safety briefings?"

Tom winced. He had started reading several of Zip's 'safety briefings' but had stopped after the headings that were filled with casualty counts and vivid descriptions of dismemberment. The military was full of horrors that he never wanted to encounter. "Are there any that are particularly relevant to this mission?" Tom was playing the odds. It seemed highly unlikely that Zip had ever been to a theme park asteroid before.

Zip clucked her tongue, mulling the question over. "Not specifically, but it never hurts to be prepared. If you're not up for reading, maybe try to get some weapons practice. We have no idea what's down on Kedasi other than Jack and his goons. That alone is a reason to take a few practice shots."

It all came back to weapons, society's greatest obsession. Tom loved machines, gadgets, and gizmos, but never understood those created with intent for bodily harm. On Crustacea, there had been plenty of leaders who asked him to use his technological prowess for such an application, and he had refused. Aggression was a silly business that often led to unnecessary death.

"Tom?"

"Yes, Zip?"

"I know you don't want to fight, but there's a good chance it's going to be necessary."

Tom contracted. "I understand."

"If it helps, remember that the lives of your team may depend on it."

It most certainly didn't. "I will try."

Zip raised her hands. "That's all I can ask. And Tom?"

"Yes, Captain?"

"Read my briefings. That's an order from your captain." Her stern tone was only slightly cut by the glazed look in her eyes.

Tom squirmed. On the one hand, he didn't want to look at warp, and on the other, he had no desire to learn about the bug planets Zip had visited. "Yes, Captain."

"And while you're at it, wake up Lars, it's time for his shift."

Tom vacated the co-pilot's chair, feeling a mix of dread and relief. Zip wasn't exactly a mean drunk, but she certainly wasn't a pleasant one either. He left the cockpit and keyed in a shift alert for Lars on the way out. Maybe the mechanic would be able to convince Zip to take a few hours of rest.

Tom took his worries about warp and Zip, carefully packaged them into a neat mental box, and filed them away for later. Likely, the box would spring open at the slightest provocation, but for the few steps it took to get to his cabin, the mental exercise worked.

He pressed an appendage to the door's scanner and stepped inside. The space was small with a bubbled porthole looking out at the technicolor vomit of warp. He pressed a button and metal shutters snapped shut, cutting the room off from the rest of the universe. Originally, the space had consisted of nothing more than a bunk and a small folding desk, but after a few trips, Tom was able to afford adjustments. Rather than a bed, there was an empty tank that covered an entire wall. Well, tank was a strong word—several pieces of glass carefully held together with industrial-strength glue was more accurate. A few hours at a shower surplus store and a fortune to a plumber had made it functional.

Tom slipped out of his hydration suit, being careful with each limb. He'd learned the hard way that the suits were fragile and warranties didn't cover accidental appendage punctures. Customer service was his least favorite technical discovery since arriving on Prota. He placed the suit in a sanitizing box and moved to the tank. As he approached, the glass panel slid open, and he stepped inside. The door closed behind him. A rain of cold, briny water spattered him from above, quickly filling the tank to a depth that allowed him to be submerged.

He sucked in water through his gills, feeling growing ease as it ran through him. A hydration suit did a lot, but it could never mimic the feeling of getting a good full breath. The temporary peace alone was worth the destitute state of his finances. *Maybe after Kedasi I can make some more upgrades.* The thought of an active filter and simulated water current was enough to make him feel giddy.

That feeling slid away when he tapped the large glass panel to open Zip's report. The side of his tank turned into a screen of documents running floor to ceiling. If he was going to read about terror and violence, he might as well do it in comfort. From word one, gruesome death was a clear theme. As headers, Zip had listed the casualties, manners of death, and mistakes the crew had made. The first report he pulled up was headed with bold letters reading: ***Colony world, infested by bugs, no survivors.***

It was some solace that Crustacea, his home, was likely still considered a 'bug planet'. Crustacea could be brutal when it wanted to be, and he had seen firsthand what the worst citizens of a good society could do.

Focus. He spooled through the report trying to find a good jumping off point and settled on a link to the origin of bug planets. There were no peer-reviewed papers on the subject because corporations paid to keep them quiet. Instead, he was directed to an online post. The writer was a former scientist, now disgraced, and based on the stark angles of his hair, in a state of mental distress. Tom supposed anyone who thought too long about killer bugs from outer space would be.

At the beginning of humanity's ambition to reach the stars, we were naïve in thinking they would welcome us. Open arms and ticker tape parades were the stuff of fantasy. Instead, what we found were rocks, much like our own. We were interstellar refugees, looking for—

Tom skipped ahead, bristling at the term refugee. Humans had destroyed their planet and decided the only workable solution was to spread to as many other planets as possible. They sounded a lot like the bugs they feared so much.

While contact was made well before we reached for the stars, our first real conversation happened when The Founders journeyed to Prota. They were intercepted by an international committee. Not many are privy to what exactly was said, but some suspect this is how the rules and regulations for our expansion were put in place. Specifically, don't settle on a planet that already has residents. I'm not sure how keen The Founders were on repeating our past mistakes of colonization, but in any case, they took the advice to heart. But there was one problem: Not all planets that looked empty were empty.

Tom felt a chill run through him and adjusted the temperature on the tank ever so slightly. Outside, he heard the clank of Lars's heavy boots as he made his way to the cockpit. *It's just history,* he reminded himself. *History can't hurt you.*

The first bugs were discovered by an ill-fated colony headed to a perfectly inhospitable world. New Terra, not known for its clever name, was a planet that had the potential to support life but required significant terraforming. The original colonists were to live in biodomes for the first twenty years while machines made the atmosphere habitable. It wasn't a glorious assignment, but back then, people took anything for a seat on a ship headed off planet. Prota was a mere fraction of what it has become today and held little appeal.

A hundred levels of poverty didn't hold as much appeal to Tom as they did for the writer. Prota was an interesting settlement, but far from perfect.

The colonists lived in relative bliss for the first few months. Problems arose when terraforming began in earnest. Once oxygen levels rose even a fraction of a percent planet-wide, something else rose with them. All interstellar bugs are different, but if they have a commonality, it's that they don't like being disturbed. Whether evolutionary or cultural, we may never be sure, but the convictions are strong, and the results bloody. The colony at New Terra was slaughtered over two days. Without proper equipment, the colonists mounted little resistance.

The origin of the species at New Terra is unknown, but a later orbital scan revealed a hollow network of catacombs beneath the planet's surface. One attempt was made to recover the assets from the colony. The biospheres were found destroyed and covered in acidic webs. The recovery team did not survive. Short bursts of video from their mission made it back to the civilized world, and they were horrifying enough that New Terra was condemned, never to be visited again.

Tom scrolled. It seemed that no one could talk about bug planets without thoroughly diving into the detailed carnage that went along with them.

So, why are bugs so widespread? It's simple: Evolution repeats good ideas, even on an interstellar scale. Bugs are hearty, breed quickly, and survive. We know from anecdotal evidence that bugs can colonize asteroids, lying in wait for the right conditions or the right planetary impact to wake them. Knowing this, it is not unthinkable that Prota will one day have to deal with such a problem. On that day, we can only hope to be more prepared than we are now. With current estimates, the capital city would last a day and a half before complete annihilation.

Tom closed the document. Bug-ridden asteroids that could strike at any time were where he drew the line. It was the fifth time he had closed Zip's briefings without gleaning anything of use.

As a distraction, he shifted his display to *The Hog's* performance monitors. Traditionally, pilots didn't bother looking at readouts at warp. Physics didn't cooperate, and it was a technological miracle that any system worked at all. *The Hog* was not a typical ship, and its captain was not a typical pilot. Despite the nearly unusable data, Zip ran *The Hog's* sensors at full for every second of every flight. Tom scrolled through his list of operating checks, ignoring flags about gravity and other bits of reality misbehaving.

Somewhere, on the belly of the ship, a gauge showed a depth equivalent to the deepest ocean on the darkest planet. Traditional navigation displays looked like a jumble of wavy lines trying to make a topographical map of a child's mess. The only thing that was working was the warp drive. It was standard issue and came with sparse features: on, off, and course-plotting. Drive maintenance was a nonstarter. In every case it was cheaper to buy a new warp drive than attempt to fix the old one. Somewhere, off a cliff behind the docks at Prota, there were hundreds upon thousands of spent drives collecting dust and slightly altering the reality around them as they decayed.

It was with this uneasy thought that Tom drifted away from the screen. His antennae drooped in front of his eyes and the world lost focus. Had it been that long since he rested? He supposed it had. Slowly, he drifted to a neutral position in the tank and consciousness faded, leviathans and bug planets forgotten for the time being, he dreamt of a vast ocean, blue and sparkling.

2

Message in a Bottle

Zip felt herself fading in and out of sleep but refused to leave the captain's chair. It was unrealistic to stay awake the whole way to Kedasi, but she was going to be damned if she would follow her advice and trust the others on the ship. Exhaustion settled over her like a heavy blanket, aided by a bottle of whisky that had miraculously survived their aerial pursuit. She could still feel the shards of the puffin rum bottle beneath her boots and cursed herself for not securing it. Just a dreg of the hallucinogenic substance would have done the trick.

Lars was a pleasant companion for her morose stupor, content to sit in silence and stare out at the looping interstellar spaghetti.

Zip didn't realize she'd been giving him a glassy-eyed stare until he turned to match it. Immediate shame blossomed in her, but she didn't look away. Instead, she pivoted, finding her inner captain through the haze. These were strangers and she needed to learn more about them, that's all. "Why did you fight for Tom back on Prota?"

Lars leaned back a little in his chair and clucked his tongue. "Because I don't like bullies."

"Marines teach you that?"

"Nah. Met my fair share of bullies in the service."

Thinking back on it, Zip had as well. "It takes all types. So, where then?"

Lars searched her face, his eyes dull and grey, lost somewhere far off. He seemed on the verge of telling a polite lie but sighed and settled on the truth. "I learned it from my brother. Never was much of a fighter."

Normally, Zip would have been content with that answer and returned to silence, but the booze or the lines on Lars's face prodded her forward. "What happened?"

"You want to know? I thought we were just a means to an end here."

Zip pointed to the slow ticking of the warp clock. "We have nothing but time." She reached down and passed him the whisky bottle.

Lars took it and had a small swig. "Now that's true kindness."

Zip snatched it back. "Your brother."

Lars grimaced. "Benny. I loved him, but he was a bit of a dumb shit. Always trying to impress our father, even though the old man never did much other than drink his pension and give us bruises. So, what does the kid do?"

"He signs up for military service."

"Aha! The great planetary defense force. See the galaxy, win honor for the UCP, and impress our dear deadbeat dad. I tried to convince him not to, but with an application that's only a page long and a two-day turnaround, he was enlisted before I could do much. So, I did the damned fool thing and joined him. Figured I'd been messing up his bullies long enough that he would need my protection. The recruiter took one look at me and asked me to name my price." Lars looked down at his lean muscle and chuckled. "Back in the day, I must have seemed quite the fighter. But anyway, I got myself assigned to Benny's platoon. We trained together, we bunked together, and when the time came, we shipped out together."

Zip knew where the story went, she had heard it a hundred times. No one knew exactly how bad the Planetary Defense Force was until they suddenly and violently became boots on the ground. She passed Lars the whisky again.

"Thank you kindly." This time he took a longer pull. "So, where do we end up? Some backwater conflict world that's gone against UCP regulation. These yahoos are held up tight. They've got bunkers, makeshift tanks, artillery, you name it, and to top it off, they've also got the high ground. Some pissant general decides he wants a promotion and that the odds don't matter. He's going to send our whole platoon, fresh out of training, up that hill to take out those separatists, no matter the cost. Prick.

"So, we go. We fight for two days in the dust and the heat, and we lose almost everybody. But when I'm standing at the top of that hill, Benny is with me. We look out over the barren landscape and despite everything, know that we've done it. Mission accomplished." Lars closed his eyes. "Then a fucking sniper bullet catches Benny right here." Lars put a finger to his temple.

"Kid never saw it coming, never felt a thing. One minute he's there, the next he's not."

"God damn the service."

Lars nodded. "God damn the service is right."

Zip sat in the silence this time. Lars could have been lying, but she didn't think so. They had gotten lucky.

"So, what about you? How does someone like yourself end up serving our great planetary commission?"

A blinking blue light and a trill of an incoming signal snapped Zip out of the moment. Thankful for any excuse not to talk about her past life, she turned her attention to the console. "What the hell? I thought we were at warp."

Lars eyed her for a second but turned to squint at the cosmic mess beyond the cockpit window. "Unless that whisky is something stronger, we are. Still, we have an incoming signal. Must be either really good or really bad news."

"You think someone is going to give us good news today?"

"OK, fine, it's bad news. Want me to put it through?"

Zip nodded and fished around in the side compartment on her chair. She found four white cylinders: sobriety shots. Realistically, they were ninety percent amphetamines, but they worked. She placed the smooth edge of the cylinder just above her left wrist and squeezed. There was a sudden cold pain as the drugs were administered in a high-pressure puff of gas. An immediate wave of clarity rushed in, followed closely by a resolute sense of purpose. *Damn, that feels good.*

Lars looked at her a second too long, maybe with pity, maybe something else, and then turned back to the co-pilot's console. The glass of the cockpit window became a screen, briefly blotting out the mess of warp and replacing it with a familiar logo: a serene blue planet surrounded by black orbits, and the words *UCP: For Every Planet* written beneath it. Around the edge of the image, a red and yellow banner read: *Official Distress Call.*

"Shit!" Zip slammed her fist on the edge of her chair. Either the amphetamines were making her angry, or that was an actual UCP distress call. "Lars, check the encryption on that message, and please tell me it's an elaborate fake."

Lars looked at the console and then back to Zip. "Check the—"

"Get Techni or Tom."

Lars stood up and walked out of the cockpit still muttering, "Encryption?"

Zip sat in her chair, massaging her hand where it had impacted the hard leather. *Can this day get any worse?* She took a deep breath and looked up at the message again. It took all her willpower to not slam her fist into the chair for a second time. An official UCP distress beacon mandated a response, or at the very least a flyby. Failure to do so could result in a hefty fine, jail time, or worse. What the worse was, Zip didn't want to know. Given the reach and bankroll of the UCP, it probably involved a pitch-black planet with triple gravity and rocks to break.

Techni walked in and strapped into the co-pilot's chair. "Distress signal at warp? That's expensive. Expensive isn't good." She tapped her fingers on the station's screens. The sound it made was mechanical and sharp.

A tension headache was already creeping in at Zip's temples. "I wouldn't put it past Jack to fake a distress signal." She hoped to hell it was Jack. There were a million things that could have caused a ship to send a warp-level distress signal, and most were variations on horrifying. Every ship had an official UCP transponder built in, but the cost of using it was astronomical. Sending an official distress call was usually a pilot's last action, if not because of their death, but because of the financial ruin that came after.

"Source is official," said Techni, teeth gritted. "We have to stop."

Zip groaned, the amphetamines already wearing thin in the wake of anger and sleep deprivation. "Shit, shit, shit."

"A verbose assessment of the situation."

Zip growled.

"Maybe the other team took a similar flight path."

"Should have planted a tracker on that bastard when I had the chance. If I had to guess, he's not stopping."

Techni raised an eyebrow.

Zip waved a hand at her. "Yeah, I know. When you have as many ships and as many hideouts as Jack, laws are guidelines, and guidelines are easily forgotten in favor of convenience."

"Sounds like a bad bar-side tattoo."

"I wouldn't be surprised if he had that somewhere on his person." Zip knew every inch of Jack's person. She brushed off the memory and turned on the ship-wide comm. "Unscheduled pit stop, everybody. Lars, Tom, set up an anti-breaching party in the cargo hold. If these are pirates, we're playing dead. I don't intend to trade one form of indentured servitude for another." *The Hog* was equipped for short battles but couldn't hold its own against a true outlaw frigate.

Techni's fingers danced over the controls with repeated metallic clicks. "Course plotted to pull us out of warp. As usual, the success rate is listed as 99.9%."

Zip rolled her eyes. Warp calculations never changed. They were always 99.9% accurate. The 0.1% was where ships disappeared, and captains were never heard from again. "I like those odds." She firmly didn't. In fact, she wasn't entirely convinced they were true odds.

"Right, five minutes," said Techni.

"How's your project coming along for Tom?"

"Do you think we're going to meet resistance?"

"That wasn't an answer."

Techni's eyes darted back and forth. "It's coming. I need more time."

"Well, Tom's going to need a rifle in his hands either way. He's not going to like that."

"He is an odd creature." There was no menace in the words, only uncut honesty.

"You're right about that."

The WARP button blinked green, and a countdown started on the main screen. Zip's brain was occupied with two warring ideas. On the one hand, she had no desire to investigate an expensive distress call that likely meant danger. On the other, she never felt bad about leaving warp. "Might as well warm up the antimatter guns."

"I thought I wasn't supposed to use them."

"Yeah, that was then, this is space."

Zip took deep breaths and pulled up a video feed of the cargo hold. Tom and Lars were already setting up temporary breach barriers. *The Hog* was designed to limit incursions to a single doorway off the cargo hold leading to the main ship. The idea was that pirates could take everything in the hold, and the pilot could claim a loss for insurance. Zip wasn't much for hiding, but whatever pirates did to deep space captives was worse than bruised pride.

Techni spooled through the code behind the UCP distress call. "I don't like this."

"Yeah, me neither. Best case, Jack blew right by it, worst case he gets there while we're boarding the ship and puts a few rounds through the hull."

"Accidents happen." Techni shook her head. "Prick."

"We can agree on that."

"Is your past relationship with him going to be a problem?"

Zip paused, calming her defensive instinct. *And how did you know that?* "I've got a bullet with his name on it."

"Good."

Zip watched the warp timer click down. "How did the Manchesters get you? You're supposed to be one of the best hackers on Prota." When in conflict, flattery was always an option for peace.

Techni stiffened—more than usual—and sat in silence a moment before answering. "I still haven't figured that out. My best guess is someone sold me out, but there are very few people I trust."

Zip understood that emotion. Trust wasn't easy, and it got harder each time it was betrayed. "This job should get you enough money to find out."

Techni smirked. "Oh, I don't need the money, I just need time. Prison cells don't have a data connection, or I would have gone willingly and worked it out in there. A little bit of solitude might be nice."

Zip fumbled for a response, but the warp timer clicked to zero and the intergalactic spaghetti disappeared all at once. Space, in all its vast emptiness, took its place. *The Hog's* cockpit screen magnified and shifted, searching for the distress signal until they had a clear image of the ship they were approaching.

The craft was dark, barely illuminated on one edge by a distant sun. There were no lights, no radio traffic, nothing. Zip switched to a heat map and saw a hazy outline. The ship looked like an elongated brick with spikes coming out one end—the brutalist style that military contractors preferred.

"There's barely any heat." Several lines swept over the craft's edges as Techni scanned. "Could be an exceptionally thick hull."

"Or it's a stealth ship." It wouldn't be the first Zip had seen that could run almost entirely dark.

"Stealth ships don't put out galaxy-wide distress beacons."

"Fair point."

As Techni's scans continued, the image of the ship got clearer. "No signs of damage or struggle. No external heat means no engines. I'm not even getting an electrical signal aside from the distress beacon."

Zip's neck tingled. Something about the dark ship scared her more than she wanted to admit. "I'm going to approach slow; it could still be a trap. Keep the long-range scanners running, I don't want anyone popping out of warp to surprise us."

Ships coming out of warp were impossible to see until they suddenly weren't. A brief disturbance in space-time could be detected in the minute or so before a ship appeared, but no earlier.

"Yes, Captain."

Zip opened comms to the cargo hold. "Leaving this channel open. We're approaching the ship now, no signs of a battle, no signs of foul play."

"Creepy," offered Lars.

Zip silently agreed. "We're moving closer. I don't like it, but one way or another, we're probably going to have to board. On the bright side, the UCP will give us standard compensation for doing so."

"Standard compensation," hissed Techni. "A free lunch and a shitty beer."

Zip pulled up a quick terminal with the going rate for responding to distress calls. It was indeed low. "Well, you're not that far off the mark, but it beats jail time."

"Why is the alternative always jail?" asked Tom.

For Zip, the alternative almost always seemed to be jail. So far, she hadn't spent more than a night there, and she was keen on keeping it that way. "Let's focus less on the alternative and keep to the task at hand. Prep those fancy vac suits from the Manchesters. Might as well see what money can buy."

3

A Shrimp in a Vacuum

TOM WAITED IN THE cargo bay and scrolled through the protocols that came along with an official UCP distress beacon. There were too many to read in one sitting. For brevity, at the top of the list, a summation read: *You have to stop*. From what Tom could read in their short approach, crew members were required to attempt communication, and if they received no response, board the distressed ship. There was a vague clause that allowed for a retreat in the event of 'undue danger', but with the maddening lack of clarity, it wasn't a real option.

To avoid the headache that followed reading UCP paperwork, Tom switched over to specs of the distressed ship. Its call sign was the *Bison-M*, but the craft looked nothing like a beast of burden. Some ships, it seemed, favored functionality over style. Shaped like an oblong brick, the *Bison-M* was made up of guns and minuscule crew compartments for those who manned the guns. At one end, a slightly larger than average room was reserved for the bridge. The crew manifest wasn't listed, the mission wasn't listed, and the captain wasn't listed.

"*Bison-M*, this is Zip Turbine of *Nana's Hog*, do you read me?" They were well within boarding distance, but even so, Zip continued to try the comms.

"No one's home," said Lars. "But whatever caused that distress signal might be." He pulled the slide back on a large assault rifle with an audible click.

"That's what I'm afraid of." Zip checked her weapons.

Tom held a standard issue UCP Peacekeeper, the favored rifle of all 'diplomatic' missions throughout the galaxy. Zip had more than a few stashed away that she'd conveniently 'lost' every time they were sent out on a government job. She never used them herself, because she "liked guns that sound like guns, not toys." Fortunately for Tom, the lower caliber meant he could fire it without snapping his limbs in half. Still, he viewed the rifle as performative, hoping there would never be an occasion to fire.

"*Bison-M*, last chance or we're coming aboard." Zip paused. Five long seconds passed. "Right, I guess we're doing this. Prepare to breach, two by two formation, everything goes by the book. No one splits up, no one gets lost, and if we see something we don't like, no one plays the hero. A UCP distress call only mandates that we do a welfare check on those inside. Nothing more, nothing less."

Techni holstered two submachine guns that were attached to her arms by a series of chrome cables. "We'll be model citizens."

Zip cracked a smile. "I'd expect nothing less. Helmets on, let's get this over with."

Tom went to grab the oblong helmet for his vac suit, forgetting that he was holding the rifle. The weapon fell to the floor with a loud clatter. He scrambled to pick the weapon up, but in his haste, accidentally kicked the helmet, sending it rolling across the cargo bay where it landed at Lars's feet with a hollow thunk.

Lars shook his head and picked it up. "Try not to drop this too many times. One hairline crack and you won't have time to remember that you made a mistake."

Tom grabbed the oblong helmet with multiple appendages, making sure he had it in a firm grip. "Thank you. I will be careful." He lifted the helmet onto his head, and it attached to his vac suit with a snap-hiss. In a turn of luck, everything fit. On Prota, there were tailors for every species imaginable. The problem was the universe was big, and human imaginations were small. While there was nothing quite like Tom in 'polite society', there were always people that were willing to try. Usually, he ended up with some ill-fitting mess that drained his bank account. The vac suit from the Manchesters was tailor-made. A cool mist drifted out of the interior pores, moistening his skin, and making his nervous anticipation comfortable if nothing else.

"Well, this is nice." Tom jumped backward, shocked to hear his voice aloud. His translator box still hung around his neck, but with the suit on, he couldn't use it.

Zip turned. "Was that you, Tom?"

Tom looked down at the suit and rubbed his appendages together in the way that normally produced speech. "I think so. Fancy suit." Technology was astonishing. He felt a pang of remorse for not using *his* translator box, his last piece of home.

"Being rich has its perks."

"Indeed." Tom picked up his rifle between several limbs, treating it like a fussy toddler that might suddenly throw a tantrum and blow a hole in another crewmate. Then he made his way to the airlock. The chamber was squat, square, and had a single glass window in the center. They were close enough that the only view was the polished black surface of the derelict ship. In the reflection, *The Hog's* approach lights looked like the eyes of an angry god. Fear, plain and simple, rushed through Tom. Looking out the porthole, he had the all-encompassing sense that something had either gone wrong or was about to.

"OK, just a short walk between ships. No big deal." Zip pushed a large red button at the edge of the air lock. A metal door slid shut behind them, sealing off the cargo bay, and a hiss filled the room as the air left. Gradually, the sound died, replaced by the silent austerity of space. The airlock door opened.

In his year aboard *The Hog*, Tom had performed a few spacewalks, but never in high-pressure situations. As a rule, Zip didn't like directly docking with other ships and preferred approaching from a distance. It made for quick getaways and conformed to her rule of "no one comes on my ship." So, Tom trained in vacuum often. Staring out at the reflective surface of the *Bison-M* was different. The ships were only a few hundred feet apart, but in the intervening gap, there was nothing but stars. The sleek surface reflected them, giving the impression that Tom was about to dive headlong into the void.

Zip jetted forward, small puffs of compressed air coming out the back of her suit.

Tom visualized diving deep beneath the ocean. In a way, space wasn't that different. Of course, in a million other ways, it was. He left *The Hog's* hold, feeling his stomach turn as gravity gave way to float. A wave of dizziness swept over him, so he focused on Zip. The black suit only reflected light from a distant sun off its glinting metal clasps and the curve of her helmet. Before he knew it, she was nothing more than a reflection within the larger reflection of the dark ship. Stars, everything around him were stars.

Keep calm. The world spun, slow, but noticeable. Tom adjusted his jets, attempting to slow his rotation. Each pulse only made things worse. Twinkling starlight blurred to bright white lines arching across the sky. Muffled voices echoed from a thousand miles away, swallowed by the void. *There are so many stars.* Tom felt sick and scared. He reached an appendage out, looking for something, anything to steady himself. There was nothing. Space was empty, the same as it had always been.

"Tom!" Zip's sharp voice cut through the haze.

She sounded aggravated. Why would she be aggravated? Tom found it hard to remember why he was outside the ship in the first place. Stars rushed towards him, fast, far too fast. The fear of falling forever gripped him, sending his heart into a mad flutter. How long would the oxygen last before he simply went to sleep and froze to death?

"Tom, slow your approach!"

Tom's eyes snapped forward. The shining black surface of the ship was far too close, he was going to hit it, he could see that now. Tom reversed his thrusters in a panic. The top of his suit kicked backward, reversing his spin and sending him into a tight backflip. Overhead, he watched as the black form of the derelict ship passed by, sliding through space like a silent leviathan. Tom stopped his thrust, but the spin continued in a sickening, ever-turning spiral. "I can't—" he started, but the nausea and g-force were too much to make coherent words.

"I've got him," came a voice that might have been someone he knew, but it was impossible to say.

A series of small, aggravated beeps sounded in Tom's suit, followed by a mechanical voice saying, "Exterior override. Exterior override."

That can't be right. The world continued to spin, the stars and the dark ship fading into an equal void, all black, devoid of anything but the deep need to not be awake any longer.

All at once, the world snapped back into existence, cold and disorienting. Zip's face floated before his, lit by the glow of her helmet lights. "Tom, you with us?"

"His vitals say he's with us," answered Lars.

"I... Yes." What had he been doing? He could barely remember. His head throbbed. Looking around, he saw the black surface of the ship once more. *Ah, yes, that's right.* The stars were still there, but he was close enough that he could see the metal surface reflecting them.

"Thank hell for that." Zip blew out a sigh of relief.

"Thank hell for me," responded Techni.

Zip put a hand on Tom's suit. "Techni just saved your life."

Tom looked to Techni. Her eyes were implacable. "Thank you, Techni."

She nodded, the gesture muffled by the restrictive motion in her suit. "We've still got Kedasi, and we can't afford to be down a team member."

Suddenly, Tom remembered the danger they were in and looked for his gun.

Zip shook her head. "You let go of it in the spin. Luckily, we have spares. Stick close and stay behind me. You're going back to Spacewalk 101 when we get back to Prota."

Shame bloomed in Tom's heart. "Yes, Captain."

There was apology and pity in Zip's eyes, but it flickered and died as the captain in her returned. "Everyone, form up on this lock, we're wasting air."

4

The Last Party

Zip's heart hammered. Stimulants waged war with the depressants she had been using at warp, and neither side was close to victory. Adding insult to injury was the adrenaline from nearly losing Tom in a routine spacewalk and the foreboding jet-black airlock in front of her. Several low-level alarms let her know that her biometrics were elevated, but not yet dangerous.

Small miracles. Deep breaths. She tried. Failed. Tried again. Her breath came in ragged little impulses, hardly enough to keep her brain alive. Thankfully, the vacuum suit steadied her trembling hands. "Keying in the airlock override. Let's see if anyone is home."

Switching to her suit's computer, she said, "Requesting UCP distress signal override protocol. The ship is locked."

There was a trill indicating the computer was processing. Zip suspected the computer had no need to process, but humans were so used to waiting that an instantaneous response would be unnerving. Scientists specialized in making technology appear exactly good enough to impress the masses while placating their existential dread of its eventual rule. "Unlocking forward airlock, permission to board granted, Captain."

A green light illuminated the circular edges of the airlock door, and a puff of white gas hissed out from the cracks. The door irised open, revealing a dark airlock chamber, not unlike *The Hog's*. "Suit lights on," called Zip.

One by one, the rest of the crew clicked on their lights, bathing the airlock in stark white. "Still has pressure," said Lars. "At least there's that."

"That just means whatever killed them can survive in oxygen. Helmets stay on. Don't want to inhale anything that's going to ruin your day." The options for hazards on an abandoned spacecraft were limitless, and none of them were pleasant. Zip had heard a story about a mercenary that had come into contact with the wrong interstellar spore and hadn't realized it until years later when a mushroom burst through his chest at a dinner party.

"Yes, Captain."

Zip jetted forward. "Tight formation behind me, but not too tight. If I catch a bullet because one of you assholes gets jumpy, I will haunt every ship you're on to the end of your days."

"Don't shoot the captain in the ass." Lars gave a small salute.

"Idiot," muttered Techni.

"Basic idea was right." Zip entered the airlock. Her boots thumped as they hit the metal surface, a low-level magnetic current pulling her down in an imitation of gravity. She approached the inner airlock window and shone her light through it. The glass was scuffed from years of use—or a fight—but she could make out a messy corridor beyond. Objects free-floated through the ship. "Gravity is off, this should be interesting."

Tom was the last to enter, being a little too careful with his thrusters.

"Please cycle inner airlocks," Zip asked the computer.

Another trill. "Of course. UCP protocol mandates that you do not use force against the occupants of this ship unless necessary. Please nod your head to assent that you have heard this mandate and intend to comply. A similar message is being broadcast to your team members."

Zip grumbled and nodded. There was a flash as the mask illuminated her face, scanning it for verification.

"Thank you, you may now enter the *Bison-M*."

Behind them, the outer airlock shut, locking mechanisms sliding into place with a dull thunk. Air hissed up from beneath their feet, pressurizing the room, and bringing sound back in a slow wave. The inner door opened with a snap-hiss. Zip raised her rifle to look down the corridor. It ran the full length of the ship, with doors and corridors leading off the main arterial. Crates of supplies hung in the air, some turning in a slow, infinite spin.

She moved forward. "Techni, left side, Lars, right side. Tom, behind me. Make sure we don't get surprised."

Techni and Lars fanned out accordingly, jetting their way through the debris with ease. While most ships had artificial gravity, everyone was required to train in zero-g at least once to be able to ship out. Gravity systems didn't often fail, but when they did, it paid to know the feeling of weightlessness. If nothing else, it taught tourists not to slam themselves into bulkheads at suicidal speeds.

Zip pulled up a schematic of the ship on her heads-up display. The ship was spartan, designed for efficiency and nothing else. The long corridor from the cargo hold had breaks for cabins and stairways. Between them was nothing but polished grey walls. They were on the primary housing deck. One deck up was the mess, and one deck beyond that was the bridge and weapons control. "We need to make our way to the bridge. That's where the signal is coming from, and it's the only way to prove we did our due diligence."

Zip scanned down the rows of cabins. If anyone was around, they were being real quiet about it. "Take the first stairway on the left."

Techni moved through the corridor, sticking close to the wall. When she reached the stairwell, she peaked through, light flashing in the darkness, and then pulled her head back in a snap. She repeated the gesture twice before calling, "Clear. Also, not that it matters, but I'm not picking up any heartbeats on this ship that aren't us."

"Thick walls," answered Lars, never lowering his own rifle. "This is a military ship. It's designed to confuse invaders. We wouldn't see a heartbeat if they were screwing each other in the next room."

"That's comforting," answered Tom.

Tom's sarcasm is getting better. "Check every corner." If there were any survivors, Zip suspected they wouldn't be in a friendly mood.

"Yes, Captain." Techni glided up the stairs with practiced ease. Her rifle swept methodically from side to side, never ceasing movement, covering as much area with the light as possible.

A small benefit to having trained killers for temporary shipping companions. "Alright," Zip said, "I'm going next, then Tom. Lars, you bring up the rear."

Lars put his back to the wall and alternated shining his rifle left and right. "Yes, Captain."

Zip waited for Techni to be halfway up the stairwell and followed. Rather than jetting from side to side, she let her magnetic boots do the talking, clomping up each step like an approaching bogeyman. If there were still survivors on the ship, she didn't want to catch them by surprise.

When she got to the top of the stairs, Techni was standing stock still just outside the doorway. Initially Zip thought nothing of it—Techni's general mechanical nature often begat moments of robotic stillness—then she saw it.

The name 'mess' was more apt than usual. Several figures sat hunched around a table in various states of decay, some still clutching their last bottles of beer. Orange foam sat in crystallized clumps on the floor, dribbling from the mouths and wounds of the dead. At first glance, one thing was clear: No one on the ship had gotten off alive.

"Are we dealing with a biotoxin?"

"No." A cold sheet of dread settled over Zip as she approached the corpses. While some were sporting clear wounds, barely hidden behind bandages now puffed out with the foam, others looked relatively unharmed.

Zip pulled out a scanner from her side holster and brought it up close enough to take a small sample of the substance. The scanner opened, grabbed a tuft of foam off the side of a dead man, and pulled it in. She held her breath as the machine whirred and beeped, never letting her rifle drop from her free hand. Eventually, the device finished its analysis and spit out a warning that only meant one thing. "Shit."

"Captain?" asked Techni, a hint of genuine fear creeping into her voice.

Zip sighed. "It's a biologic, which means one thing."

"Bugs."

Zip nodded. "Bugs."

Techni jetted over to her, keeping a careful distance from the bodies. "No signs of struggle."

Zip's head swam with sudden images of spindly squirming bodies inside the walls of the ship. She took a deep breath. "No, they were celebrating. Whatever they fought, it wasn't on the ship." Zip said the words to remind herself more than anything.

A small orange light blinked, letting her know that her heart rate was elevated. She tried to focus on the facts. The fact that the goop hadn't burned through several levels of the deck was a good sign. "Whatever this is, it isn't corrosive."

"Unless you're organic material."

Zip looked at the wounds, still dripping goop. "Yeah, I wouldn't touch it."

"Wasn't planning on it."

"Oh dear," said Tom, emerging from the stairwell.

Lars followed close behind. "Well, shit."

Zip pushed away from the mess, floating backward. "Not a good day for these people. Still, a chance it might not be a bad day for us. Let's find the bridge, tag this ship as a lost cause, and get the hell out of here." Suddenly warp seemed like a much friendlier place to be.

"Agreed." Techni was already jetting back across the room to the stairwell. "You heard the captain, let's not stay around long enough to find out if ships can be haunted."

"Ghosts are not—"

Lars put a hand on one of Tom's appendages. "Not the time."

"Right."

Zip moved past them. "Keep an eye out. Just because the wounds happened elsewhere doesn't mean we're not going to run into trouble here."

"You'll get no argument from me." Lars went back to sweeping the room.

Zip moved through the stairwell, feeling suddenly cramped. She wondered how many more bodies were hiding around the ship. *Where the hell did they get those wounds?* The answer was simple, but she didn't want to say it out loud.

She exited the stairwell and quickly crossed the short distance to the bridge. A long panel of glass ran across the length of the ship, giving unobstructed views of the space around them. Below, banks of stations were attached to the wall in neat order. Raised in the middle of the room were three command chairs and a central console. A slumped figure took up the main chair, its right hand still on the control stick. A video screen played a repeating message, casting the figure in a stark silhouette.

"This is Captain Kane of the *Bison-M*. If you are finding this message, then my crew and I are long dead."

5

An Interlude with Kane

KANE COULD FEEL THE fire in his guts. The others were celebrating their survival, probably thinking they had a little too much to drink, but they would figure it out soon enough. He staggered toward the bridge, his hand held over the wound on his chest. In theory, the laceration was nothing the ship's medic couldn't manage. In practice, he'd bled through every bandage they put on him, and the pain grew with each passing second. He spat and was surprised to see it was orange. "That's not great."

His voice echoed thin in the empty corridors of the *Bison-M*. A decade as captain, and it was all going to end because of a goddamned theme park. The universe was a messed-up place.

Each step toward the bridge was harder than the last. They had been off Kedasi for around twelve hours, and while the wound had never stopped hurting, the agony was new. The others would feel it soon.

The ship's analyst said it was biochemical acid that fed on organic matter. No cure. *Ain't that a trip.* Trouble was, the analyst had been there in the fight, same as everyone else. No free rides on Kane's ship. When the kid saw the results, he wouldn't stop blubbering. Kane had snapped his neck, put him out of his misery.

No point in letting the crew know they were doomed. Let them have their party.

He stumbled his way towards the captain's chair, thoughts focused on the vintage whisky concealed in its arm. He'd drink the whole thing when he was finished recording his message. They'd burn the ship when they found it anyway. A perfect record kept spotless by cleansing fire.

He slumped into the chair, surprised by a sudden wave of

exhaustion. The bridge was empty, nothing to look at other than the expanse of stars. He doubted they even had enough crew to fill the place anymore. More than three quarters of the original team died on Kedasi.

Dillon, stone cold killer, Dillon. Last words "one click out." They never found his head, just a corpse spouting a fountain of orange goop from a rotten hole of a neck.

Maybe leaving the world behind wouldn't be so bad after all. Endless sleep would put a cap on the horror show he saw whenever he closed his eyes. *God I'm tired of this shit.*

Kane tried his best to look presentable. Orange pus leaked out from beneath his bandage. *So much for my regal image.* "Begin recording. This is Captain Kane of the *Bison-M*. If you are finding this message, then my crew and I are long dead." *I've listened to a hundred messages like this.* "I'm filing an official UCP distress beacon. You will find there are ample funds from our ship's employers." That was of course assuming the Manchesters didn't get there first. Evidence, that's what the ship was now.

"We were on a routine mission to retrieve precious cargo for a wealthy employer from a dangerous place. You'll notice I'm being vague. Well, I've got a family." Technically true. He hadn't seen his wife in almost a decade, and the son they had together was a stranger, but that didn't stop the Manchesters and their threats. "All you need to know is that you are at no biological risk from the bodies on this ship. I mean if you decide to go around licking the corpses… Just don't." *Rambling, John. You're rambling.*

A knot twisted in his guts sending tendrils of pain through his stomach. He grunted. "It appears I need to wrap up. I'm not sure how much time this shit takes to set in. "To our employers: Don't send another team to this rock. There is no way to recover what you lost. Do the right thing, and nuke it from a safe distance. There is nothing there but death, and the rotting steel of your ambition." *Waxing poetic?* Death did funny things to people, especially when it was slow and creeping.

A fresh round of tight pain looped around Kane's insides, squeezing them with burning fire. "Yup, that's my cue. Whoever finds this, I hope you're having a better day than I am. End recording." The screen went blank and then popped up the blue logo of the UCP. Below it was a simple question: *Do you want to send your official UCP distress signal?* Below that were two check boxes, yes and no. Below the yes was a dollar amount that would have been enough to make Kane contemplate his life even if he hadn't been on his deathbed. He tried not to think too hard about where the money went and clicked yes.

The UCP logo blurred away as a cartoon rocket sped across the screen, leaving a vapor trail that spelled out *Help is on the way*.

"I swear, our government is run by children." That made Kane chuckle, and the spasm that followed made him wish for death. He doubled over in pain, gripping the edges of his chair.

In the distance, he thought he could hear screaming from somewhere else on the ship. *So, it's started for them as well.* Gentle in his movements, Kane leaned back and opened the chair's side compartment. He ripped the stopper out of the bottle hidden there and tossed it to the floor.

"Was saving you for a great victory, but hard times." Kane lifted the bottle to his lips and took a long pull. The harsh vapor made him splutter and cough, sending a rusty knife of pain through his guts.

For a moment, he could see the chittering brown bodies charging at them in a sickening wave. "Yeah, fuck you too."

6

Contemplation Leads to Death

TOM SAT IN THE cramped confines of his cabin, trying to find some measure of safety. There wasn't enough time to fill the flotation tank, and even small tasks were taxing. Every time he lost focus, even for a second, he saw Kane's message on repeat juxtaposed against a headless corpse, rotting, and covered in orange goop. When it wasn't that, he felt the tight spinning sensation of space as he slowly drifted away from his companions forever. There were infinite ways to die in space, and in the last few hours, Tom had become acutely aware of several more.

An alert chimed and Tom tapped the side of his tank to open it. It was a short message from Zip: *Crew meeting, in the galley, fifteen minutes.*

Tom contracted. A crew meeting meant they would be leaving for Kedasi soon. Originally, Tom had hoped to make an argument for abandoning the mission, but after a few cursory searches on the Manchesters' wealth, the lack of options became clear. There weren't many things in the universe money couldn't buy. If they chose to run, they'd all be dead within a week, and that was a conservative estimate.

Another chime filled the room and Tom felt it like a gunshot. There was someone at the door. He tapped at his terminal, heart still pounding in the sides of his head. Techni was standing outside, tapping her foot and staring at the camera like she wanted to fight it. Tom straightened and walked over to the door, but not before there was another chime as Techni pressed the entry button again. *Impatient, but at least she did not hack the door.*

Tom knew that Techni could lock them out of all *The Hog's* systems in under an hour if she wanted to. He might not have read Zip's files on bug planets, but he had certainly done his homework when it came to their new shipmates.

Tom pressed a button and the door to his compartment slid open.

Techni was midway to pushing the button again but pulled her finger back. "I have something for you."

Tom wanted to ask if it could wait, but Techni had other plans. Before he could respond, she was walking down the corridor at a brisk pace without so much as a look to see if he was following. Tom scrambled to catch up, limbs clicking along the metal flooring, mixing with the hum of the ship's engines sitting perpetually primed for warp.

Techni made her way down the spiral staircase that led into *The Hog's* hold.

Tom followed. Long work benches had been set up in what was previously an empty storage space. Lars was in the far corner, inspecting welding lines that ran across *The Hog's* hull. They were remnants of a Crustacean patch job after a group of renegade lobsters had blown a hole in the side of the ship. Tom had told Zip many times they needed to get them fixed, but the money never seemed to find its way toward repairs.

"Hurry up, we only have a few minutes before the captain wants us." Techni motioned for Tom to come over to one of the work benches.

He scuttled then stopped, unsure of what exactly he was looking at. Sitting on the table was a bundle of metal rods and wires surrounding a gun barrel and magazine. From a distance, it looked like a confused metallic spider.

Techni stood back, looking as close to content as she ever got.

"What is it?" If they were short on time, there was no harm in being blunt.

"This might be the only weapon that someone like you can fire."

Tom reached out a tentative appendage toward it. All at once, the metal sprang to life, curling around his limb and then snapping around like an exoskeleton on his back. The rifle whipped around in front of him, dual triggers extending to meet his limbs.

Techni took a step back. "Hmm. I didn't know it could do that."

"Didn't know?" The barrel twitched and swayed.

"I didn't have time to read the AI manual. I gave it some parameters, and it looks like it's doing what it's supposed to."

"You put artificial intelligence inside a gun?" There were several treaties and laws against that, and for good reason.

"LIGHT artificial intelligence. It's not going to talk to you at a dinner party. At least, I hope it won't."

Tom couldn't tell if Techni was joking, but he was acutely aware of the weapon now in his hands. With it, he could deal death, and he did not like it. "How do I take it off?"

As soon as he said the words, the bundle of metal leaped back on the table where it collapsed into a form no larger than a briefcase.

"Alright, we'll call it medium AI."

For someone so interested in technology, Tom couldn't help but feel Techni had little respect for it.

Lars approached and looked down at the jumble of metal. "Cool toy."

Techni scoffed.

"Ah relax, only joking. Tom, who did these repairs?" He motioned to the welding lines he had been inspecting.

"Crustaceans," answered Tom.

"Huh."

"I have told Zip to get them fixed."

Lars grimaced. "They'll hold for now. I wouldn't go poking them too hard."

"Noted."

"Captain wants us in the galley."

"We have five minutes," answered Techni.

"And here I thought we were short on time." Lars headed for the stairs.

Techni waited for him to be a good distance away before muttering a hushed curse. Then, she turned her attention back toward the weapon, eyes sparkling with delight and after-market cosmetics. She looked at Tom. "So?"

Tom fidgeted. The idea of a weapon that was custom-made was endearing, but it also put him one step closer to having to use it. "Thank you, Techni."

She waved a hand. "I don't need your thanks. Can you fire it? Can you kill to stop something from killing me? That's what I care about."

"I—" Tom's hands fumbled with the translator box, unsure of what to say. In the end, the truth spilled out without too much thought. "I have never killed anything."

"Never?"

"There were a few pests in the palace on Crustacea that needed to be—"

"You've never been in combat."

"I have been combat adjacent." Tom had seen more death secondhand than he cared to talk about, and all that in the last few years alone. Zip was a wonderful captain, but she was quick with a trigger, and to the outside eye, not discerning about when it was used.

Techni seemed on the verge of several curse words but smoothed her composure at the last second. "First rule, only point it at things you want dead."

Tom nodded. "That is simple enough."

"Second rule, try not to screw up the first."

Tom looked down at the mechanical bundle and back to Techni. "Thank you for this, Techni."

She looked at him, calculating. "I don't want to die at a theme park. I have some affairs to settle with whoever sold me out on Prota."

Before Tom could respond, Techni had turned and was heading toward the galley. He was left alone, standing in the packed cargo bay—well, not entirely alone. A part of him felt as though the weapon was watching his every move. The jumble of metal twitched with an expectancy that made Tom uncomfortable. Thankfully, he did not have long to contemplate. A chime played from his terminal; it was time to go to the galley.

He followed Techni and did his best not to think about the killing to come. As he walked, he listened to the ambient sounds of space, looking for the calm in their regularity. *The Hog* was home, and right now it was protecting him. The comfort was enough to quell the rising panic in his gut.

The rest of the crew were already seated. To call the mood tense would have been an offense to the word. Zip sat centered on the holo table, staring at a rotating image of Kedasi. Lars was beside her, massaging his temples. Techni was scowling in the corner. Tom moved to sit across from Zip.

Lars leaned in to look at the image of Kedasi. "I really don't want to go there."

"Scared?" asked Techni.

"You bet. Ever been to a bug planet?"

"No."

"You'd be scared too."

Tom felt more than enough fear for all of them.

Techni clucked her tongue. "We could try to run."

"There's nowhere far enough to get away from the Manchesters," said Zip.

"If we split up, we'll stand a better chance. I know a few tricks to hide us."

Lars chuckled. "Split up, we just die slower. I don't care what tricks you know, with enough money and enough time, we'll be found. The Manchesters have plenty of both."

"There isn't anyone better than me."

"It's a big universe, Techni."

Techni stepped off the wall looking like she was ready to start a fight when Zip slapped a firm hand on the table. "Enough. You two need to figure your shit out before we get to Kedasi. If I die because of a squabble, I'm going to be pissed. Now, let's focus on what we can do rather than what we can't. Our odds of surviving this mission are slim, but I'll take slim over none. I've been to several bug planets, and I'm still standing."

"Several?" asked Lars.

Zip nodded. "I've sent you all a packet of briefings. I suggest you read over as many as you can before we get to Kedasi."

"I have read them," said Tom.

Zip raised an eyebrow. "Tom, we can travel through warp to distant galaxies, do you really think I can't see read history on my documents?"

Tom fiddled with his hands but ultimately decided not responding was the best. There was a tension in Zip he hadn't seen before. He saw sweat dripping from her brow despite the chilled air in their suits.

"Before I was paranoid, now, I'm sure: Kedasi is infested. I've been to infested planets before, and it doesn't end well. The only way to stay alive is to be there for as little time as possible and then get the hell out."

"And bring the biggest guns we have?" asked Lars.

"I like the enthusiasm, but we're going to need to be able to run. High caliber, low weight wherever possible."

"Dress for the occasion." Lars smiled. "I think I have something."

"I'm sure you do."

"What if we run into Jack?" Tom hoped there was an answer that involved negotiation, but even as he asked the question, he knew the response he would get.

Zip's lip curled into something halfway between a sneer and a smile. "The guns aren't just for the bugs."

Tom bobbed his head, hoping he didn't look too uncomfortable, knowing he did.

"We've got twenty-four hours in transit to Kedasi, do your reading, prep your weapons, and let's try not to die."

7

Leave Your Cares Behind

ZIP WOKE TO THE sound of a blaring alert, heart racing, covered in a cold sweat. She shot to a sitting position and smashed her head on the low ceiling. Stars blotted her vision, followed closely by pain, cursing, and regret. It took a few seconds for her eyes to focus, but as they did, she realized she was in her cabin, and the terrifying alert was the alarm she had set. She pressed a panel on the wall next to her bed and the incessant beeping stopped. The alarm meant they were close.

She rolled out of bed and onto the floor where she immediately began her morning workout routine. Push-ups, crunches, pull-ups, jumping jacks, repeat. Being the captain of a ship didn't leave long for exercise, but every minute counted. Fat captains didn't make it to retirement age. Besides, the sweat and endorphins felt good at times when nothing else did. Staring down the barrel of a bug planet, she took what she could get. With each repetition, her muscles burned and her mind quieted.

Fifteen minutes later, she stepped out of her cabin, freshly showered, and blood pumping. It was a new start, dulled by the remnant of amphetamines in her system from the previous day. *Small price to pay.* She walked the ten steps from her door to the cockpit and opened it. The room was already full. Tom was in the co-pilot's chair staring out at warp with a familiar terror, Techni was in one of the engineering jump seats continuing her constant fiddling with the circuit board in her arm, and Lars was opposite her, running diagnostics on systems that had already been triple checked. It was enough to give Zip a sliver of hope, but not enough to let anyone know about it.

She took her seat right as the countdown for exiting warp hit one minute. A small machine built into the flight console chimed and spit out a fresh cup of steaming coffee. The aroma filled the cockpit with its delicious and strong scent. She took the cup and brought it to her lips. They were about to enter Hell, but at least the coffee was good. "Who's ready to go to a theme park?"

"Spoken like someone who has had sleep," said Lars, yawning.

"You should grab a cup. I brew it strong."

Lars made a shooing motion. "Never liked the stuff. If I want motor oil, I know where to find it."

And that is why things would never work out between us. She took a long and savoring sip from her cup and watched the warp timer click down. A nagging sensation in her brain reminded her of the dangers they were about to face, but she focused as much as she could on the coffee.

Outside, warp disappeared in an instant, becoming afterimages and faint hints of looping matter before fading to nothing. An orange gas giant loomed large in its place, glowing brilliant in the light of a distant sun. Chaotic storms raged in colorful swirls that looked beautiful from a distance but would rip anything that entered the atmosphere to shreds.

Kedasi, by comparison, was nothing more than a black spot against the planet's surface. To *The Hog,* the spec was a bullseye. As they approached, the asteroid took shape, growing from a shadow into the craggy surface of a derelict rock. From the far side, it wasn't much, but even long-range scans showed something odd: atmosphere. At a distance, it showed up as a hazy bubble. Zip brought up a tactical display of the asteroid's surface and shot off one of *The Hog's* survey probes just to be safe.

A technical layout of Kedasi's main park and adjacent lodging complexes filled her screen. The Opus was the most obvious landing site. Somewhere deep in its bowels was a jewel worth enough for the Manchesters to hire two mercenary teams. *Three, maybe more,* she corrected. Who knew how many mercenary bones littered the asteroid in front of them? She shuddered, remembering Kane's final message. Bugs were never pleasant, but whatever was on Kedasi sounded like it was straight out of Hell.

Zip set *The Hog's* autopilot to direct them toward a VIP landing platform adjacent to The Opus. While most guests would have had to use the park's main landing pads—there were nearly a hundred of them—wealth was always king with the Manchesters.

"Doesn't look like much," offered Lars.

"Nothing does in the shadow of a gas giant." Zip had seen plenty of planets, but there was something about the impossible scale of gas giants that still gave her pause.

Kedasi continued to grow before them, artificially magnified at first, but switched to real-time the closer they got. Most of the asteroid was barren and covered in shadow. *The Hog's* angle of ascent brought them in over the dark side, just on the edge of sunrise. The ship bumped and shuddered as it entered atmosphere, but far less than on a typical planet. There was a loud WHUMP as it dropped several feet, adjusting all at once to Kedasi's artificial gravity.

The probe returned with a suite of green readings. "And there's the confirmation that there was never a gas leak. The air down there is fully breathable." Breathable was an understatement. The planet's temperature was a perfect seventy degrees with a slight breeze and air clean enough to make the wilderness jealous.

Tom tapped at the screens on the co-pilot's console. "Not picking up any signs of movement. We should be coming up on the main park in less than a minute."

"Always wanted to go to one of these places as a kid." It was one of the many dreams Zip had let die in the depths of the income-reduced districts where she grew up.

"I wanted to be as rich as a Manchester maybe," replied Lars. "Money, power, telling other people to get lost for a living. I'm not sure where I went wrong."

Techni scoffed. "Didn't start your life with a billion credits hidden in your diapers?"

Lars nodded. "That probably would have helped."

The chatter died as *The Hog* neared the edge of the dark side of the asteroid. Despite being in atmosphere, the flight was eerily smooth. With Kedasi's size, they passed out of darkness in little more than an instant. One moment, they were in the equivalent of night, and the next, the sun was shining bright on the surface. Gleaming in the distance, Zip saw The Opus's towering glass helix. Long tendrils of railway lines ran high above the ground and gave spectacular views of the park beyond. Towering metal rollercoasters silhouetted the skyline, reaching up like the tentacles of a frozen elder god. Beneath them, a strange hodgepodge of buildings and icons formed a makeshift city.

Lars whistled. "Alright, I'm impressed."

"People would ride those rails for fun?" asked Tom.

"Tom, people would have paid a couple thousand credits just to spend the weekend here."

Tom vibrated. "Some days, I'm not sure I'll ever understand humans."

"You and me both," agreed Lars.

The Hog banked left, the ship's autopilot taking them on a smooth curve toward The Opus. Zip looked at the gleaming theme park and keyed in an override to take manual control. The ship shuddered as she adjusted their course, flying low toward the rollercoaster. "Might as well get a lay of the land and see what we're dealing with."

She would never admit it, but a part of her was curious to see just what the hell the Manchesters had managed to build. A dormant sense of wonder and childlike curiosity bloomed in her heart. It was a feeling she didn't realize she had missed until it returned.

Tom raised his chair and leaned it forward, looking down through *The Hog's* orb-shaped canopy. His bulbous black eyes shone. "Wow."

As they neared the edge of the park, Zip saw the backsides of elaborate facades stretching up into the sky. "Wow is right." From the ground, they would block the view of the asteroid beyond, completing the immersion that Manchester parks were famous for. On the outer edge, long industrial buildings spread out connected by spiderwebs of maintenance roads. The park looked nearly finished. There were several idle construction machines and crates scattered around, but the Manchesters couldn't have been more than a year out from opening.

Zip flew over the façade and slowed their approach. The back roads gave way to a cobblestone street, lined on both sides with tall wooden buildings. The sun glinted off shining shop windows with brightly colored goods just behind them. A series of planters ran down the center of the street filled with rainbows of blooming flowers. Green trees rustled in the asteroid's calm breeze.

"An idyllic representation of Old Earth," said Techni, now standing behind Zip's chair. "This is meant to mimic a time well before humans left. The 1800s maybe, early settler shit."

Zip turned to look at her. "Oh?"

"There was a time when I wanted to study ancient history. We forget a lot about the planet that gave birth to our species."

Zip sat in silent surprise, resisting the urge to pry. Knowing Techni, one too many questions would lead to *The Hog* getting hacked, or Zip's bank account being drained.

Instead, she focused her attention out the window and watched as the wooden streets gave way to a towering red rock canyon. Multicolored pools shimmered in deep rock wells crisscrossed by rollercoaster tracks. Dusty paths led towards large cave entrances, carved into a rock face at the center of the canyon. The rollercoaster dipped between geysers and weaved through the canyon. A foolhardy part of Zip wanted to ride it more than anything else in the world at that moment. *Probably filled to the brim with bugs.*

Below, the canyon fell away, giving rise to a generic big city street with a towering rail station. Long single rails extended from it in four directions.

Lars tapped a few keys and brought up a map of the park. It was stylized, made for guests, but still gave a decent representation. "Those rails would have led to landing pads and hospitality buildings."

A train, silver and shining, sat forever halfway to its destination on one of the rails.

The Opus stood sentinel beyond. Even surrounded by the barren nature of the asteroid, the building was breathtaking. Every inch looked delicate and on the verge of collapse. Luckily, without so much as a gust of wind on Kedasi, there was room for delicate.

As they approached, the chasm upon which the hotel sat became clear. It was a long, dark scar on the asteroid's surface. Unlike the friendly canyons of the theme park before it, the ground here looked old and uninviting. The asteroid was pitted and craggy. Landing would be a challenge, traversing would be another hassle entirely. *The Hog's* distance to target slowly clicked down, and Zip eased back on the throttle. They were almost in the shadow of The Opus when she saw it.

Lars unbuckled and stood up from his chair. "Well, so much for Plan A."

The steel beams that would have made up the landing platform's superstructure were bent and torn, pieces of debris hanging above the chasm. The glass where The Opus connected with a walkway to the landing platform was cracked and shattered. In short, no one was landing at the front door. Zip slowed *The Hog* to a hover, keeping a careful distance.

"What's the next closest landing site?" Zip looked out at the craggy mass of grey rock beneath them. They could attempt a landing on the surface, but if the bugs had truly hollowed the asteroid out, the surface could be unstable. Not to mention the dust that would get in *The Hog's* vents. There was a good chance they would never take off again.

Next to her, Tom scrolled around the map of Kedasi. He hesitated, but eventually responded. "The park's front gate has a drop off center for incoming tourist ships."

"The Manchesters provided override codes for the train systems," hissed Techni.

"They knew." Zip looked back toward the derelict train, sitting placid, glinting in the sun. "I hate this place already. Everyone get suited up, it looks like we're going in on foot."

Lars groaned. "Of course we are. I'll go check the guns."

8

The Plaza

Tom stood in the *Hog's* cargo bay staring out at the smoldering wreckage of six practice dummies. Training rounds or not, the effect had been real. The acrid stink of gun smoke filled the air, and his appendages still vibrated from the rifle's kick. At its core, Techni's contraption was a series of elegant stabilizers that clipped a gun to Tom's body and helped hold it steady. The effect was simple: He could fire it, and his whole body took the effect of the recoil rather than a single arm. Tom operated the triggers with a simple twitch from one of his lower appendages, and the rest was pure instinct—well, instinct, and the AI hiding somewhere beneath the gun's surface.

Techni sat on a crate nearby, double-checking her vacuum suit. "Better than expected."

Tom let go of the rifle, the sudden shock of the moment starting to wear off. The rifle hung in the air for a second, attached by magnetic guides to the stabilizers, and then whipped around to his back. Tom jumped slightly.

Lars came up from behind and put a heavy hand on his shoulder. "Hey, take it easy. With shots like that, we might stand a chance."

"Do you think so?" Tom felt a wave of relief wash over him.

"Eh, maybe, maybe not."

The relief died.

"Just try to keep yourself as calm as possible. Nothing can prepare you for your first fight, but if you keep a level head, you'll stay alive."

"Thank you."

Thankfully, the new Manchester translator didn't convey the fear in Tom's voice. Levelheadedness was not one of his strong suits; planning was. The trouble with hostile asteroids filled to the brim with bugs was they were impossible to plan for. In the intervening time between the derelict ship and Kedasi, Tom had read every single one of Zip's reports, cover to cover, just like she had asked. In short summation, there was no planning for an enemy that was superior in every way, which left only the obvious course of action: Panic.

Lars moved around Tom to face him eye-to-eye.

Tom stared blankly back. He suspected there was supposed to be some degree of emotional significance in Lars's gaze, and he tried to convey with his own bulbous eyes that he too found meaning in the gesture. In reality, he was more struck by the detailed lines creasing the corner of the man's eyes than anything else. The human body was a strange thing.

Eventually, Lars spoke. "No one wants their first battle, and those that do often find it's their last. Walking toward death isn't something people were made to do, human or otherwise."

"I was designed for eating detritus off the ocean floor."

Lars looked Tom up and down. "Sure, but they don't know that."

"They?"

"Bugs, people that want to kill you. What they see are carapace and claws. They see a killer."

Tom flinched. "That would explain certain attitudes on Prota."

"People will always be scared of what they don't know. Right now, that's an advantage."

Tom vibrated, uncomfortable and unsure of what to say.

"I know you're afraid, or at least I assume you're afraid. That's good, keep it close."

"Fear is good?"

"Fear *can* be good. If you give it too much thought, fear will consume you, but if you let a little in, that's just smart. There are plenty of ways to die out here, and acknowledging them, or even just noticing them doesn't make you weak. It makes you hu—Well, it makes you a person anyway."

"I am very afraid." Very afraid was an understatement. Tom felt as though at any moment the very gravity of the asteroid would crush him into oblivion.

"So am I, but you, shooting like that," he pointed to the practice dummies, "that helps me more than a little bit. Out there, I need to know that you have my back, and you need to know I have yours. If we can get trust, there's a chance we'll make it off this rock alive." Lars favored him with a grin.

Tom did his best to approximate something similar by wavering his antennae back and forth. "OK, Lars, I will watch your back."

The metallic click of heavy boots interrupted the conversation as Zip strode into the cargo hold. She was in her vacuum suit with two guns strapped to her back; they looked like crossbones. A long knife hung on her left hip, and several explosives were buckled to the other. Despite the fear of the situation, she wore a look of pure joy. "Who's ready to go to a theme park?"

Lars shouldered a rifle of his own and picked up a loose bandolier of grenades. "What's got you in such a fine mood, Captain?"

"It's not often I get to take this many guns out for a walk. Get your vac suits on, I'm opening this cargo door in five."

"You got it, boss."

Zip walked over to the door and set about checking her weapons. The process was methodical, bordering on obsessive. Rifles were disassembled, cleaned, reassembled, and then cleaned again for good measure. All the while, Zip's face was stretched in a permanent grin.

Lars turned to Tom. "That normal?"

"Weapons checks, yes, the smile… Not for a bug planet." Tom had never seen Zip display anything but abject terror and vitriol at the mention of bug planets.

"Probably a psychotic break from exposure to repeated trauma," chimed in Techni as she passed by.

"I heard that!"

Tom put on his helmet and felt the cool sensation of water circulating through the suit. *Small comforts.* He followed Techni to the cargo bay door.

Lars was close behind, fidgeting with his vacuum suit with each step. "They can't have gotten the right measurements for this. It's pinching in all the places it shouldn't be."

"That suit is the only thing between you and whatever that crap was that killed the crew on the *Bison-M*," replied Zip.

"At this point, I might prefer it." He pulled at the back of the suit where it had bunched in a sensitive area. "One more joke from the Manchesters before we all die for their greed."

"You keep talking like that, I might shoot you myself." There was a joke to it, but not enough to make Tom feel comfortable. Lars, it seemed, also picked up on the tone and stopped fidgeting.

Zip unslung one of her rifles. "Techni, you and I take the front, Tom and Lars, keep an eye out behind. Constant sweeps and attention to detail. Got it?"

Tom's heart pounded in his head, his vision pulsing. He understood well enough, but the panic coursing through him had other plans. In his head, visions of hundreds of bugs clawed their way out of the earth and charged to rip him limb from limb. His carapace crawled with the idea, and he shivered. *Deep breaths.* Tom sucked in a lungful of recycled water and held it. Eventually, he let it out and said, "Yes, Captain."

Zip pushed a button, and the hangar lowered, becoming a ramp and revealing the momentarily blinding bright light of Kedasi's distant sun. Tom felt his appendages curling around the end of his weapon's trigger. As his eyes adjusted, he saw a sprawling promenade with ticket booths at the far end. Golden flags stood above each, flapping in the asteroid's gentle breeze. Beyond them, the towering giants of rollercoasters and themed buildings cut intimidating silhouettes. There was a loud THUNK as the cargo bay door hit the ground, becoming a ramp for them to walk down. Then there was only the quiet rustling of the wind and the slow ticking creaks of *The Hog's* metal cooling after its brief reentry.

Zip stepped forward, the sound of her metal boot heels echoing across the empty plaza. It would be impossible to travel unnoticed in a place with such silence.

Techni followed, her footsteps quiet despite their stilted mechanical nature.

Lars looked at Tom, and they set off across the plaza.

Pristine red bricks spread out in a wide path from the landing pads toward Kedasi's main entrance. Tom could feel their contours through his boots, like stepping into something out of a storybook. As they approached, he could make out a sprawling flower bed on a sloping green hill just beyond the ticket booths. Despite being abandoned, the flowers were blooming, wild and overgrown.

Lars tapped him on the shoulder and motioned toward his eyes, then behind them, and followed it with an exaggerated sweep of his rifle.

Tom bobbed his head. *Right, we are the rear guard.* Many of Zip's reports had ended in tragedy because the rear guard 'got lazy'. He pivoted, facing the back. *The Hog* looked out of place, sitting in an empty parking lot. Over a hundred unused landing pads were spread out behind it like lilies on a pond. Tom wondered what Kedasi would have been like, fully open to the public. He probably could have spent an entire day watching the unique fleet of humanity's ships flying in.

Another tap from Lars.

Tom cursed himself for getting distracted and returned his attention to sweeping. While many of his species were blessed with bifurcated vision, Tom was stuck with forward-facing orbs. They did give him an unprecedented view of what was before him, but he had to turn his entire body to look at his sides. It was never a problem in an ocean or a cockpit, but already, he could feel the strain of needing to twist constantly. To his surprise, the rifle in his hands bounced back and forth on its own accord. Even if he forgot to sweep, it seemed the gun Techni had constructed had other plans.

They approached the ticket booths. There were no gates or anything to keep out intruders, only simple scanner systems that stood black and unpowered.

Zip's voice cut the silence like a knife. "It's going to be impossible to be completely silent out here, but I want everyone on high alert. Whatever it is that killed those men is still here, and it knows we're here."

"Bugs would have felt the vibration from our ship landing," offered Tom.

"Gold star," said Zip. "I see you read the reports after all."

Tom allowed himself an internal moment of pride but kept his attention on their surroundings.

"I didn't see Jack's ship on the landing pad, so at least we have that going for us," said Lars.

Zip shook her head. "Jack would never leave his ship where I could get my hands on it. My guess is that it's autopiloted to hide somewhere nearby."

Lars looked back at *The Hog*. "Any reason you don't share that same fear?"

She laughed. "Anyone who tries to set foot on *The Hog* without my consent is in for a world of hurt."

"If you want, I could hack a quick autopilot for you, antimatter guns and all," said Techni.

"Don't touch my ship."

Techni raised her shoulders. "Your loss. Could come in handy."

"You heard me."

"I said your loss."

Zip bristled. "Alright, everyone, through the turnstiles. After that, we take the most direct route to the park's train station. The path is wide open and should give us decent sightlines."

No dark corners, no tunnels, no caves, recited Tom internally. It was a simple summation of Zip's reports. While useful, it also brought back the other gruesome details of her writing. Tom felt fear seizing at his limbs. He wanted to curl up under a rock somewhere deep in the ocean where neither the Manchesters nor bugs could ever find him.

"Tom?" asked Zip.

Tom stood at sudden attention, wondering where in the conversation he had dropped off. "Yes, Captain?"

"Your vitals are elevated."

Tom looked at the readings at the edge of his helmet. Elevated was an understatement. "Yes, Captain."

"Do the breathing I taught you, and if it helps, think of this as observation for your future ambassadorship."

Tom mulled it over. "Like dissertation prep." Already, he could see details in the environment he had missed before. Symbols of status, organizational principles for the human condition, all hidden in plain sight. "I can do that."

Zip moved to one of the turnstiles and split open a large palette of brochures in shrink wrap. She pulled one out and handed it to Tom. "And if that fails, remember you're on *The Happiest Asteroid in the Galaxy*."

9.

The Happiest Asteroid in the Galaxy

Every muscle in Zip's body was taught and ready to snap at the slightest provocation. Looking out at the brightly colored flowerbed flanking two short tunnels leading into the park, she was struck by the juxtaposition of reality and feeling. Despite being abandoned, Kedasi was cheery. Gold statues flanked the entrance tunnels, guiding visitors inside toward the time of their lives. Even the warmth from the sun was reminiscent of a summer day somewhere nice. The peace warred with the images in her mind of the death lurking beneath the surface.

Then, in a disorienting span of a few seconds, Zip noticed the shadows growing noticeably longer. She looked up into the sky. Despite their brief time on the asteroid, the sun was already starting to set.

"Kedasi is the happiest place you will find among the stars. Come one, come all, and engage with your dreams in a place where they can become reality," said Tom, reading from the brochure.

"Hell of a promise," said Lars.

Zip grunted in response, grabbed another brochure from the turnstile, and flipped it open. In the corner was a blue-purple panel in the shape of a conjoined sun and moon. Beneath it was a list of times, reminiscent of a show schedule. She read out loud: "Kedasi's day-night cycle is only four hours, meaning you get the thrill of seeing the park change after dark twice a day." She looked up. The sun was growing red on the horizon.

"Well, that's eerie." Lars strode to the middle of the plaza, never letting his rifle drop. He looked out at the buildings just beyond the main entrance as they turned from red to purple to shadow. All at once, the park's lights sprung to life, bathing the entrance plaza in an artificial glow. Multicolored lights illuminated the rolling green hillside with the colors of the flowers that dotted it. Beyond, the two entrance tunnels suddenly shone with welcoming yellow light. "And I don't like that either."

"Better get moving. I want to get to The Opus by the next light cycle, and who knows how reliable the trains will be."

Tom stepped up beside her, his rifle twitching back and forth on its own accord like a hound on a scent. He patted it gently with one of his limbs, and the rifle slowed its movement slightly. "In my scans, the trains appear to be solar-powered. So long as the batteries are functional, there should be no issue."

"Small blessings. Thank you, Tom." Despite genuine thanks, the words came out flat. Every ounce of Zip's energy was being used playing high-stakes mental whack-a-mole with the panic at the edges of her mind.

She turned on the flashlight at the end of her rifle. It pulsed with an almost indetectable strobe designed to capture any and all movement at a distance. Even the slightest flicker behind a dark windowpane would stand out like a beacon.

In silent obedience, three more lights clicked on behind her.

"Tight formation, let's move quick." Zip started off toward one of the entrance tunnels, each footfall feeling too heavy. Something horrible was moving beneath them, deep or shallow; she knew that for a fact.

Approaching the tunnel felt like stepping into the maw of a great beast. Despite its twenty-foot length and welcoming, saccharine atmosphere, Zip saw it as the point of no return. Ornate frames of attractions that would never open hung on the walls. One depicted a blocky time-travel vehicle passing through a vortex of shining lights. It read: *Journey to Old Earth.* To its right, *Adventure Canyon* displayed the rocky ravine they had seen from above and a cavern filled with skeletons. The poster read: *Journey to a place humanity should have forgotten and try to escape with your life.*

Tom came up beside her. "Fitting."

Zip twisted her head to check that someone else had taken the rear guard. Techni and Lars were sweeping behind them. "The appeal of these attractions was always faux danger. People need to feel like they're just on the edge of catastrophe while still being perfectly safe."

"I see the appeal."

That made Zip laugh. It felt good despite everything else. "We must seem so strange to you."

"More often than not, yes, but looking at these attractions, I think I would very much like to ride them."

Lars slapped him on the shoulder. "Maybe there won't be any bugs after all, and we'll get a sneak preview." His sarcasm was heavy but not mean.

Zip shook off her focus on the posters and put her attention back on their grim reality. Every inch of the Manchesters' parks were made to make guests forget about the real world. Even in extreme danger, Zip felt the pull toward the fantastic. She too wanted to experience the rides and visit this place as a tourist rather than a mercenary on a suicide mission. The cobbled tunnel gave way to smooth black pavement as they exited. Beyond that, tall buildings illuminated by bright spotlights gave the impression of the world's quietest bustling street. Vacant shops boasted warm windows and multicolored wares made from infinite combinations of refined sugar.

The main square spread out before them with a magnificent fountain at its center. At the far end, three gates were built into the sides of buildings. Each towered large enough to accommodate even the biggest species in the galaxy. Above them were plaques with gold lettering labeled 'Past', 'Present', and 'Future'. The gate to the Past was made of grainy wood and hung open, revealing a passageway beyond. The Present was an ornate wired gate that only just obscured a modern-day metropolis on the other side. The Future was made of metal that looked like it shifted in the shadows. Both stood firmly shut.

"I like it when the choices are made for me." Zip did not. The fact that the gate was already open likely meant it was the same route the ill-fated mercenary team of the *Bison-M* had taken, or worse, Jack.

"The past it is," answered Techni. She looked around the square, never dropping her submachine gun from firing position. "This place is unsettling."

"You can say that again." Zip moved forward, careful to watch for any sign of danger on the ground in front of them. There was nothing. Every patch of pavement, every cobblestone, every plank was pristine. The lack of dust was unnerving in its own right. Still, bugs always cleaned up after themselves. Wasteful species did not often move on to become the pinnacle of evolution.

Standing in the doorway to the Past, Zip felt small. The sense of wonder returned to her as she read a silver plaque hanging beneath the archway. It read: *Leave the present behind and travel back to a golden age of humanity on Old Earth.*

Techni scoffed. "Golden age on Old Earth?"

"It's where the Manchester fortune began," replied Zip. "Of course it's a golden age to them."

"There is nothing behind us," piped up Tom.

"Thank you, Tom."

"You are welcome, Captain."

"Am I going to have to walk backward through this whole damned park?" Lars turned around to look at the sign. "It's a unique perspective, to be sure, but I—"

"Eyes on the park. There's a reason this gate was open. Likely the other mercenary crews took this route."

"And whatever killed them too," added Lars.

"And whatever killed them too." Zip walked into the tunnel, leaving the main square behind. Inside, the modern aesthetic faded, giving way to old wooden plank. The polished concrete beneath their feet transitioned abruptly to cobblestones. Zip hated the noise her boots made as they clicked on the ground, unavoidable as it was. Any sound in a silent place was an intrusion.

Ahead, the tunnel sloped up, revealing the same city street they had flown over on their path toward The Opus. An idyllic Old Earth town stretched out before them. Pristine wooden buildings stood proud in the amber glow of the park's lights. Manicured topiaries ran down the middle of the street, honed to pristine edges. Two bronze statues flanked the end of the tunnel, depicting a man and woman in wide hats and strange leather garb. A sign between them read: *Welcome to Earth as it was almost a thousand years ago—a time of wonder, exploration, and merriment.*

"Funny, in all my reading, I never saw anything about precise hedges. Most people were concerned with dying before fifty, disease, or the rampant gun violence." Techni snorted.

"Sounds a lot like where I grew up," replied Zip.

"Some things never change," Techni said. "More often than not, we try to whitewash the past and forget its effect on the present. A thousand years ago, bacteria in the water killed thousands, but I'm guessing that's not the idyllic representation they wanted."

Who were you before all this, Techni? "What about the merriment?"

"Well, that at least was partially true. When life is short, there's nothing to do but live."

Zip had to agree with that. She had seen a similar sentiment in the marine corps, where life expectancy was significantly shorter. "Tom, what's our route through this area?"

Tom scuttled up beside her and pulled up a holographic

map on a hand tablet mounted to one of his appendages. The display was cheery and cartoonish, made to appeal to childlike sensibilities in adults and youth alike. Attractions were drawn double the scale of the general path information, but it was enough. "We should be able to cut through this section about Old Earth and make our way towards the midway. Just beyond that, we'll find ourselves headed toward the train station in the park's central hub. No more than a kilometer or two."

"Nice and easy. Just a little stroll through the past." Zip stepped out of the tunnel and onto the city street. It really was incredible in the planet's night cycle. Bright yellow bulbs ran in long strands along the edges of every building, giving the impression that the entire city street was glowing. In the distance, she could hear the trickling of one of the many fountains they had seen from above.

Then, cutting through all the glitz and the glitter, she heard an audible click, followed by the last voice she wanted to hear.

"Evening, Zip. Why don't you all put your weapons down and we can have a little chat." In emphasis, several red dots appeared on Zip's chest, refracting off her vac suit in a twinkling display.

"Ah, hell."

10

Mercenaries, A Territorial Bunch

Tom watched Zip's hands raise above her head and felt his heart rate increase to a violent pounding. *Jack beat us here after all.* He felt the weight of the rifle in his hands—well, the metaphorical weight anyway—and wondered if he would have to use it. Fighting for his life was one thing; killing fellow citizens of Prota was another. Instinctively, he raised his limbs. The rifle hovered in front of him for a moment, aiming back and forth across the street. Then, with some reluctance, it snapped away, rotating onto his back.

He did the slowest version of a scuttle he could manage and moved out of the tunnel. The glittering street was momentarily blinding, filling his vision with bright spots. His warm feelings about the park evaporated as he spotted silhouettes on the rooftops and the faint red lasers coming off their weapons.

"Nice and easy there, shrimp man," called Jack, his voice low and friendly.

"My name is Tom." Even saying the words brought a wave of nausea and anxiety, but it felt like the right thing to do. The twitch of pleasure at the edge of Zip's face confirmed it.

"You're right, that was impolite. Nice and slow, Shrimp Man Tom."

Rude. Tom did not retort again and instead moved up beside Zip. A small laser dot appeared on his abdomen. The light was harmless, but its mere presence felt like it burned at his abdomen. A few guns had been pointed at him in the last year, and he found that he carried an intense dislike for the experience.

"Now, the other two in the tunnel. Tiny has a sniper trained on you, so don't try to make a break for it. If you believe its boasting, they killed a politician from a mile away with that thing. While I'd love to see that, there's no need to add any corpses to this shithole."

Tom had never seen such a pleasant place described as a shithole, but he supposed everyone had their aesthetic preferences.

Lars and Techni stepped out of the tunnel, their hands raised. From prep, Tom knew they had several weapons concealed on their person, but the threat of a distant, unseen rifle seemed enough to ensure they didn't use them.

"And here I thought this was supposed to be a friendly race to the finish," called Zip through gritted teeth.

Jack hopped down from the rooftop and walked out into the center of the street. Crossing the distance between them, he cut a spitting image of a cinematic cowboy. Despite the centuries of difference, Old Earth suited him. A long, black leather coat hung down to his knees, open around his chest, revealing high-tech armor beneath. His face was unobscured, his hair ruffling lightly in Kedasi's gentle breeze. All at once, it clicked for Tom: The man wasn't wearing a vac suit.

"I see you all haven't tested the air. It tastes great, just like the real thing if you don't think about it too hard." He took a deep breath and let it out with a pleased sigh. "Much better than the crap that comes in through those Manchester-issued vac suits.

"I play it safe. Learned that in the service."

"Oh, the service. Bad memories, didn't care too much for the boot polishing."

"Didn't care too much for any of the rules as I remember it," said Zip.

Jack ignored the barb. "Funny where playing it safe lands you. You walk into this place on tiptoes, sweeping behind you in classic formation, and where did it get you? Walked right into a trap. How about that? I knew I was good, but I didn't realize how good. The great Zip Turbine, surprised by a past-his-prime mercenary captain. That is what you called me back when, right?"

Even beneath the vac suit, Tom could see the clear twitch of Zip's muscles. They were either about to have a fight, or she had actually read the books he sent her on self-control.

"I called you a lot of things back when. As much as I love catching up, what do you want? Am I about to get two to the chest, or can we discuss this like friends?"

Tom looked down at the red dot still boring a hole in his abdomen. He wasn't sure what damage a bullet would do to his carapace, but either way, it was going to hurt. "Do I get a vote?"

"Course you do, Shrimp Man Tom." Jack's smile was winning, pleasant, and always just on the edge of violence.

Tom looked at Zip.

"Yeah, sure, Tom. In fact, the whole crew can have a vote. Raise your hand if you'd rather not die in the middle of the street."

All the crew already had their hands in the air in a traditional sign of surrender, so nothing changed except an uncomfortable silence. Tom raised what extra appendages he could, hoping they were counting each one rather than one per person. Humans had strange customs when it came to their hands. One day, if he lived long enough, he hoped to understand at least half of them.

Zip spread her hands. "Unanimous, who would have thought? Want to call off your dogs? This laser sight is making me twitchy."

Jack brought a pair of fingers to his lips and blew out a long, loud whistle. The red dots disappeared.

Zip relaxed. For a half-second, Tom waited for her to draw a concealed pistol, but she didn't. Instead, she let her hands down and walked straight up to Jack. "You really should be quieter."

"Why, bug planet?" He laughed. "There's nothing on this rock but us. Whatever spooked the Manchesters is long gone."

So he doesn't know. If Jack had read Zip's briefings, he would know that bugs were nearly impossible to detect without specialized equipment.

"Well that puts me right at ease. What do you say we hold hands, skip to the diamond, and split the Manchester's money eight ways?" Zip smiled broadly.

Jack chuckled again, but the humor was gone. "Yeah, I never really learned how to share. Broken home and all, tragedy. Why don't you step into my office?" He motioned toward an old building labeled 'Saloon'.

Tom had no idea what a saloon was, but judging by the double doors that swung outward, it was a place one often had to leave in a hurry. Glass bottles adorned the windows, shining in the overhead lights and refracting multicolored spots onto the pavement.

"Don't mind if I do." Zip motioned for the crew to follow and stepped through the double doors.

Tom followed and tried his best to make a friendly glance at Jack on the way.

Jack grimaced. "Yeah, I'd prefer if you didn't do whatever that is, Shrimp Man Tom."

Tom contracted, embarrassed, but pushed the feeling

down and turned away without saying more. Zip always said it was better the enemy knew less about you than you wanted. At this point in time, Jack was the enemy, and based on his clear confusion, the man knew nothing about Tom.

He pushed the double doors open and stepped into the saloon. Inside was a wide room where nearly everything was constructed from wood in various states of distress and polish. The bar was dark, sanded, lacquered, and polished to a shine. The floor looked like it was not far from the forest it had come out of. It was a contradiction of ideas that somehow felt like they belonged together.

Zip was already seated at a table in the corner beneath a hanging chandelier with burning bright bulbs adorning its various levels. The floorboards creaked as the others joined. Tom sat next to Zip, training his eyes on the door like she had taught him. Jack came through first, followed by the Cheri, who barely fit through the door and looked just as pissed as the first day they had met. Next came Big and Tiny.

"Well, look at that, the gang's all here. I'd offer you a drink, but the Manchesters didn't see fit to stock the bar."

"Cut the shit, Jack. Why aren't we in a firefight right now?" Zip crossed her arms and kicked her boots up on the table.

Jack walked up and put his face right next to Zip's helmet, speaking quietly enough to barely be heard. "Because you and I got history. It's not polite to shoot history like a dog in the street."

"Polite, never a word I would have used to describe you." Despite the venom in her words, Tom caught a hint of a flush on her face.

"You keep talking like that, and I'll start to get the right idea about us again."

Zip smiled and stamped a heavy boot heel on Jack's foot.

He reeled backward. "Bitch! So, it's like that, huh?"

"It's like that."

Tiny started to raise its rifle, but Big put a hand on the creature's shoulder, stopping the escalation.

Tom noticed there was still a white bandage on one of the slithering creature's limbs and felt a pang of remorse.

Jack's eyes were full of fury and hatred, but he smoothed them over. "Well, Zip, I guess we can't do this the easy way, so I'll put it simply: We don't want to be here anymore than you do. The galaxy is big, bullets aren't cheap, and I have a big heart."

Tom's limbs vibrated momentarily like he had experienced a miniature earthquake. He looked around the room, but no one else appeared to have felt anything. Carefully, he put two more limbs on the floor. With Jack's unfamiliarity with shrimp anatomy, he likely would assume it was a normal gesture. Tom lost the conversation and focused all his effort on the ground.

Almost imperceptible vibrations coursed through the earth beneath them. Whatever it was moved in a straight line from the saloon doors towards the back wall. Tom tried his best not to show his discomfort. Eventually, the tremor passed.

"And I'm supposed to rely on your better nature?" asked Zip.

"All I'm saying is stay clear of the midway if you know what's good for you. I'm trying to throw you a lifeline here, Zip."

"Why don't we just kill them now and be done with it?" grumbled the Cheri, cracking four sets of fuzzy knuckles and staring right at Tom. Its oversized face was pulled into a mixture of a grimace and pure delight.

"Because I am a polite and honorable man."

Zip laughed. "That story might fly at a low-level Prota bar, but it's not working with me. Tom, do we have options aside from the midway?"

Tom reluctantly pulled his eyes off the Cheri's massive, angry face and looked down at his terminal. "There is always more than one path." He searched the map to make sure the platitude was true. "Some are less desirable than others." There were two paths to the main hub that didn't involve unlocking the huge gates in the entry plaza. Doing so would make noise, and noise attracted bugs. Tom thought back to the vibration and the general direction it had moved. He couldn't be sure, but it felt like it was going straight toward the midway.

"Tom, I'm going to need an answer. Keep in mind, the wrong answer makes this little chat turn bloody real quick." There was no warning in Zip's voice. A part of her clearly wanted the second option despite its predetermined suicidal outcome.

In response, the creature known as Tiny lifted a long rifle, putting three red dots on Zip's chest. "Try me."

"Tiny, put that thing away. Just because we'd win the fight doesn't make it worth picking. I would think you'd have learned that lesson."

Reluctantly, the creature lowered the rifle with a hiss, its eyes glowing red in the cowl of its trench coat.

"Tom?" asked Zip again.

The only other path ran right through Adventure Canyon's artificial cave system, which they had seen from above. *No caves*. Did artificial caves count? The brochure said they were supposed to be a thrilling family experience. On the other hand, bugs liked dark places.

"Yes, there is another path." Saying otherwise meant immediate death, but at least Adventure Canyon gave them a chance.

"We can work with that." Zip slapped a gloved hand on the table. "Why don't you get out of here, Jack? We'll stay clear of the midway and see who makes it to the diamond first."

Jack cracked a wide grin that said he'd already won. "That sounds just peachy, Zip. You heard the lady; we're getting out of here. Let's go get us a diamond."

The Cheri grumbled in intense dissatisfaction, and Tiny hissed, but both moved toward the door. Big was entirely silent but fixed *The Hog's* crew with a penetrating stare as he walked out.

Jack started out after him but stopped at the doors. "Zip, I like you—despite my better instincts—but next time, there won't be a warning shot."

Zip stood from her seat. "Likewise."

"Charming as ever." Jack gave them a wink and walked outside.

Once the double doors swung shut, Lars let out a long breath. "Well, he seems nice."

"Doesn't he?" Zip rubbed her gloved hands together, massaging out the tension.

"We could have taken them," answered Techni.

"I didn't like our odds," answered Lars.

Techni pulled out the submachine guns at her hips. "These fire faster than the human eye can blink."

"Yes, because the speed of the bullets was going to be the issue."

"Excuse me," interrupted Tom.

"Yes, Shrimp Man, Tom?" asked Zip with a grin.

Tom did not return the gesture. "We may have a problem."

11

A Walk Through the Past

Zip's heart was a kickdrum, vibrating the vacuum suit with each furious pound. She had barely heard Tom finish his sentence before the panic set in. Numbness crept up the tips of her fingers, and a dark tunnel closed around the edge of her vision. She tried to touch thumb to forefinger and ground herself in the moment, but she could only visualize millions of armored bodies moving beneath their feet. She saw orange goop spilling out of her guts after an errant slice from a horrible pincer—her team dead in the road, their last view a rich family's homage to a time they knew nothing about.

"Are you alright, Captain?" asked Tom.

From experience, Zip knew there were two ways out of a panic attack. One was curled up on the floor, waiting for it to end, and the other was taking control, usually with pharmaceuticals. Option two wasn't always feasible, but she did her best. With herculean effort, she sucked in a deep breath and held it. Then she let it out, long and slow. The room brightened as the tunnel at the edge of her vision dissipated. Her heart did not slow, but it no longer felt like it would explode. *One step at a time. Come on, old girl.*

"Captain, with all due respect, if what Tom says is true, we should be moving." Lars's voice was soft, the gruff mercenary on temporary hiatus.

Zip resented the tenderness. *You are not your fear.* "You said it was headed toward the midway?" Her words were shaky, but she managed them. *One word at a time, one breath at a time.* The room was clear now, crystal in the palette that only adrenaline could paint.

"I can't be sure. The vibrations were faint. I think they are far below us."

"At least we don't have to worry about them coming up through the floorboards." She forced a laugh. No one else did.

"Yeah, at least there's that." Lars let out a heavy sigh and shook his head. "This place is fucked."

Zip ignored him. "What's the second path, Tom?"

"That is the other bad news. We have to travel through the artificial cave system in Adventure Canyon." Tom brought up the map on his terminal to show her.

Zip looked down, none of the excitement from earlier leaking through. According to the map, Adventure Canyon was home to a state-of-the-art rollercoaster careening through haunted mines and an active underground volcano. The cave systems were a more family-friendly experience. Gem-filled caverns served as a winding path through the Past and Present portions of the park. "Of course it goes through a cave."

"Is this the point where we take a vote about running and never coming back?" asked Lars.

"How many times are you going to try and start that conversation?"

"A few more, depending on the circumstances."

"I've read the reports, I'm going," said Techni. "Bugs have weak spots, just like everything else."

"A positive attitude." A complete misunderstanding of the reports, but positive nonetheless. Zip's breath grew easy. "If the caves are our only path, they're our only path. Hopefully, Jack and his team will make enough noise to give us a window to slip past."

"A Cheri is incapable of walking softly," said Lars.

"That's putting it lightly. We also have an advantage."

"We do?" asked Tom.

"Well, let's see how well you've read my briefings. What do you see here that bugs don't like?" She pulled out the paper map and laid it on the table before them.

Lars, Techni, and Tom started like students caught napping in a lecture.

"Cover to cover, my ass. Bugs don't like artificial structures. If they can help it, they'll burrow into real rock before they hit the fake stuff." It was only a theory based on a few observations, but it seemed sound. They weren't going to get anywhere without a little false confidence.

Lars's eyebrows raised. "Well, that is good news."

"Maybe the only good news we're going to get today." Zip stood from her chair. "Now, we're on the longer trail than Jack, which means if he survives the midway, he's going to get to the diamond first."

Techni unholstered her submachine guns in response and grinned.

"Love the enthusiasm. Just remember to stay sharp out there."

"You know us, Captain." Lars stood and headed for the saloon doors.

Techni followed suit.

Zip was on her way out when a sharp tap on her shoulder held her back.

"May I have a moment, Captain?"

Zip turned to Tom.

"Are you going to be alright?"

Zip stiffened, immediately finding a defensive posture, but then she searched the watery globules of Tom's eyes. Emotions weren't easy to read off a shrimp, but Zip knew she was looking at a friend. "Sometimes, when you see one horrible thing, it comes back when you least want it to. I've seen a hundred horrible things, and when they come back, they mean business."

"I am sorry."

"Me too, but sorry doesn't keep us alive. Still, thank you for checking."

Before he could respond, Zip was moving out the door. Emotions had no place on the battlefield, even if they were between friends. Zip silently thanked Tom again for his kindness and filed that kindness away for another time. When she emerged on the street, it was with a singular focus: Don't die. Her breath was regular, her senses were alert, and her rifle was raised.

Lars and Techni were already in a defensive posture, covering both sides of the cheery street. It was an odd juxtaposition. Zip could picture the families walking with their children and the bustling crowds of people. Looking out at the wooden buildings, it was easy to forget where they were. She expected that was the park's intention. The universe was a scary place, and most would pay a premium to escape.

"On your lead, Captain," said Lars, sweeping his rifle back and forth across the street. "Looks like Jack kept his word after all."

The back of Zip's head itched where a hidden sniper could have easily put a round. If Jack was lying, then it was already too late. She kept her rifle forward, sweeping her eyes back and forth. Jack might not have shot her in the back, but there was plenty more to be worried about up front. "Continue up the street and stay in the middle. Could be tunnels under any of these shops. If something comes out, I want to see it coming."

The street was silent apart from the distant hum of the electricity powering all the lights and the constant trickle of water in fountains. There were no creaks, moans, nothing. While the street was meant to look old, everything was brand new.

Ahead, it was easy to see where the Old Earth street ended and Adventure Canyon began. The main street split in two. On the left, the cobblestones gave way to a rough dirt path, and the orderly buildings ended abruptly, replaced by tall spires of red rock. On the right, the buildings shortened and changed style gradually, the cobbles replaced by faded wooden planks. A tall rollercoaster ran along the rooftops of a midway filled with all manner of games and sideshow attractions. Bright neon lights pulsed in the same eerie silence. Without barkers beckoning passersby, the midway felt more like a gaudy tomb.

"That's Adventure Canyon on the left," said Tom, double-checking his terminal.

"You think?"

"Yes, I—Oh, sarcasm?"

Zip nodded, curt but approving.

"I see. If we follow the path, it should lead us straight to the cave passage."

"Thank you, T—" The creak was like a gunshot in the silence. Zip spun on her heel, orienting toward the noise. She held her finger a hair's breadth off the trigger. On autopilot, she moved the barrel toward any shadow that looked like it might hold a bug.

No one made a sound, but Lars and Techni turned in the same direction, taking up flanking firing positions. Tom continued to bumble with his map, unaware that anything was wrong.

Zip hissed, not wanting to remove her finger from the trigger to snap and get Tom's attention.

Tom jumped and spun around, his rifle leaping into his hands. "Are we shooting at something?"

Zip let her breath out in short bursts, watching the buildings. "I heard a creak."

"A creak?"

"Yeah, a creak," answered Lars. "No sound in this whole damned street. A creak stands out."

Zip nodded. "You see anything, Techni?"

"Nothing. Heat scans are negative. Can bugs be cold-blooded?"

"I'd give my favorite gun for a reptilian right about now. And I really like that gun," answered Zip. "Bugs produce a heat signature, but their carapace can mask it to a degree. They don't run totally cold but aren't easy to see either." She waited a few more seconds, and when there were no more noises, she lifted her rifle. "Let's get the hell out of here."

"No argument." Techni moved back to a leading position.

Zip turned and followed toward the towering canyon. In Kedasi's night cycle, the rocks were lit up in bright shades of red and orange, emphasizing their majesty. Blue-green pools bubbled and shot up water alongside a set of steel rollercoaster tracks that wove in and out of the canyon walls. The tracks disappeared into dark tunnels, likely leading into the deeper cave system they had seen on the map.

Lars cleared his throat. "I think we're all wondering, so I'm just going to say it: Why is everything on?"

The words put a chill down Zip's back. The question had been on her mind, but she hadn't put the words to it. "Automatic timers?"

"Kedasi was designed to run almost entirely off solar power," offered Tom.

"Even that has a cost. The Manchesters didn't get where they are by letting costs run on forever."

"You got a theory?" Zip had a few, none of them pleasant.

"How intelligent are the bugs?"

That alone was enough to return a note of panic and fear in Zip's mind. "Did you read my report?"

Lars laughed. "You can harp on it all you want; it won't make it more read. I skimmed most of it. Besides, I've been on a bug planet before. You see more than one, you know each is its own shit-covered snowflake."

"You're right about that."

There hadn't been anything about bug planets in Lars's file, but Zip supposed there wouldn't be. The military didn't like reporting losses, and with a government as corrupt as Prota's, they didn't have to. Likely, the casualties had been attributed to political rivals rather than the creatures that had actually caused them. People liked enemies they could hate, not super species that would eventually be the death of them all.

"Short answer, maybe?" asked Techni.

"It's possible," admitted Zip.

"Why would they want the park turned on?" asked Tom.

Lars grimaced. "To attract prey."

12

An Interlude with the Designer of Adventure Canyon

"THIS IS ADVENTURE CANYON!" Joe beamed, sweeping the cloth off a 1/10th scale model of his greatest achievement, a themed thrill experience unlike any other. Towering columns of red rock interspersed with colorful pools set the stage for a land straight out of an Old Earth postcard. He had poured his heart and soul into every detail, and the real thing would be awe inspiring. They might not be able to visit the derelict home of their ancestors, but Adventure Canyon would be damned close. Joe pushed the model to the middle of the table where the assembled members of the board could observe it properly.

Some stood, but most remained seated, observing with mixed reactions. Joe could see twinkles of delight in their eyes, but as the board were corporate goons, they kept their emotions deep down. The Manchester board didn't appreciate expressions of elation, or anything beyond profit calculation for that matter. As long seconds passed, all heads turned toward the woman sitting at the head of the table: Angelina Manchester. From her position of power, she loomed over the room, towering in stature and influence.

Joe had worked in the amusements industry for his entire life and knew a trick of perspective when he saw one. The signs were slight, but noticeable to the trained eye. Upon entering, he had spied that the boardroom was ever so slightly angled, meaning the CEO of the Manchester corporation was literally above everyone else. As an added cherry, the table was tapered, and the seats lowered as they went farther away from her. It was an effective trick, but he did not let it deter his enthusiasm.

"I've read over your budget for this proposal. You're asking for a multi-million-dollar section of the park without a single thrill ride." She steepled her fingers and fixed Joe with an intense stare. "I'm not sure I see the appeal."

The rest of the board nodded their heads in sycophantic agreement.

Joe smiled, tight and professional. He had anticipated the question. "Adventure Canyon makes up for the lack of a traditional thrill ride with story elements and putting a sense of discovery at the forefront. People are going to pass time in this area, stay immersed, discover new stories of their own—"

"Discovery doesn't look very good in an advertisement." Short, cold, and a planned attack.

Joe didn't falter. "Yes, but Kedasi already has plenty of marquee attractions that can easily fill an ad slot."

"It never hurts to have more."

Money, it always comes down to money. Joe liked to think he built for delight and wonder, but at the end of the day, credits were what made the worlds go round. "What's the main problem with marquee attractions?"

The board looked at one another as if trying to come up with a collective answer. They were more likely to eat the table than speak out, but appearances were important. It was ironic to see creativity and free speech barred in a meeting supposedly about innovation. Only one person had an opinion that mattered, and it was clearly Angelina. "I don't see an issue," she said.

When was the last time you spent a day in one of our parks? "Lines," he answered. "Lines that snake on forever keep your guests in one place and keep them from experiencing the other things your park has to offer." He paused, chewing the next words before finding the will to spit them out. "Other things like concessions, souvenir shops, and premium experiences." He wanted to vomit. Why couldn't he pitch a land of exploration without the corporate bullshit?

Angelina's eyebrows raised.

You've got her attention. "Adventure Canyon will serve as a main causeway between two of the most important sections of your park: the Past and the Present. It will delight guests, keep them entertained, and offer more opportunities for them to shop." The current model only had one retail opportunity built into it, but there were several places where more could be added. Anything, so long as they didn't make him add another goddamned rollercoaster.

Angelina leaned forward. "A place in the park that will draw guests, keep the lines shorter, and have retail. Well, now that does seem like something."

He had her. "The budget is large, but I promise you, this will be one of the most wondrous—"

"Put a rollercoaster in it, and we've got a deal."

"But—"

"Kids love rollercoasters, Joe. Now, put one in the next model or you're fired."

"I—"

"Send in the pitch for Journey to Old Earth." She made a shooing motion, ending the conversation.

Hot shame crept up Joe's cheeks, but he picked up his model and turned around before he said anything he would truly regret. As he walked into the hallway, he found Pressler, another designer, holding an ungainly model of what would no doubt be another thrill ride.

Pressler shifted from foot to foot, clearly struggling with the model's weight. "How did the pitch go?"

Joe sighed. "They want another rollercoaster."

"But we already have five!"

Joe nodded. "Good luck in there." He walked away. *Another pointless rollercoaster to add to my resume of cheap thrill rides. I used to make experiences.*

He thought of the plans for Kedasi and the looping metal monstrosities that made up most of the park's skyline. People were obsessed with thrills, but Joe wasn't convinced. He believed that if presented with something more, something beyond the ordinary, they would understand.

"Fine," he said to himself. "I'll build you a rollercoaster, but I'm using all the budget we have left."

13
Adventure Canyon

Tom stared up at the canyon walls with wonder and delight. Even at night, they were illuminated in bright orange and red hues, giving the already towering structures more impressive scale. Unfortunately, Tom's awe did not last. Ahead of them, the path continued straight through the red rocks and into a cavern lit with softer blue and purple hues. Everything felt meticulously placed, from the boulders to the stray mining equipment against the outer cave walls. Rail tracks led into long tunnels crusted with sparkling gemstones. Stacks of shrink-wrapped crates tried to dull the illusion, but even so, Adventure Canyon was an inspiration.

Cold air blew out from the caves, smelling of distant water and minerals. Tom knew it was artificial and purposeful, but it felt real. The smell was that of an old, dark place, the perfect hiding spot for killer bugs. Stalactites hung from the entryway, making the cave appear like some long-dead monster's jaws. His gun bobbed in front of him, more eager than nervous, twitching back and forth, looking for something to shoot.

"Have I mentioned my disapproval for entering the dark and scary cave?" Lars swept his flashlight in tight arcs along the cave walls.

Zip did the same. "Your objections are noted. Our other option is to face off against Jack and his team. Given that they already got the drop on us once, that's a trap I'd like to avoid unless we're the ones setting it."

"On the bright side, the cave is not actually that dark," said Tom.

Lines of multicolored string lights hung from the ceiling, creating branching pathways that followed the cave's many twists and turns. Ahead, they split into three distinct paths. The left climbed into the rock and was illuminated in green. The right curved down and glowed red. The center tunnel was wide and plain white.

"Which way?" asked Techni.

Tom pulled up the map. "It only says that Adventure Canyon is full of—well—adventure." He lifted his limbs in an approximation of a shrug. "Perhaps there is a sign we can follow."

"Negative," answered Zip. She flashed her light on several exposed studs along the walls. "It seems signs were the last thing they were planning to put up."

"You would think the Manchesters would give us a full schematic," hissed Techni.

"They never planned on us coming to this part of the park. We were supposed to land at The Opus, get the diamond, and get out."

There was a sudden crash from the left tunnel, followed by an unmistakable scuttling. Four rifles shifted at once, illuminating the shadows in their stark light. The tunnel was empty.

"What did you say about bugs not liking artificial rock?" asked Lars.

"It was just a theory." Zip held up a finger and pointed toward the middle path. "Brightly lit tunnel it is."

Before Tom could process what was happening, everyone broke into a run. The scuttling from the left tunnel grew louder, and once more, he felt the low-level vibrations beneath his feet. That alone was reason enough to run the other way. Tom scuttled, keeping pace with the humans only through sheer exertion. Strictly speaking, shrimps were not designed to run on land, but Tom had learned during his time away from Crustacea. Zip often put him in situations with moving quickly on one end and mortal peril on the other.

The four of them rushed down the brightly lit hallway, easily following its bends and curves. False gems were stuck in the cave walls, glittering in the ceiling's bright lights, casting multicolored prisms along the ground. Ahead, a small viewpoint was cut out of the tunnel, looking down at a vast inner chamber. Tom only just caught a glimpse through the window in their hurry, but he thought he could see the tangle of tracks that was Adventure Canyon's main attraction, a rollercoaster.

The sound of heavy vac boots on stone drowned out the sound of their pursuers. Tom was looking behind them when a curse from Zip drew his attention. The group skidded to a halt, blocked from further passage by scaffolding and building supplies. Tall wooden barriers with the words *Pardon Our Dust* blocked the path to the Land of the Present.

"Shit," hissed Zip, turning on her heel to face the tunnel behind them. "Any other ideas?"

Techni swept the beam of her rifle back and forth. "I don't hear anything anymore."

"Yeah, me neither, but that doesn't mean it's not there."

Tom pulled up the map. "One option is going out the way we came."

"And potentially catch a bullet from one of Jack's trigger-happy goons. Next?"

Despite the fear, excitement rose in Tom's stomach. "There is a third option, but it carries some risk."

"Tom, we're on a bug-infested asteroid, every option carries risk."

"Point taken." Tom inhaled deep, the suit's water coming through stale and overworked. "We follow the rollercoaster track. According to this, it briefly comes out the top of the canyon with a view of the Present." Tom had pulled up the image of the map once again. It showed an oversized image of a family having the time of their lives as a rollercoaster crested Adventure Canyon's tallest peak.

"We're going to risk our lives based on an artist's illustration of what a rollercoaster might do?" asked Lars.

"Do you have a better idea?" replied Zip.

"Nope." Lars smiled. "Just saying it out loud, so I can remember why I died later."

"Alright, let's go for a ride."

"There is a chance the track hasn't been finished."

Zip turned to look over her shoulder. "We're not actually going to ride it, Tom, but I appreciate your concern."

They started back in the direction of the rollercoaster. Tom kept his breath measured and watched the edges of the tunnel for any sign of their pursuers. There were none. The artificial cave walls were unblemished and brightly lit, making him feel like a child searching for monsters beneath the bed.

When they came back to the point where the path diverged, the lights in the left tunnel were out. Inky darkness had swallowed the formerly bright green light. Tom stopped and listened while the others continued moving toward the red tunnel leading toward the rollercoaster. The ground beneath him was still, but something was moving in the darkness. Tom swept the light back and forth one more time. There was a brief glint, a pinprick in the darkness, but it was gone when Tom moved the beam back. *Probably one of the gems.* They were everywhere and caught the light easily.

"Keep up, Tom," called Zip.

Tom turned away from the dark tunnel and followed the red light with the others, checking over his back with each step. Metal rails formed the attraction's queue, snaking back and forth through the narrow tunnel. Several digital signs were erected with bright block letters reading: *Only this much longer until you can ride The Ghost Train*.

Tom imagined what the queue would be like at full capacity. It seemed more stressful than fun.

He continued forward and came to a bend in the tunnel. A hole in the rock wall provided a view into a well-lit cavern below crisscrossed by even more metal queue posts. At the edge was a loading station. A shiny, unused rollercoaster shaped like a train sat on the rails, ready for guests. Its wooden panels and futuristic gold inlay made it the perfect blend of the past and present. At its front was a miniature locomotive captained by a grinning animatronic skeleton. At least Tom hoped it was an animatronic rather than some poor soul that hadn't survived Kedasi's evacuation.

Zip had stopped next to the viewpoint. Beside it, the queue ran into two tunnels that wound their way down toward the station. Both were so narrow that only one person could walk through them at once. Runes and faux skulls adorned the walls.

"Yeah, this is going to suck," said Zip in response to the question no one was asking. "One by one, only the front and the back shoot. I don't need a bullet up my ass because one of you got jumpy."

A chittering roar echoed out from the tunnel behind them as if in answer.

"Ah, shit." Zip hopped over the queue bars and ran full tilt into the passage.

Techni followed.

Tom looked at Lars.

Lars sighed. "You and I both know we stand a better chance if I'm at the rear. Go."

"Lars."

"Tom, I know you're not a sentimental creature, so don't get started now. Move."

That was entirely untrue. Tom felt a deep sense of sentimentality, but apparently, he didn't show it outwardly. *Something to improve another time.*

"GO TOM!"

Tom released the rifle, sending it whirling around his torso and snapping onto his back. Then he hopped the rails and moved into the tunnel. While most of Kedasi had been made to accommodate larger creatures, there appeared to be limitations. The tunnel was cramped and confined, and Tom felt his suit scraping against the edges as he moved. Grimacing skulls stared out from the walls, red lights glowing behind their eye sockets like tiny fires. As he passed one, it cackled and shot a burst of compressed air. Tom jumped and tripped, sliding forward on the polished stone floor. The world filled with the horrible sound of his helmet scraping as he slid forward. *Please don't crack, please don't crack.* The suit flared several orange warnings, but none of them turned red.

Behind him, flashes of gunfire erupted, swiftly followed by their deafening reports. All at once, the tunnel was a strobing mess. Tom recovered quickly and pushed further, his vision obscured by a long scuff across the front of his helmet. Luckily, a tactical display appeared, outlining the corridor in front of him in neon lines. The vac suit's makers had thought of everything.

"Go back to hell!" Lars shouted before letting out another burst of gunfire.

Tom wanted to turn back to help but followed Zip's instructions. He pressed forward, following the tunnel's twists and curves until eventually it widened, revealing the station they had seen from above. Illuminated in bright red lights, the ghost train looked like something straight out of Hell.

Zip and Techni were already at the platform's edge, taking up defensive positions. Tom scrambled down to join them, carefully avoiding their lines of fire. When he got there, he looked back and realized that somewhere in the chaos of running, the gunfire had stopped.

"Lars?" called Zip.

There was no answer.

"Hundred credits says he's dead," answered Techni.

Tom did not try to hide the look of disgust on his face. It was unlikely Techni would recognize it for what it was, even if she were paying attention.

"We don't bet on our teammates," answered Zip, cool and final. "Lars, you alive? Techni here is about to owe me a hundred credits!"

Silence.

"I'm telling you he's dead."

A loud BOOM shook the cavern, and the tunnel illuminated in a flash of light. Acrid black smoke drifted out, followed a second later by Lars. He ran out of the tunnel and slid behind Zip and Techni, panting. Aside from the soot covering his vac suit, he seemed unscathed. "I don't think Kedasi was closed for a gas leak."

"Did you kill it?" asked Techni.

"Not it," answered Zip. "Them." She shone her light toward the platform that overlooked the rollercoaster loading station. Bright eyes glittered back at them from the darkness.

Tom tried to count them but quickly gave up. At a certain point, too many was too many.

Lars pushed himself up to one knee and stared up at the creatures. With his free hand, he made an obscene gesture at the assembled hoard. "I know we said we wouldn't, but what are the odds that rollercoaster still works?"

14

The Ghost Train

Zip was still processing the idiocy of the idea as she knelt in one of the rollercoaster's cars. Above, hundreds of bulbous eyes stared down at them, eerily still. A slow wave of sound buzzed around them as the clack and buzz of mandibles filled the air. Despite looking death straight in the face, Zip couldn't help her childlike excitement. They were about to ride a rollercoaster. *What the hell is wrong with me?*

"Techni, how long until we can get this thing moving?"

"Don't rush perfection." Techni was up against the front rollercoaster car, fiddling with her wrist-mounted computer, rifle discarded in the seat next to her.

"Where I come from, perfection is the enemy of good."

Techni ignored her.

Zip's heart pounded in her chest. "Lars, did you manage to kill any of those things in the tunnel?"

Lars ejected his clip and reloaded. "I didn't have time to check for a pulse. But judging by their reaction, their diet doesn't normally consist of grenades."

Several creatures scuttled out of the entrance tunnel, looking just as soot-covered as Lars but otherwise uninjured. "Are you sure about that?"

Lars looked at the creatures. "I said I didn't have time to check."

The sight of them was enough to send cold waves of fear across Zip's body. Each bug stood at least six feet tall and walked on four legs. Their bodies were armored exoskeletons, mottled brown in color, supporting an oblong black head with too many eyes to count. Orange bile dribbled from between razor-sharp mandibles that buzzed in constant saw-like motion.

"Techni, let me rephrase my request. We need this thing

moving NOW."

Zip moved her rifle back and forth, first to the creatures coming out of the tunnel and then to those at the overlook. Neither moved. They were waiting, warbling to one another.

"This isn't exactly my expertise."

"I thought you were supposed to be the bes—"

The attack happened all at once from both sides. One minute, the bugs were standing still, the next, they were sliding down the walls in a brown wave. The only sound was an eerie crackle coming from where their appendages pierced the false rock.

"Alright, executive decision." Zip turned her rifle toward the ride's control box at the end of the platform and fired. The booth exploded in a shower of sparks.

"What the hell?!" shouted Techni.

"Sometimes that works!"

"That's not how tech—"

The skeleton at the front of the train gave a maniacal cackle, and the train lurched forward.

A sudden roar from the bugs drowned out Techni's curse as they leaped from the walls to the ground. This was followed by the thunder of gunfire as both Zip and Lars began shooting at the same time. Chitinous bodies rushed across the faux rocks with incredible speed, heaving roars of violent madness.

Zip sighted one of the beasts and fired in a short burst, carefully watching its reaction. Several of the bullets hit their mark. The creature's head jerked and spasmed as the metal ripped through its armored exterior and splashed out the back. Zip waited for the bug to fall. Orange goo dribbled from its torso, but it continued charging. Its movements were jerkier but otherwise unchanged. *Shit.*

Zip was thrown back in her seat as a restraining bar came down over her legs, and the train accelerated. The coaster banked left, whipping away from the loading platform and into a dark tunnel.

The skeletal conductor cackled. "This mine will be your tomb!"

Zip was pressed into her seat as the coaster rounded a sharp corner and then slowed. The tunnel gave way to a cavernous room filled with stalactites, stalagmites, and pools of multicolored water. And graves. Rectangular funeral plaques lined the walls at even intervals with words carved in stone. Cool air rushed past, and green lights illuminated along the track's edges. "The miners of Adventure Canyon never had time to bury the dead proper, so they put them here. A deep hole dedicated to those digging even deeper holes. Fitting, isn't it?" The skeleton laughed.

Zip was more focused on the tunnel behind them. The creatures hadn't reappeared, but the train was practically crawling; it wouldn't be long. She looked at the others, all twisted awkwardly in their seats to look back the way they had come. The situation was about as bad as it could be for a firefight.

"Can this thing go faster?" asked Lars, wriggling in his restraints.

"Not when someone shot the control panel," answered Techni.

"Hey, it worked, didn't it?"

The train moved slowly forward to the edge of the room. On the far side, Zip heard a growing chittering that could be only one thing.

"What the miners didn't know was that this wasn't a place where all good spirits came to rest—quite the opposite, in fact."

"Enough with the god damned story; start the ride!" yelled Zip.

The first of the bugs made their way out of the tunnel at the far side. They cut even more monstrous figures in the shifting light of the pools.

"I'll give an extra five percent to whoever figures out how to kill these things first," shouted Zip and then sighted another bug. *Alright, headshots are a no-go; where else are you bastards weak?* Even at a distance, it was clear to see the armor plating covering almost every inch of the bugs' bodies.

"You're on," replied Lars. A single booming report echoed from his rifle, striking one of the bugs at a joint in its leg. The limb blew off, hobbling the creature, but it only roared and continued to advance.

"While the miners were buried here, they would not stay here. Why don't I introduce you?"

Zip exhaled and let out another controlled burst of gunfire. At the same moment, the lights went out. Projections of skulls and spirits coated the walls, shrieked, and flew toward the individual graves.

Zip couldn't tell if she had hit anything through the din and darkness. "They can probably see in the dark, don't stop firing!" She let out several more bursts in the direction of the bugs. Her muzzle flash illuminated the room in strobing pulses. The creatures were only thirty feet away now.

"I don't want to do this," said Tom as he pulled the trigger on his rifle. A fiery whip of tracer rounds cut through the darkness. To Zip's surprise, each round hit its mark, finding the breaks in the bug's armor, blowing through them, and moving on to the next bug. The effect was a chaotic string of bullets moving with no rhyme or reason that were somehow more efficient than any of the other team members. "I'm sorry!" Tom yelled as he held down the trigger.

"Techni, what the hell kind of gun did you—"

Crashing booms filled the cavern as the plaques fell off the wall, and skeletons burst forth, screaming and hissing. Zip jumped.

"I told you, this place will be your tomb!"

The train rocketed into darkness. Zip held on to the safety restraint with one hand, doing her best to keep her rifle trained in front of them with the other. Ahead, the only light was from the glowing orange embers of the skeletal conductor's eye sockets.

The train dipped, sending Zip's stomach up into her chest, and despite herself, she let out a whoop.

"Don't tell me you're enjoying this!" shouted Techni.

Zip smiled in the darkness. "You aren't?"

"What are the odds the track is finished?" asked Lars.

"They would not put the train on the tracks until they were ready to test," answered Tom.

"THESE SPIRITS WILL EAT YOU ALIVE!" shouted the conductor. Flashes of ghostly apparitions appeared on the walls. As each one illuminated, the train would turn sharply away and down another bending path.

"We're going to need to get off this thing at some point. Can anyone loosen their restraints?!" Zip pushed against the bar. It didn't budge. Her legs were pinned to the seat beneath her. As the rollercoaster whipped through the dark, she was thankful for it, but there would come a time soon when the restraints would be more of a hindrance than anything.

"Would have been easier if someone hadn't shot the control box!" shouted Techni.

"Be helpful or shut up!"

"I'm working on it!"

"YOUR SOUL IS MINE!" Faux flames illuminated the sides of the tunnels with blinding brightness, and jets of heated air blasted up from beneath the train—giving the feeling they were baking in the flames of Hell.

In the next instant, they shot out of the tunnel and into the sparkling hills of Adventure Canyon. The train careened along the hillside, twisting among fountains and rock formations.

Zip tried to look ahead and saw they were quickly running

out of time. The track bent sharply upward, riding the rock wall toward Adventure Canyon's jagged peaks. "Techni, I'm going to need you to release those restraints right now."

"Or what?"

Zip grimaced as the g-force sucked her into her seat as they were launched up the side of the canyon wall. On the bright side, she couldn't see any bugs.

She looked back at the others. Tom was wide-eyed as usual, but she thought she could see a hint of excitement in the shrimp's eyes, or maybe it was nausea. He gripped his rifle and its detached triggers with several appendages, pointing it down toward the canyon. *Finally learning.* She then turned her attention to Lars. He was struggling with the restraints and, in a moment of frustration, pointed his rifle right at the edge of the train door and fired. Sparks flew up, and his restraint popped open.

Techni turned toward him. "No faith."

Lars gripped the sides of the train for support. "If it works."

Zip looked down at her own restraints and followed suit. There was a loud bang, and the bar constraining her lifted free.

"Fine, if everyone's doing it." Techni fired.

"This is not safe," stated Tom.

"None of this is safe. Just do it, Tom!"

"OK!" Tom struggled with his rifle, trying to aim it down at the restraints. The gun bobbed and weaved of its own accord, looking for a target amidst the chaos flashing past them.

Zip was aiming her own rifle to help when the train crested a hill. The sudden change in elevation lifted her out of her seat and into the air. She floated, weightless, as the others passed beneath her, and then she fell. The ground rushed up to meet her. Zip shouted a curse and flailed with her arms, struggling to catch anything. Her outstretched hand struck against metal, and she grabbed it on instinct. Her shoulder ripped violently in its socket but somehow managed to stay attached. With her free hand, she held onto her rifle.

There was a sickening crunch as she slammed into the rollercoaster's track. White spots blotted her vision, but she gripped the track with every ounce of her being. *Don't you dare pass out on me.* Slowly, she blinked away spots, getting her bearings back. The world was a violent blur of orange and grey. Zip looked up and saw that she was hanging from the mountain's edge just before the coaster tracks leveled out.

She swung her gun onto her back, clipping it to the harness there, and started to climb. How her arms had any strength was beyond her, but she suspected adrenaline was part of it, and she'd be paying later. Feats of extreme exertion had a way of coming back to bite.

Hand over hand, she worked her way up the tracks, pulling herself up. With each rung, her limbs burned, and her heart pounded. "I am not going to die on a damned rollercoaster." Inch by inch, Zip made her way up the canyon wall. Soon, she scrambled over the lip and sprawled forward, panting. For a moment, she lay there, hugging the tracks, thankful to not be a smudge on the canyon below. Then, reality set back in.

Zip rolled onto her back and let out a long wheezing breath that turned into a laugh. "Holy shit." Through the scuffs on her vac suit helmet, she could just make out some figures standing at the edge of the canyon wall. "We made it."

As unlikely as it was, they had all made it. Zip pushed herself up to a seat with one hand. The world was rendered blurry by the spiderweb cracks in her visor. "Anyone else want to go for a second ride?"

There was no response. Zip unlatched the seal on her helmet and pulled it off. The view really was breathtaking from atop the canyon. She could see Kedasi's lights in all of their glittering glory—but something was wrong. Looking at the figures at the canyon's edge, her heart stopped. There were only two of them. Lars and Techni were looking down at the hole where the rollercoaster tracks disappeared. Zip stood, shaky, fear blooming in her chest.

"Where's Tom?" she asked, her voice a dry dusty rasp.

Lars and Techni looked at her, their faces masked by the reflection of their helmets.

"Where's Tom?!"

15
In the Dark Below

Tom listened to the screaming of the train's skeletal conductor and the hiss of the wheels against tracks with abject horror. He had missed his chance. The train passed through an open cavern filled with faux lava. From beneath, a massive animatronic demon reared its head, spewing steam and heat and fogging Tom's visor. It barely registered. The only thing on his mind was the fact that his gun hadn't cooperated in shooting the restraints, and now he was going to die. Helpless, he sat back in the train car, feeling his heart pound.

The rollercoaster slowed as it passed through a final bending tunnel. "YOU WILL NOT SURVIVE NEXT TIME!" shouted the conductor as the train rounded a corner and emerged back on the loading dock. It hissed to a complete stop, and the restraints around Tom's waist popped open. He scrambled to stand as quickly as he could, keeping the rifle in his hands. Splashes of orange goop littered the platform from the firefight, but the bugs were nowhere to be seen. Tom made sure to give the substance a wide berth.

Which way would the bugs have gone? The last he had seen them, they were flooding into the crypt cavern, which was only a few rooms away. Whatever he was going to do, he needed to do it quickly.

Tom found himself turning in circles and liking none of his options. There were the two rollercoaster tracks leading forward and backward, the entrance tunnel, and a red exit tunnel back to the caverns beyond. Following the tracks backward could lead him to the top of Adventure Canyon, but the incline had been steep, and he wasn't sure he could climb it.

Tom, think, think fast, please. He always found that his mind performed better when he addressed it politely. In a swift decision, he chose the exit tunnel, remembering the pile of bug bodies most likely blocking the entrance. He hurried as quietly as he could, his appendages only making the slightest clicking.

Just off the main platform there was a bank of monitors with the words *I survived!* above them. They were all off, but a sample photograph showed a delighted family at the top of the hill as they crested Adventure Canyon. Tom wondered what his photo would have looked like.

Rustling. Tom heard rustling. It was coming from the platform, and while he was not entirely familiar with the noise, he suspected he knew exactly what was making it. *No time for distractions.* He turned away from the photo bank and continued moving through the exit tunnel. It sloped up, gradually increasing in illumination until he was back at the original divergence. To his left, he could see the red tunnel leading back to the rollercoaster and, directly ahead, the path out of Adventure Canyon.

Options were limited, and while he did not want to deal with Jack and his mercenaries, he was even less inclined to stay in Adventure Canyon. He walked back toward Old Earth, toward freedom. Hope surged as he moved farther and farther away from the rollercoaster. He would laugh about this adventure with Zip someday. Finally, he would have a story, something to talk about when they went out for drinks at Marvin's.

Rustle.

Tom spun, looking back down the tunnel, the light of his rifle illuminating it in stark white. It was empty. *Jumping at shadows.* He knew very well there were good reasons to be jumpy, but blaming it on simple fear made reality a little less scary.

He turned back toward the entrance tunnel and froze. Where there had been an empty path leading out moments earlier, now there was only a sea of bulbous eyes staring back at him. Shoulder to shoulder, packed to the brim, a hundred bugs or more gazed at him, their mandibles vibrating and clicking.

Tom's limbs turned to lead. Out of instinct, he turned around, thinking he could escape back the way he had come. His heart sank further. He should have expected it. The tunnel behind him was also blocked, the creatures forming a wall of shiny armored bodies.

I do not want to die here. Instinctively, he raised his appendages, the rifle swinging free and snapping around to his back. The time for fighting was over.

The bugs whirred and clicked, advancing slowly. There

was a rhythm to the noise, a hint that could be discerned as language. It wasn't all that dissimilar to how he communicated back on Crustacea. Tom held out two limbs and rubbed them together, trying to mimic the creatures' vibration, but struggled through the fabric of the vacuum suit.

The air is breathable. Slowly, not wanting to startle the creatures into a full attack, Tom reached up and lifted off his helmet. The stench was unbearable. Ordinarily, Tom found that his sense of smell on the surface was inadequate, but it was more than enough in the presence of these creatures. Trying to hide his disgust, Tom lowered his helmet to the ground.

The bugs did not advance. Without his helmet, Tom felt like he was really looking at them for the first time. Their shells were a mix of light and dark brown and interlocked, leaving few weak spots. Their eyes were clustered around a central focal point in front of them: predator's eyes. Their mandibles were long, serrated, and capable of vibrating at the frequency of a buzz saw. In short, they were creatures made for violence.

Tom desperately wanted to run despite having every egress blocked by these horrifying creatures. Instead, he tried to calm himself, one breath at a time. *You are not dead. There is a reason you are not dead.* Tom looked out at the sea of bugs and tried to take an analytical approach. Despite the obvious fear they inspired, their anatomy was not all that dissimilar to his own. *Perhaps they're not sure what I am either?*

The creatures parted before him, making way for a larger bug shuffling out of the darkness. While most were a uniform shade of brown, this one bore red stripes along its abdomen and mandibles. It was also considerably larger, with a bulbous thorax that dragged along the ground with each step. Each of its eyes was the size of Tom's head, and he felt the weight of their gaze.

What are you thinking? He imagined it was something along the lines of: useful or food? Keen to interject his own opinion on the subject, Tom peeled off the top half of his vac suit, careful to keep his motions slow and deliberate. While the risk of getting bug goop on him was higher without a protective layer, getting eaten immediately was worse. *I'm just like you. No need to eat me.*

The creature watched with interest but did not advance.

Tom attempted to speak by rubbing his limbs together. "Hello."

The creature twitched slightly and slowly approached. Soon, it towered over him. The stench was that of a thousand shorelines at low tide. The bug leaned down, resting on its forelimbs and bringing its maw to Tom's head level. At such a close distance, two things were clear: Being eaten by this bug would be painful, but it would also be quick.

The creature roared, blasting Tom with its vile internal stink.

"I am Tom," he tried again, the fine movements difficult with his nervous trembling.

The creature clicked and whirred in something that was just on the edge of language. Fortunately, or unfortunately, for Tom, it required no translation. The bugs behind him closed in, wrapping limbs around his midsection and pushing him forward, deeper into the depths. A collective roar rang out from the assembled bugs.

Oh dear.

16

Rage, Pure and Simple

Zip smashed her fists into anything that would remotely buckle. Despite the faux rock's solid appearance, it cracked and revealed the wireframe structure beneath when it was pounded hard enough. Her knuckles were bruised and bloody, and poking through the gloves of her vac suit. Alarms rang out, letting her know that seals had been breached, that she was in a state of high stress, and that things were generally not going well in her body.

What punching inanimate rocks solved was unclear to her, but the pain was at least focusing in a way that helplessness wasn't. *I let Tom down.* Her fist smashed into the raw wires poking out from the rock face, sending a dull throb of pain up her already aching wrist. *He's going to die because of me.* Another punch. *I should have left him on Crustacea.*

A hand stopped her, delicate in stature but firm as ice in its grip. Through the blurry haze of rage, Zip made out Techni's mechanical features. Whether it was good sense or plain exhaustion, Zip did not turn and redirect her anger. Instead, she slumped to the ground, allowing Techni to hold her hand back from further damage. A snap-hiss followed by a cooling sensation ran up her arm. Zip looked down and saw blue foam spreading over her hand.

Techni didn't say a word but continued applying the foam to both hands and then stepped away as it sizzled and popped.

Thank you, Zip wanted to say, but all that came out was a low grunt. A few more punches and her trigger finger might have been beyond repair without serious medical attention. *Neglecting your crew.*

"Captain?" It was Lars, kneeling next to her, rifle still held in a defensive position—a man who knew how to stay alive even when leadership fled sanity.

Zip lifted her head, taking in their surroundings. At some point, they had descended the rockface, but it had been a blur. The grapple tether still attached to her waist was a strong indicator that she had done it in relative safety. *Thank you, autopilot.* Often, in times of exceptional stress, Zip's body would take the wheel, bypassing the pesky red tape of the brain. It felt like blinking. One moment, the danger was there, the next, she was safe and often covered in someone else's blood. She looked down at her vac suit to check. Dirt, grime, and a single splotch of bug blood, nothing new. *How the hell did that get there?* The lack of a helmet was disturbing, but there were bigger problems.

Zip searched for her voice, eventually finding it in a deep, ragged tone. Had she been screaming? "Lars, I know what you're going to say, but—"

"We're not going to leave Tom behind."

Zip looked into Lars's eyes, seeing kindness, hurt, and fear wrapped in a single gaze. "We're not?" Zip would have given Lars the keys and gone after Tom herself, but the company was a nice surprise. She turned her attention to Techni.

Techni looked up from her wrist-mounted computer. There was no compassion in her eyes, only calculation. "We are not. He's moving toward the diamond and leaving here without the stone is a death sentence."

"So sentimental," said Lars.

"Sentimentality has no place in a life-or-death situation. I thought the service would have taught you that."

Lars stood. "And what would you know about the service?"

"How do you know he's on the move?" asked Zip. The last thing they needed was infighting.

Techni looked at Lars, the urge to fight clear, but let it go. She held up a map just above her wrist. It showed three red dots blinking at variable speeds and a fourth blinking at a significantly faster rate, moving through the park at alarming speed. "His heartbeat is elevated—more elevated than usual—and whatever took him is moving him."

"Didn't answer my question."

"You all should be more careful about what you eat."

Lars spluttered. "You fed me a tracking device?"

"In a galaxy with people like me, there's no such thing as free donuts."

Zip's stomach rumbled—that donut might have been the last thing she'd eaten. Techni was clever, but Zip would be more careful about her intake moving forward. "So, two birds with one stone." Zip pushed herself to a stand. Pain stabbed at her wrists and forearms. She grimaced but made no sound. "How far have we got to The Opus?"

Techni switched her screen to show a different view of the map. "Five kilometers."

"Any of you fancy a sprint?"

Lars hissed out a curse as if the mere mention of exercise were a cardinal sin in some religion Zip wasn't familiar with. "Why would we run when we have a perfectly good train?" he asked.

"Because some shithead mercenaries probably took it."

"So, we take the next train."

"And then they shoot us when we get to The Opus."

Lars shrugged. "We're going to The Opus anyway. Either they shoot us when we're out of breath because we decided to run like high school gym class, or we can ride a nice train and have a proper firefight."

Techni looked at Lars like a scientist examining a specimen. Her eyes ticked back and forth, processing. "He's not wrong."

Lars flapped a hand. "Of course I'm not wrong. Run? What kind of idi—" He stopped, suddenly remembering his role as a crewmate. "We should not run. Besides, Jack didn't shoot us the first time; maybe he's still feeling generous."

Zip wiped her hands on her vac suit, clearing the foam from her knuckles. "Jack's a coward. The only way we get by him alive is if he needs us."

"Well, thanks to Tom, we know where the bugs are going," said Techni.

"We know where *some* of the bugs are going," corrected Zip. "But that might be enough." She flexed her hands, feeling joints pop and muscles strain. There was pain, but everything was in working order. The ragged holes in her gloves were bloody, but the flesh beneath was clean. Medical foam was another miracle she didn't need to understand to appreciate. "So, we catch a train, get to The Opus, see if we can bargain our way past Jack and his goons, and then hope we can follow the tracker to Tom. Simple, might get us killed—probably will get us killed—I like it."

"The alternative is standing here exactly where a swarm of bugs took our friend and nearly killed us," said Techni. "Care to flip a coin?"

"I did like the rollercoaster," offered Lars.

Zip looked back up at the tracks snaking over the cliff's edge. "Yeah, that was fun until it wasn't."

"Most things in life are."

"Fair enough." Zip oriented herself toward the train station. "Let's go; we have a train to catch."

Part III - A Bug ~~Planet~~ Asteroid

1

All Aboard

Zip looked up at the magnificent train station; it was even more lavish than the park's already extravagant surroundings. The building was encased in what appeared to be an intricate lace basket made of multicolor glass that shone with interior lights. A single metal rail extended from both ends of the station. One direction led back toward the launch pads and around the edge of the park, while the other left the world of fantasy behind and headed out over the open expanse of asteroid desert. Several wooden struts and wire structures adorned the end of the walkway leading up to the station. Based on context, Zip guessed they would have become another faux rock formation, blocking parkgoers from seeing the asteroid until they were on the train.

Lars whistled. "They seem to be betting there won't be any angry teenagers with rocks at this park."

"I'd be worried about someone breathing on it wrong."

The whole building looked fragile. From the outside, it was impossible to tell if there was a train in the station or not. Zip turned back toward the park. The rest of their journey had been uneventful and eerily quiet. Something about Tom was keeping the bugs interested, and for the moment, that was a good thing. A small blinking light on Zip's wrist assured her that Tom was still alive. As long as he was alive, there was a chance of rescuing him.

Tom's heart rate was fast but back down to a non-critical level. His location showed that he was almost directly below The Opus, somewhere in the wide chasm the Manchesters had used as a diamond mine. The hotel's brochure displayed an automated tour of the mines in small hovering carriages. Their only hope of retrieving Tom was that these carriages had already been built. Otherwise, Zip would take down the entirety of The Opus with *The Hog's* antimatter guns, land in the hole, and ask for forgiveness later. She had yet to inform the rest of the crew about her plan, but that was one of the benefits of being captain.

"The computer system shows two operational trains," said Techni. "One is here, and one is currently at The Opus."

Zip looked up at the single rail. "One track, two trains."

Techni nodded. "It's a swivel model, allowing the train to travel on both the upper and lower portion of the tracks in some segments."

"Fancy. I'll take point. Watch my back." Despite the building's extravagant exterior, Zip didn't trust enclosed spaces. Likely, the glasswork would be too fragile to support the lifestyle of armored bugs, but it wasn't worth the risk. The thought of a firefight ending in a suicidal rain of glass shards was similarly unappealing. Zip moved toward the building, following a set of stairs that led up toward a pair of sliding glass doors at the base. As she approached, they slid open. Sterile air wafted out in a cool wave, and she stepped inside.

Technicolor, blown glass hung down in rivulets from the building's central support beams. It felt like being inside the ribcage of a fish tripping on hallucinogens. At the center was a freestanding sign with arrows pointing toward *Parking* and *The Opus – RESERVATION REQUIRED*.

The others filed in behind Zip. "A reservation? Well, we might be walking after all." Lars chuckled. He might have only been making himself laugh, but he clearly enjoyed it.

"What do you know? We're on the list." Techni pulled up the terminal on her wrist and showed them a shining reservation card.

"That was quick."

"Big dreams, big oversight. This place is a cybersecurity nightmare."

Zip wondered just how bad *The Hog's* security profiles had looked under Techni's shifting mechanical eyes. If the Manchesters had lackluster security, whatever backwater junkyard had put together *The Hog* was likely worse. Stifling that feeling, she moved in the direction of The Opus. A spiral staircase made its way up, following the edge of the building, and leading to the second-floor train platforms. The building's curved glass reflected strange patterns on the stairs, giving her the impression she was ascending a rainbow.

At the top of the stairs, they came to a train platform occupied by a jet-black carriage with gold inlay. It looked like something a fancy child might have designed to show their friends to prove their parents were wealthy. The doors were open. Inside, a plush interior lined with further shining gold accents exuded status. Zip kept her rifle trained on the doors and approached. Knowing Jack, it could easily be a trap.

"Any chance he's just strapped a bomb to this thing and hoping we'll give him the easy way out?" asked Lars.

Techni held out a hand, a faint light coming from her palm as she swept it back and forth over the train. "I'm not seeing anything. Judging by the quality of his team, I doubt any of them would have the subtlety to hide something like that from me."

"Seeing as how you're feeling confident. Would you like to go first?" asked Zip.

Techni shrugged and walked into the train without hesitation, holding her palm out to scan and one of her submachine guns in the other. Upon entering, she swept both sides, quick and efficient. Seeing nothing, she lowered herself into a plush armchair and holstered her weapon. "It's clear. No heartbeats."

Lars moved up beside Zip, still facing backward to cover the rear. "It's annoying when she's right, isn't it?"

"Usually, I'm the only one that gets to be right."

"Tight ship."

"Small crew." In the past there'd been no one to tell Zip she was wrong because the operating capacity for the crew had been herself, a bottle of puffin rum, and illegal cargo. It had been lonely, but consistent.

"Are we getting on the train?"

"Yes, Lars, we're getting on the train."

He sighed. "I don't want to say it..."

"You think we're all going to die?"

"Yeah, pretty much."

"Well, might as well die with a really big diamond."

Zip left him standing at the station to ponder and boarded the train. Inside, low, soothing music played through overhead speakers. Immediately, the tension that strung her joints together eased, and her muscles relaxed. The thousand ways to die that were usually ping-ponging through her brain settled into quiet nothingness.

Techni was near meditative, sitting back in her chair. "These are Mercurian beats. Specifically designed to calm your nerves. Working on a planet that close to the sun requires a steady hand."

That explains it. Zip had met a few Mercurian workers before; they were all a dreadful bore. There was only so much self-love and occupational contentment she could take before a date went south.

Lars walked in. "Mercurian beats, fancy. Never cared for the stuff."

"Why don't you sit quietly and let *us* enjoy it then." Techni's voice was slower, the closest it had been to human in the brief time Zip had known her.

"I hate to say it, but I agree with Techni." The permanent knots in Zip's shoulders unwound, reminding her of a time when danger had been exciting rather than a constant. Why the hell hadn't she put Mercurian beats on *The Hog* a long time ago?

The answer came seconds later when the doors to the train shut with a light hiss, and they were moving. In her relaxation, Zip had briefly left the present moment. Relaxation got people killed.

"Welcome aboard the Locomotive Delight," said a bubbly voice from above. "This is one of two operating trains that move between Kedasi's main park and the crown jewel of this asteroid, The Opus."

Lars audibly groaned. "Techni, can you do anything about that?"

Techni shook her head. "I turn that off, the beats go with it."

"To hell with the b—"

"Kedasi derives from a word in ancient society that meant pleasure and enjoyment. We strive to curate both of those elements in everything we do. If you're participating in an activity on Kedasi, it's serving one of those two core values."

"Are you sure one of them isn't annoyance?"

"We are now passing over the barrier of Kedasi's main park and heading over the barren fields of the asteroid itself." All at once the walls of the train became transparent, showing the grey, rocky surface of the asteroid below. "While there is nothing here now, rest assured that the Manchesters have plans for the space. Once the main park opens, construction will begin on two expansions in the coming years, as well as retail, dining, and even living spaces for those who never want the adventure to end."

Outside, projections of buildings rose, showing city streets, towering skyscrapers, and in the distance, another elaborate theme park. Green trees and flowers dotted the sidewalks below. It was idyllic, even if it was fueled by corporate greed.

"That will all take time of course, but Kedasi will never be fully complete. The Manchester vision is an ever-evolving surface dedicated to the best experience for thrill seekers such as yourselves. Speaking of which, if I can direct your attention to the front of the train, you'll see we're about to have a head-on collision."

Zip turned her head toward the front wall, which magnified to show an oncoming train on the tracks just in front of them. Her heart skipped a beat despite knowing exactly what was coming. Their entire train swiveled around the rail in a smooth motion, shifting to hang from the bottom. The train above passed by harmlessly, and they were treated to more panoramic views of the asteroid below.

"Kedasi's unique monorail system allows multiple trains to run on the same track simultaneously. It is the only place in the universe where such a train can be found."

"Because one mistake would lead to catastrophe," added Lars.

"And they copyrighted it," agreed Zip.

"But it is peaceful," replied Techni.

The train swung back up to the top of the tracks. "We are rapidly approaching our destination, The Opus. The Opus was built for our premium customers with the hope of offering a home away from home. With luxuries beyond imagination, we hope your stay will bring you back year after year. Whether it's fine dining, shopping, or the great pastime of karaoke, The Opus has something to offer for everyone."

Lars groaned. "Rich fucks and their big, small ideas, am I right?"

Zip nodded. "It's a tale as old as time. Earn enough money and you can live in a reality far enough away that you forget the people below you exist."

"People like us," answered Techni.

"People like us."

The exhaustion in Zip's limbs returned with a vengeance. Her fists were sore, but healing. Punching the rock had been on the dumber side of dumb ideas. *What the hell am I doing here?* The job was a lot easier when it was transporting contraband. Getting things where they weren't supposed to be and shooting people who asked too many questions might not have been a moral life, but it was a life. Every time she came close to shutting her eyes, Zip could see the chittering mass of millions of bugs beneath the surface. If there was a Hell, she guessed Kedasi wasn't that far from it.

"We will be arriving shortly. Please have your identification ready so we can get you and your belongings to your rooms as soon as possible. We hope you've enjoyed your journey. Have a pleasant day." The voice signed off with a trio of singsong notes before the train returned to playing solely Mercurian beats.

"Glad that's over." Zip stood, trying not to wince. The rifle was heavy in her arms, and no part of her was ready for whatever came next. Sleep, sleep was what should have come next.

The train pulled into the shadow of The Opus, passing beneath the curved structure and straight into its heart. Darkness surrounded them momentarily, and then bright light flooded the exterior as the train emerged right into the middle of a lavish hotel lobby. The doors hissed open, revealing a wide golden staircase leading down to a row of marble concierge desks. Ornate glass chandeliers hung above, reflecting prismatic stars and light throughout the lobby.

"Posh digs," admitted Zip.

"Even when it's filled with the likes of you," called a calm voice from just outside the train.

Zip let her gun drop to her side, not even bothering with the formalities. "Hello, Jack."

2

Crystalline Stink

TOM SAW NOTHING BUT the dim outlines of dark shapes moving against a black backdrop. A long time ago, his eyes had been adjusted to dim water, but after a year of bright lights and the glow of humanity, darkness was darkness. He was keenly aware of the monsters moving in the gloom around him. Their bodies clicked and rattled as they went, creating a constant echoing mess in the wide cave system. Then there was the stink. It seemed that no matter where the creatures were, they emitted the same foul odor that could have won wars and devastated societies if harnessed. Beneath him, the bodies of his captors bobbed and crunched as they carried him along, wafting up the ever-present stench with each halting movement.

In the uniform darkness, he had nothing but existential dread as company. In the absence of visual stimuli, Tom found hundreds of ways to forecast his death. It was a macabre fantasy, but it kept boredom at bay during the monotonous march. At first, his heart pounded with every jolt and jostle, but like most threats in life, captivity quickly became routine. Even the potential for sudden death felt like a cheap thrill.

The bugs let out a rhythmic thrumming that echoed off the walls, vibrating the air and Tom's carapace along with it. It was maddening, making even the simplest thoughts a muddle. Ahead, faint light glowed. For the first time since being taken, he could see the outline of the cave walls. With each step, the world grew clearer, and Tom noticed honeycomb networks of tunnels spindling off in all directions. From the looks of it, the bugs had been working long before Kedasi had atmosphere.

The sheer number of bugs surrounding him was staggering. Thousands of eyes glinted from the darkness, their carapaces no more than hints of shadows in the dim light. Infested would have been putting things lightly. Even with a full theme park above, Tom guessed the bugs would outnumber humans five to one conservatively. Given the size of the bugs carrying him, significantly larger than most, he thought the odds of quelling such a population without orbital nuclear weapons were slim.

The tunnel's glow grew to a blinding brilliance, casting the bugs in stark white light. Fully visible, the hoard was terrifying—a mass of razor-sharp pincers and armor. Yes, to some species Tom would seem much the same, but shrimps had never kidnapped anyone and taken them underground—that he knew of. This thought was interrupted by a sudden view of gleaming diamonds. Unlike the faux gems of Adventure Canyon, these stones were the genuine article, reflecting shafts of rainbow color that somehow looked ugly when projected on the bug's carapaces.

Tom had never seen gemstones so large, or with such color. The light source came from a pair of work lamps attached to an abandoned mining rig in the center of a large chamber. A black cable snaked out of the rig's back and up toward a cylindrical hole a hundred feet up in the ceiling. Still sitting in the cab was a headless operator, orange foam spilling out of his equally orange uniform, now shrunken and wrinkled from decay.

In the center of the room was a formidable diamond, free standing, and surrounded by bugs. Their eyes were shining bulbs in its reflected light. There was a beauty to the terror, but only just. Laid out before the diamond was a long, flat, stone, stained brown with the unmistakable color of dried blood. It only took Tom a moment to realize exactly where he was headed. *Do bugs have ritual sacrifice? Do they have rituals?* He supposed crabs, shrimps, and lobsters on Crustacea had developed plenty of rituals. Surely that would have been the psychic ocean's doing. Wouldn't it?

The thrumming from the bugs took on a chanting quality, buzzing briefly and then giving way to low silence before repeating itself. The sound was not unlike that of an industrial drilling machine. In fact, the more he listened to it, the surer he was they were making sounds that mimicked mining equipment. Most of the places Tom and Zip could afford to stay were near construction zones in the city, and the bug's noises were not unlike those he'd heard when he was trying to go to sleep.

The elation of his eureka moment was only slightly dampened by the feeling of being dropped onto the flat pedestal. Upon closer inspection, Tom was doubly sure the stain was blood. Luckily, it did not appear to be shrimp blood. *Maybe they only kill humans.* Tom stretched, able to move his limbs independently for the first time since being carried down the tunnel. As he did, he felt the rifle's weight, still clinging to his back. Looking out at the crowd, Tom knew he didn't have enough bullets. Maybe with Zip's Old Faithful creating ammunition from the air, but even then...

The thrumming stopped.

Tom listened in the sudden and eerie silence. He couldn't hear anything but felt a trembling vibration beneath his feet, consistent and mechanical. *It's the train.* There was no way to know for sure, but given the derelict nature of Kedasi, Tom had hope. They were beneath The Opus, and the train meant either Zip had survived or Jack's team had beaten them to the punch.

He held his breath, waiting for the sudden and shocking vibrations of gunfire. The earth went still.

The assembled bugs before him remained motionless, listening or feeling for something. A roar went up from somewhere beyond Tom's vision. The sound was deafening. All at once, the bugs before him parted, making a clear path. Tom only had a moment to wonder if he was supposed to walk down it when he saw a pair of bugs approaching. They were fatter than the others, their bulbous girth bursting from between their armored plates. As they approached, they made a hawking, gurgling noise that sounded too much like someone getting rid of a particularly nasty head cold.

"Hello," tried Tom, once again not using the voice box but scraping his limbs together.

The bugs in the front row beneath him flinched but did not respond.

The gurgling behemoths marched forward undeterred, stopping at Tom's feet.

"My name is Tom."

One of the bugs looked at him, cocked his head, and then sprayed orange gunk at Tom's feet.

"That is completely unnecessary." Tom batted at the goop with the few appendages still safe in his vac suit. It made no difference. The material solidified, crystallizing around his legs and rooting him to the stone platform. He wriggled, feeling suddenly claustrophobic.

The first bug stepped back and allowed the second to step forward. Before Tom could flinch or protest, it, too, vomited orange goop onto the existing pile, encasing Tom up to his abdomen. Tom's speaking limbs remained free, and he tried a series of curses that would have made his parents abandon him in a restaurant feeding tank. The bugs seemed to comprehend that the noise was indeed noise but didn't pay that much attention to it.

In a great wave, the assembled hoard moved, flushing out of the chamber. In less than a minute, they were gone, leaving Tom completely alone with the sparkling diamond behind him illuminating the now-empty cavern. *Well, that's odd.* He listened for the bugs but did not hear them. He could feel their trembling movement as they fled. Then, it was joined by the mechanical vibration of the train once more.

Tom tried to move again but only succeeded in tweaking his torso by twisting too far. Exasperated, he sat back to think. *Zip, wherever you are, please hurry.*

3

At Least There's Gin

Zip sat at the edge of a lavish welcome bar off to the side of reception, and she was staring into Jack's smug face. Despite that fact, she wasn't spoiling for a fight. Most of which was due to the silver drink shaker in Jack's hands. The man was many terrible things, but when it came to mixing drinks, he was a saint. Lars and Techni were beside her, Big and Tiny next to them, and the Cheri was slumped against a wall. Everyone's weapons were stacked neatly in a corner, out of reach, as a show of good faith. It was a small comfort; the air of violence was still palpable. In the meantime, at least there was gin.

Lars looked around the room. "I'll take my whiskey straight. This hotel is too quiet for my liking."

"We've already cleared out the hotel, tiny man. Sit back and enjoy your drink," replied the Cheri. It grimaced and put a fuzzy hand to its side. Orange crystals were forming on a tear in its vac suit.

Well that's unfortunate. Zip watched Jack, trying to see how much he knew.

Jack was calm and collected, mixing drinks like they were used to drinking in fancy bars. He held up the silver shaker and tossed it between his hands, the clack of ice cubes echoing in the quiet. "My furry friend is correct. It took some doing, but I think we are safe here for the time being."

"How many?" asked Techni.

Zip had been on the edge of asking the same question. On a bug planet, there was no such thing as 'cleared'.

"Fifty or more," hissed Tiny. "Turns out, they are allergic to lasers."

"That's a lot," admitted Zip, thinking back to the hoard in Adventure Canyon.

"Not even a scratch on us." Jack smiled.

The Cheri grunted.

"Sorry, one scratch, but you got that back at the park. The Journey to Old Earth ride must be a damned nest. A hoard ambushed us right before the midway. We blew up the entrance with a few charges and took out the stragglers. No more surprises." Jack tilted the shaker into a glass tumbler and slid it over to Zip. "Just the way you like it."

I wish he didn't know how I liked it. Zip took the glass in her hand and drank. There was always the chance that Jack had poisoned it, but desperate times… "We really need to start meeting in better bars."

"You and I both know all you have to do is name a time and a place."

Despite Jack being a shithead, there was still an instant where the offer sounded appealing. Zip quelled the urge with a gulp of Jack's drink. It *was* damned good. "Cut the shit, Jack. If you cleared this place, then why are you still here? What happened to no second chances?"

Lars gave Zip an unsubtle glare.

"It's the truth."

"I wanted to," said Big, fingering his empty knife holsters longingly.

Jack laughed. "Yes, you sure did. But what have I told you about our friends?"

"Not to trust them."

A flicker of annoyance crossed Jack's face. "Yes, but what else did I tell you about our friends?"

"We could use them."

Jack raised the cold silver shaker to his temple and sighed, exasperated. "You'll excuse Big; he's not one for subtlety or understanding the finer points of language."

The Cheri groaned, the sound long and low coming out of its massive mouth.

"Is he going to be OK?" Zip knew full well he wouldn't be.

"He's fine," snapped Jack. "What we're talking about here is more important anyway. I'm proposing a temporary alliance."

Zip leaned back in her chair and whistled. "Wow, that diamond is crawling with bugs, isn't it?" With fresh eyes, Zip noticed large stacks of furniture against each door leading out of the lobby. "When you say this room is clear, do you mean you barricaded yourself in here like a bad zombie movie?"

Jack let a hissing breath out between his teeth.

"Wow, I'm not far off the mark. Let's say, just for a minute, that we agree to the truce. What happens if we do fight our way through the bugs and get that diamond back. We're both going to take it to the Manchesters and hope they're feeling generous?"

"I was going to say we see who lives through the ordeal first and worry about numbers later."

Zip shook her head. "That's a recipe for getting shot in the back the second we walk out of here."

"What do you want, Zip? My word?"

"I think we both know what that's worth."

Jack threw up his hands. "Well, what then?"

Zip thought about it. In the vast expanse of galaxies, there was nothing you could trust less than a mercenary you weren't paying. Even then, things got dicey. "How about access to your bank accounts?"

The Cheri let out a snorting laugh that quickly turned into another grunt of pain.

Zip would never get over how exaggerated facial expressions looked when the face was that damned big.

Jack laughed. "Alright, you want me to sign my will and testament over to you at the same time? No dice."

A crash shook the lobby as one of the doors buckled under a great weight.

Zip forced herself to smile, hiding the sudden adrenaline coursing through her exhausted body. Bugs were coming, lots of them. *Use it. Negotiate.* She took a breath and let it out slow. "I think we'll take our chances with the Manchesters. Techni, Lars, we're out of here."

Jack spat but gave a nervous sideways glance at the door. "You wouldn't leave your man behind."

A roar emanated from the far side of the lobby, muffled but not by much.

Zip stood up and turned to leave. "A, he's probably dead already; B, he's a bug, and you know how I feel about them." *Sorry, Tom.* Even as a negotiating tactic, it felt dirty. Still, she held her calm and walked toward the train platform. "Lars, Techni, did I stutter?"

Lars wiped a look of mild shock off his face and stood up. "I guess I'll be taking my whiskey to go."

"I can't give you access to my accounts!" shouted Jack, a little too much desperation creeping into his voice.

Ah, but you can give me something. The fear was plain to see on Jack's face if one knew where to read. The Manchesters had something on him, and it was bad enough that he was going to continue a suicide mission to get rid of it. "Alright, I'll take your ship's access codes then." The second thing mercs loved after money was property. Work for hire wasn't enough to own land, so a ship was a close second.

"I can't—"

Zip held up her middle finger. "Bye, Jack."

"You can't outrun the—"

"Good luck," whispered Techni, retrieving her guns and walking away with Zip.

"Fine, fuck it!" Jack slammed a fist down on the bar top. "You can have the ship's access codes."

Zip stopped. "See? Compromise is good, Jack."

"Don't get too excited; you're getting them on a dead man's switch."

"You're going old school on me?"

Jack paced behind the bar. "You know me. So, if you die, the codes go to your next teammate, and so on and so forth."

"And if we're all dead?"

"Then I'll... I don't know... donate the ship to charity." He looked as though the words tasted vile.

Seeing Jack struggle was worth it. "Now that is an interesting proposal."

A crash echoed, and a large bookcase fell like an oversized domino, slamming into the marble floor and cracking it.

"Zip? We don't have time for a counteroffer!" shouted Jack.

"Fine, Techni, get it coded."

"Hell no, she isn't going anywhere near my—"

A roar shook the doors.

"Fine."

Zip nodded to Techni, who tapped furiously at her wrist terminal. "Don't worry, it's not my first time coding something like this."

"That's what scares me." Jack held out his terminal.

"Pleasure doing business with you, Jack." Zip lifted her rifle towards the door. "Let's kill some bugs, for old time's sake."

4

Out of the Frying Pan

Tom struggled against his bindings. The orange goop was tight around his abdomen, and for the second time that day, he found himself wondering about the seal on the vacuum suit. The top half of the suit dangled behind him, but somehow the legs continued to circulate water, keeping his lower body relatively cool and hopefully protecting against the foul substance surrounding them. Removing any of the suit had been a stupid idea, but he did wonder if it had saved his life. All the same, his top half was running dry, and he desperately needed moisture. Tom could survive for hours outside the comfort of his tank, but ordinarily, he wore protective gear to keep his eyes and face hydrated. It wasn't dangerous yet, but it was uncomfortable.

The cave around him sparkled like something out of a child's dream. Beams of light bounced off the diamond behind him, filling the room with its crystalline light. *I don't understand all the fuss.* Two teams and an obscene amount of money for a stone, a pretty stone, but still a stone. The universe was filled with vast curiosities and unknowns, and yet humans chose to covet shiny rocks. *I'm going to die for greed.*

"No." He surprised even himself by speaking aloud. Even more surprising was that he had used the old translator box still dangling around his neck. Force of habit. The mechanical noise echoed around the room, bouncing back to him. "I am not going to die here." The echoes made it sound like there were other Toms encouraging him. It was just the push he needed to wriggle at his constraint anew. The goop was hardened but far from a perfect bond. Like all pastes, it would break under extreme pressure, and if there was one thing shrimp were good at, it was wriggling.

Tom undulated his body, pushing at the hard substance and working until there was enough space for his lower limbs to move. To his surprise, they loosened easily. The real problem was his abdomen, firmly encased. Then, he remembered the rifle on his back. His front two arms were free. *This is a terrible idea.* Tom held his hands out before him in a gesture of preparing to fire. The goop behind him buckled and shattered in an instant as the rifle leaped around Tom's upper body and came to rest in his hands.

Tom remembered Techni's advice: Never point a firearm at something you don't want to kill. Looking down at his encased body, Tom was cognizant of the fact that what he was about to do could be classified as very stupid. Still, he carefully aimed the rifle at the edge of the hardened mass. Taking a deep breath and a firm hold, he pulled the trigger once. The shot was deafening, and the impact of the bullet was immediate. He winced, waiting for the pain that would tell him he had severed something vital. It never came. He looked down and saw a hole in the rock beneath him where the bullet had embedded after shattering the resin around him. It wasn't enough, but it was a start.

Carefully working his way in a circle, Tom blasted off various pieces of gunk. Each jolt brought fear, but it lessened with the successive cracks of the rifle. Eventually, he found that he could wriggle his torso enough to shatter the rest of the material. He stood. Crusted chunks of orange goop still clung to his vac suit, but for the most part, he was free. Careful not to pierce the lining, he brushed the remaining pieces off with the end of his rifle, letting them clatter to the cave floor. Then, he released the rifle and worked his upper body back into the suit.

When the last seal was closed, Tom felt immediate life-saving water circulate around his body in a cool wave. His eyes were still dry, but some hydration was better than none. He vibrated with a sense of pride and joy. *I did it! I can escape!* Just then, he looked around the room and noticed the pair of brown bugs standing at its edge, watching him. They looked on with a dull curiosity. The pair were bigger and had arms that grew out longer as well, ending in large, bladed pincers.

Tom extended his arms once more. The rifle jumped into them, eager and bouncing like an excited puppy. "Hello, friends?"

The first bug roared and charged.

So much for diplomacy. "I really am sorry about this." Tom pulled the triggers.

The cacophony of the weapon was deafening. The rifle bucked back and forth in a schizophrenic impression of aiming.

Tom tried to hold it steady, but eventually gave up and let the machine do what it wanted. He held down the trigger until a small sensor on top blinked red with the word 'Overheat'. The gun's barrel sizzled, and a small trail of smoke drifted toward the cavern ceiling. The barrel dipped toward the floor from apparent exhaustion.

Tom wondered how in the hell one was supposed to deal with 'Overheat'. He waved the rifle back and forth in the air, lamenting his lack of proper weapons training. As his vision cleared, he realized the motion was unnecessary. The two charging bugs were nothing more than shattered limbs and blood splatters.

A wave of nausea crept up inside Tom. *I killed them.* It was a strange feeling that washed over him, competence mixed with extreme shame. He had fired at bugs in Adventure Canyon, but that had been in the dark. Here, in close detail, he could see the results of what he had done. Bullets were not kind to creatures. *At least I tried to say hello first?* No, that didn't help. *Stupid Tom, stupid.*

What would Zip do? Tom scanned the room for additional enemies and waited. The red sensor on the top of his rifle clicked green. *No more overheat.* The tunnels around him remained silent despite the racket he had made killing his captors. Wherever the other bugs were, they were busy, presenting Tom with an opportunity.

He turned and looked at the diamond. It seemed that the Manchesters hadn't thought through the physical logistics of getting the diamond free of its resting place. Still, despite his exhaustion, Tom was strong, and despite its weight, he was resourceful. Leaving caution to the wind, he shuffled to the derelict excavator, trying not to look at the headless occupant.

For the most part, the vehicle was untouched, other than a few scuffs where it had burst through the roof of the diamond's main chamber. The machinery was made for heavy-duty extraction and painted in grey tones that hid scratches. Tom poked around the exterior, looking for any kind of an emergency kit. To his delight, there was an easy access panel on the back of the vehicle just between its main treads. He popped it open and found tethering cables. *I can do this.* He unspooled the wires and checked their length. If anything, they were a little too long, but they would suffice.

He moved back to the diamond and began lashing it to his back. In a matter of minutes, Tom was firmly tied to the diamond. All that was left was to see if he could lift it. Roman had said "it will be heavy, but not overly so." There was only one way to find out.

With considerable effort, Tom leaned forward, leveraging his many appendages on the floor to lift the diamond free. It slid out with ease and Tom tested its weight. The cables held, and while heavy, he could still move. Careful to keep his balance, he scuttled forward.

Alright Tom, time to save the day.

5

This Is Why We Can't Have Nice Things

ZIP HELD DOWN THE trigger until her finger went numb. Her knuckles were white, her ears were muffled from the chattering gunfire, and her arms burned. Bullet after bullet bounced off the behemoth bug in front of her, ricocheting into the hotel's lavish wallpaper and sending spurts of white dust into the air. "Can you just die already?!"

She leaped forward, sliding on the ground and turning her rifle up, trying to find the gaps in the bug's armored plating, and fired. One shot found its mark, blowing apart the armor from the inside and sending a spray of orange goop out with it. Zip focused on the newly exposed skin and concentrated her fire. In a few seconds, the bug was left with a gaping hole where its midsection used to be.

The bug staggered and fell forward with a wet thud.

Zip breathed a sigh of relief and looked for her next target. She didn't have to look far. Off to her right, one of the smaller bugs was approaching, mandibles vibrating at a frequency that told her she wouldn't even feel them pierce her skin. Zip took aim and pulled the trigger. The rifle clicked. One of the many problems with removing her helmet was no heads-up ammunition counter.

"Shit." She reached for a fresh magazine, but before she could even get it out of her belt, the creature was on top of her. The first thing she noticed was the stink. The second was the orange puss oozing from between the creature's jaws. "Shit, shit, shit."

Zip fought, kicking with her legs. The weight was too much, and her boot heels bounced off the armor plating. Hot, stinking breath turned Zip's world into a putrid nightmare. *Never take the helmet off.* She would die by disobeying one of the rules she put at the top of every mission briefing.

"Hey, ugly." Zip didn't have to look to know the silky-smooth voice was Jack's. "Where I come from, it's not polite to hit a lady."

Zip didn't see much other than the bug's head jolting suddenly to the side as the back end of Jack's rifle swung into it. There was a blur of motion, a cacophony of gunshots, and the creature was dead. *At least he had the courtesy to get it off me first.* Not wanting to push her luck, Zip scrambled to her feet and popped a fresh magazine into the rifle.

It was unnecessary. For the moment, the fight was over. What had once been an impressive foyer was now filled with stinking orange crud and piles of unidentifiable bug bits.

Jack sidled up next to her, rifle held confidently at his side. "What, not even a thank you?"

"You almost made the last words I heard benevolent sexism. No, no thank you."

"Last time I save your life."

"I'd say you owe me a few."

Jack flashed a grin, one of his gold teeth glinting in the harsh light of the lobby. "You might be right."

Zip resisted the urge to flip him off by reminding herself that her hands needed to stay firmly on her gun. Refocusing, she turned away and moved through the piles of bodies. "Lars, Techni, you alright?"

Lars popped up from behind a particularly large bug that had been pinned to the bar with several rounds from what might have been a harpoon gun. "Alright is a relative term."

"Alive then?"

"I am that."

Techni wiped down her submachine guns, careful to get every last inch of gunk off the barrels. "Alive, but I hope I never see another place like this in my life."

"I keep telling myself the same thing."

"I don't think he's alright though." Techni jabbed a finger toward the Cheri, its hulking form slumped against a wall, huge face split in a horrified grimace. Orange bile dripped from the corner of its lips. An oversized rifle hung loose in one of its furry hands.

"Jack, you got a med kit?" Zip rushed over to the Cheri, knowing full well it was too late. The med kit would at least have military-grade painkillers to make it an easier death.

"Look at him. No point."

"Screw you," wheezed the Cheri. The words hardly came out through a heavy gurgling at the back of its throat.

Jack looked at the remaining mercenaries. "You'd do the same for me. We should keep moving. Wait around too long, and we'll be bug bait."

Zip wrapped her finger around the trigger reflexively then forced herself to relax. "Get him a med kit."

The last vestige of Jack's cool fled. "Will you cut the act, Zip? You might tell these shitheads that you've changed, but I know better. I've watched you shoot a man in the back for an extra share, and that kind of darkness doesn't just leave a person. You are a mercenary, the same as me. We were bred as soldiers and found a better way. So, spare me the sympathy play, and let's get the hell out of here."

"The med kit, Jack." Zip raised the rifle by a hair, enough to be noticed.

Jack spread his hands. "Do it. At least that will get us to the point a little quicker. If we're going to die, I'd rather do it with a gun in my hand. Take your best shot."

Zip was halfway to pulling the trigger when Techni stepped in front of her. "He can have one of ours." She pulled out a small green cylinder.

"There, see? The robot has her uses."

Techni's eyes flickered almost imperceptibly toward Jack in the smallest act of violence Zip had ever seen. Still, she held out the med cylinder. "Ignore him," Techni whispered. "We need to save Tom; we can't do it if we're dead."

Tiny slunk over with a squelching slither. "Boss?" It lifted a slimy appendage and pointed at the Cheri.

Jack looked over. "Well, it seems this conversation is now moot."

The Cheri's face was contorted in a sudden and final image of extreme pain. Swaths of orange foam dribbled their way down its front and puddled on the floor. The wound on its side had bulged out, ripping the vac suit.

Techni returned the med canister to her belt.

"Check for a pulse and log a time of death. We're going to need to report this for the insurance." The relish had left Jack's voice.

Tiny slithered over and held a scanner to the Cheri's massive face. Red lights flashed and it gave a single beep. "No pulse, time of death, whatever the hell time it is right now."

"Good enough for me. Shall we?"

"You're an asshole, you know that right?" Zip hadn't liked the Cheri, but it was still a living thing. And not a bug.

"Yeah, I've been told, but right now, I'm the asshole that's going to keep you alive and get us off this rock."

"And here I thought we were the ones saving you," said Lars.

Big held one of his oversized knives out towards Lars. "No one saves me."

"Boys, play nice." Jack's voice carried a new edge that stopped the conflict, at least momentarily.

Zip looked at her wrist terminal and pulled up Jack's ship details. Everything was still green; she had access. "Remember that if you screw us over, your precious ship is going high speed into the nearest sun."

"Oh, believe me, I can't think about much else. Now, can we pull together and get the hell out of here? Having a ship doesn't matter much if you're dead on a pleasure asteroid."

"Fine." Zip motioned to Lars and Techni, who formed up behind her. "Techni, what's the path?"

Techni pulled up a small holoprojector on her wrist showing a map of The Opus. "From the atrium, we will need to move down toward the VIP suites. These were designed to have a good look at the diamonds in the chasm below. It's also where the guided tours would have started. There's a chance the gondolas they were planning on building are already operational."

"Another ride?" asked Zip.

"Another?" asked Jack.

"Long story."

"We shouldn't need the gondolas, but we can follow the service lines to get to the display chamber." A faint green line appeared from their current position, plotting a course down toward the bottom of the hotel.

Even if it would save Tom, Zip still didn't love the idea of going deeper into the asteroid. Artificial cave systems were one thing; the belly of the beast was something else entirely. "The further down we go, the more bugs there will be. Let's try to spend as little time down there as possible."

Jack let out an exasperated sigh. "That's what I've been saying, but you keep on—"

"Shut it, Jack. Follow us." Zip motioned for Techni to lead, and they moved forward.

The door the bugs had come through was shattered. Zip passed through the debris, careful to check her corners as she went. Soft classical music played from overhead speakers on an endless loop, giving the eerie feeling that the hotel was in use. Beyond the lobby was an ornate hallway leading to a pair of spiral staircases that went down to the hotel's lower levels. Glass panels lined each side, looking out at the asteroid beyond. The view was breathtaking, even if it was barren.

The team moved fast. The sound of boots on tile clicked and echoed. There was no point in being quiet; every living thing on the asteroid knew they were there. It was only a matter of time before they got into another gunfight, and ammunition was already running low. Eventually, they came to a long hallway with wooden doors leading off both sides. Each bore a gold number and a small tap pad below it for access. "Guessing these are the VIP suites?"

Techni nodded. "The lounge and waiting area we're looking for should be at the end of this hallway."

A rumble shook the floor above, sending bits of plaster raining from the ceiling. The whole hotel vibrated for a moment before going still.

"What the hell was that?" asked Zip.

Jack shook his head. "I thought you said you checked him."

Tiny slunk up beside him. "I did. I thought he was joking."

"What are we talking about?" asked Zip.

"The Cheri had a kill switch embedded in it. Stupid son of a bitch. You were supposed to shut that shit off, Tiny!"

"I did!"

"Well, clearly—"

The vibrating restarted and was joined by the sound of a hundred scuttling limbs just ahead of them.

Zip didn't have to look to know what it was. "Into the suites, now."

6

High Rollers

The VIP suite looked like a mix between casino décor and the golden age of a civilization long past. Like the rest of The Opus, it was done in primarily dark colors with shining accents. When a design worked, it worked. With the door shut behind them, Zip could barely hear the rumble of the bugs passing by in the hallway beyond. She said a silent thank you to Techni, who had hacked the door panel in less than three seconds. The backup plan had been to break it down the old-fashioned way and hope the bugs passed without noticing. Subtlety was the better choice.

Despite the sound-dampening qualities, no one moved. They all stayed still, waiting for the creatures to pass, knowing that even the slightest vibration would give them away. Zip used the opportunity to get a better look at the mercenaries she now found herself temporarily aligned with. Jack was reclined on a queen bed, with a hat over his eyes but a hand near his pistol. Tiny was on high alert, red eyes darting around the room. Even in the Manchesters' briefings, there hadn't been much about that creature. It was a Slither, which meant foul temper and a penchant for murder, but not much else was known about the species. They all purposefully obscured their full form. What were they hiding? Looking into Tiny's dark hood, Zip saw several rungs of coiled skin beneath the glowing eyes.

A hard stare from Big stopped Zip's curiosity dead. She knew enough from the large humanoid's file to understand that anyone who hurt Tiny was going to get hurt shortly after. A loyal trait, but not when it wasn't on your side. Outside, the rumbling grew quieter and eventually faded completely. Zip imagined the bugs rounding the big spiral staircase they had come down and finding an entire room of their compatriots blown to bits by whatever device the Cheri had outfitted itself with.

Techni moved to the door and put a finger near the bottom edge. The tip of her finger detached, sliding underneath the crack between the wood and the floor and snaking into the hallway beyond. Techni's eyes flashed with video images. "Hallway is empty, no stragglers. Time to move."

"Time to move," agreed Zip.

Lars stood with a sigh. "I assume we're ignoring the fact that the bugs will have us pinned in if we continue deeper."

"It was always a risk." Zip didn't like it much either, but the surface was no longer an option. "We've gotten lucky before. Why not now?"

Lars checked the end of his rifle. "Yeah, lucky. That describes my life."

Jack stood. "I feel lucky. Ladies first."

In her head, Zip let fly a myriad of increasingly crass insults but kept her external response to a curt nod. Shouting, or any fight, would mean vibration; vibration meant more bugs. She moved to the door and signaled Techni to open it. The smooth wood clicked and swung inward. The hallway was empty, but the carpet was pitted and scored from the bugs that had just passed over it. Zip started a timer on her wrist terminal, clocking how long the bugs would take to realize the threat was no longer upstairs and return.

The group moved quickly and as one, covering the hallway in quiet strides. They passed room after room, the doors much the same as the last, only the little gold numbers changing. Eventually, they came to another sweeping marble staircase. The top was narrow, matching the hallway, but widened out into a lounge surrounded by curved glass. Outside, multicolor spotlights shone on the sparkling walls of the chasm. Plush armchairs lined the sides of the room, facing outward, each flanked by a small table for drinks. Top-shelf bottles glistened behind a dark wood bar at the far end of the room.

"Think we could have ever afforded to stay in a place like this?" asked Jack.

For a moment, Zip saw the person he used to be. A small flame flickered in her heart, but she stamped it out. "This was built to ensure the high-ups never had to see people like us."

"You might be right about that."

"Well, I think we know where they're coming from." Lars pointed a finger just beyond the bar at the room's only non-glass wall. The remains of a large, no doubt tasteful, oil painting hung in shreds on either side of a crude tunnel.

Zip looked at the hole and felt a primal sense of fear course through her. That darkness was a place no human was supposed to enter. She scanned the room, hoping for other options, but the gondola system had either been scrapped for budget or moved to another part of the hotel. "Looks like a fine enough entrance to me."

It looked like another in a long series of gruesome ways to die, but she wasn't going to let Jack know she felt that way.

Tiny slithered toward the glass wall and looked at the diamond-speckled chasm beyond. "Why can't we just take one of these instead?"

"An angry creature that can't read, how original," said Techni.

"I can—"

"Apparently not the mission briefing," finished Jack. "I don't like the robot, but she's right, it was all there. The diamond that the Manchesters had in mind for the crown jewel of The Opus was specific. They failed to mention outside the fine print that they never finished extracting it before things went sour. It's at the bottom of a mine shaft. Not a very deep one, but it's still a hassle."

"Leave it to the Manchesters. Don't worry, I brought heavy equipment," said Lars.

"It's not supposed to be heavy."

"Just in case. I like my heavy—"

Rustling from the tunnel caught their attention. Flashlights and lasers rose all at once, painting the rock in white and red. Zip silently motioned for everyone to fan out and take defensive positions. For once, no one argued.

The rustling continued from the end of the tunnel, but it was quieter than an entire hoard of bugs moving at once. Then, a new, tinny noise echoed from the end of the tunnel. At first, Zip couldn't make out what it was, but when she did, her heart soared.

"Weapons down, now."

7

Reunion

TOM MOVED THROUGH THE tunnel with great difficulty, the diamond strapped to his back weighing down his many limbs. While it wasn't heavy, strictly speaking, shrimp were not built to carry much of anything. On Crustacea, labor tasks were left to the bulkier brethren of crabs and lobsters. Tom's ancestors had evolved for an aqueous environment that didn't require much in the way of lifting. Why would you build anything when the sea provided all the hiding places you could ever want? With his limbs burning from exhaustion, he wished for the first time that his ancestors had faced just a little more adversity.

While strapping the diamond to his back had worked, it limited him to a clumsy shuffle. The lower end of the diamond kept dipping and dragging along the ground behind him. Tom hoped the Manchesters weren't paying for pristine. Getting back up the cable had been a simple manner of restructuring existing machinery. Tom liked machines; they made sense and, more often than not, eschewed the possibility of future manual labor. He hadn't accounted for the tunnel that would come after the ascent.

Looking ahead, he couldn't see anything. A dim light shone somewhere in the distance and from the hole behind him, but otherwise, he marched in darkness. With each mincing step, the stone dragged behind him, feeling just a little bit heavier. There were several points where he was on the verge of giving up, but the grim reminder of what awaited him if he did was enough to push forward. The choices were to drag the diamond out or wait and see what the bugs had planned for him. Something told Tom it wasn't in the vein of a nice meal and a chat. So, he soldiered on.

Eventually, the tunnel lightened. Tom couldn't be sure how far he had walked, instead choosing to measure distance in terms of exertion. By the time he saw the light, he was on the verge of passing out from extreme exhaustion. It was unfortunate then that the light was joined by several pinprick red laser points on the dark walls of the tunnel and a blinding white flashlight in Tom's face.

"Please, don't shoot me." The words came out garbled but audible from his battered translator. The minor electrical shocks that came along with the effort were barely noticeable against the straining cords of his frail muscles.

A quiet but authoritative voice echoed from the end of the tunnel. "Weapons down, now."

Tom loosened the straps around his midsection and let the diamond drop with a heavy thunk. Then, he hobbled to the end of the tunnel, putting his appendages up in a way that did not cause his rifle to leap into his limbs. The voice had clearly been Zip's, but he had always known her to be more than a little trigger-happy. His best chance was to remain unarmed.

Suddenly, a bobbing light burst through the end of the tunnel, blinding Tom further. He stopped moving, sinking toward the floor in an ingrained gesture of submission.

"Tom! Are you hurt?"

He looked up and saw Zip's muscular outline. Against the impossible, there she was, ready to rescue him again. "I need a proper scan and I am tired, but otherwise, I am unharmed."

Zip's arms wrapped around him in an embrace. The gesture was strictly primate in nature, but even so, Tom had come to treasure it. Zip helped Tom out of the tunnel.

"Good to see you," came Lars's voice.

Tom's eyes adjusted, seeing a much bigger crew than he had left. "Oh, Jack is here." A quick calculation showed that the Cheri was not. While Tom would never strictly wish anyone an ill fate, he was not upset to see the creature was missing. Still, Tiny and Big were lurking in the darkness, leaving death an itchy trigger finger away. Techni was beside them, keeping a watchful eye, and never let the barrel of her gun drift far from their center mass. *So, things are tense.*

"Yeah, Jack is here," agreed Zip. "Can't shake him."

"Well, I'll be damned," said Jack. "Look what we have here." He climbed into the tunnel, walked over to the diamond, and gave it a perfunctory kick. "That is one hell of a stone. Think it's the one we're looking for?"

"I have already scanned it." The idea that Tom wouldn't have checked before hauling such a load was nothing short of insulting. "This is the diamond we're looking for."

"Well, Shrimp Man Tom, I take back everything I said. Turns out you were the most useful member of Zip's team after all."

Tom knew the words were mean, but they didn't bother him. What did was the sudden twitch of Jack's hand. It was small enough to be almost imperceptible, but Tom recognized it as a habit of violence. At that moment, Jack wanted to kill them all, take the diamond, and be done with it, but something stopped him. Tom looked to Zip. She was breathing steady, eyes on his, but flickering back toward Jack every second or so. She knew. There was a sort of tenuous insurance playing out between the two.

"Ordinarily, I wouldn't let you anywhere near that thing, but you've got the muscle." Zip pointed to Big. "Would've been nice to have the Cheri do it, but you seem strong enough."

Big grunted. "Fine." That was it, no minced words. What the universe had given him in muscles, it had taken in verbosity. He climbed into the tunnel, walked to the diamond, picked up Tom's makeshift straps, and slung it across his back like a fashion accessory.

Tom felt a momentary pang of inadequacy, but it was quickly dissolved by a roar that shook The Opus on its foundation.

"I think that's our cue to get moving." Jack pointed toward a long marble staircase.

Techni pulled up her wrist projector and showed a map of The Opus. "Unlike you, I don't leave my fate to chance." Hundreds of red dots popped up, filling the upper floors and blocking any chance of getting out through The Opus's main doors.

"And I'm supposed to believe those are bugs?"

"I put sensors down as we walked."

"Expensive tech to leave lying around."

"I get paid well. The front door just became a dead end."

"No," groaned Lars.

Zip turned back toward the tunnel. "How bad is it back there?"

"Very."

Zip turned to Techni. "And how bad is it up there?" She pointed up the stairs.

"Worse." Techni held out the projector showing the red dots now moving through the hallway.

Tom could feel the vibrations beneath his feet. "I'm not a fan of worse."

"You can't be serious," hissed Tiny.

"We're all going to die," muttered Lars.

"Is there a way off this rock through that tunnel, Techni?" asked Zip.

"The bugs did manage to bring me here, but there are many tunnels. It was confusing," said Tom.

The rumbling beneath their feet grew steadily stronger.

Zip stepped toward the tunnel. "Come on, Jack. You walk up front with me. This is going to be fun."

8

Tunnels, Why Did It Have to Be Tunnels?

ZIP HAD NEVER BEEN in a bug tunnel. In fact, she had done everything she could on multiple occasions to avoid such a fate. Kedasi marked her fourth infested excursion, and as far as she was concerned, three had already been far too many. She had stuck to the surface on those previous ill-fated missions and still suffered severe casualties. The reason was simple: Fighting bugs in an open field was hard enough; fighting them on their own turf was suicidal. A better rule would be not to fight them at all, but no one seemed to listen.

Shining a light at the moist dirt walls of the tunnel beneath Kedasi reminded Zip exactly why they shouldn't be there. The tunnels were fifteen feet tall at their lowest. Bugs didn't care for aesthetics, so if the tunnels were tall, it meant there were some big nasty bastards that necessitated the height. So far, the maximum bug size she had seen was somewhere around ten feet. The thought of anything bigger made her shudder.

Then there were the holes. While difficult to see in some of the larger sections, the tunnels clearly had entrances on the sides, roof, and occasionally in the ground. It made for a precarious walking path and also an impossible watch. The result was a cadre of constantly flashing lights sweeping over the tunnel and giving the ambiance of the world's shittiest dance club.

The team did not speak; the only sound was their booted footfalls on the damp earth floor. Despite trying to explain the need for stealth, Big still plodded along like an old-timey movie monster. With each thud of his feet, Zip got a little closer to turning around and pulling the trigger. She breathed deep and slow, reminding herself to keep her eyes forward and be ready for anything.

A green alert from Techni flashed to Zip's wrist terminal. It read: *Left tunnel ahead. Pretty sure.*

Zip turned to her and mouthed, *Pretty sure?*

Techni sent another message. "The tunnels aren't exactly on the park's main map."

That was fair enough. They were aiming for the tunnel system of Adventure Canyon which seemed tame compared to the vast network that had existed long before developers arrived. The goal was simple: Get to the end of the bug tunnels and hope that most of the colony was distracted somewhere else. Unfortunately, Tom didn't remember much about his initial trip through the darkness, and what he did was more fear-inducing than helpful. Put succinctly, there had been too many bugs, and it was too damned dark.

They marched for thirty minutes without incident, moving quickly but not so quickly as to be noticed. The distance back to Adventure Canyon wasn't all that far, but the time underground was winding and passed slowly. Every step was on the edge of sudden death, and every fiber in Zip's being knew it. The lack of active pursuit made her twitchy. Either the bugs were preoccupied, or they weren't worried about their prey escaping.

Another message popped up, this time from Lars: *Are those webs?*

Even reading the message filled Zip with cold dread. Somehow, even through vast quantities of interstellar travel, spiders survived and thrived on Prota. The initial settlers had made valiant attempts to keep them off the colony ships, but six months after arrival, spiders were alive and well. Zip wasn't hard at heart, but spiders were one thing she didn't mess with. It didn't matter how small; she would rather leave a room or burn an apartment to the ground than deal with a single spider. So, when she looked down at the floor and saw the white webbing clinging to the edges of the tunnel, a vice tightened around her throat.

She opened a message to Tom, tapping quickly with her free hand so as not to let her gun go for too long: *Did you see anything that made webs?* A simple question. It also didn't explicitly call out what kind of creature she was looking for. A good happy medium that could keep her in blissful ignorance for a little while longer.

Tom checked his wrist terminal, the rifle in his hands snapping around to his back with a quiet click.

Zip made a mental note to ask Techni for something similar if they survived.

Tom's reply: *Too dark, didn't see anything. Bugs with diamond were same.*

Neither confirmation nor denial.

"What are you kids gossiping about?" hissed Jack. Even at a whisper, his voice carried through the tunnel in a way that might as well have been an alarm.

Everyone stopped moving and Zip shot him a glare that might have killed a weaker man. Together, they waited, listening and feeling for any vibrations in the ground. None came.

"Oh, come on, like they're going to hear a whisper over our footsteps. Big walks like a god damned freight train." Jack's eyes flicked around in the smallest betrayal of how nervous he felt.

Zip rolled her eyes and pointed to the webs on the floor.

Jack looked down. "Don't tell me you're still afraid of spiders."

"Everyone should be afraid of spiders," replied Zip, her voice raising slightly higher than she would have liked.

"Most bugs have armor, spiders don't. They're ambush predators, not much good against a solid rifle and someone alert."

"Spiders aren't the only thing that makes webs," whispered Lars. "Now shut up before you get us all killed."

"What he said," whispered Zip and continued forward.

Thankfully, no one wanted to continue the discussion. After a few more minutes of walking, they came to a fork in the tunnel. Zip looked to Techni who pulled up a projection. There was a bright green line that indicated the tunnel they'd been walking followed by an immense blank space between them and Kedasi's main park. Techni pointed in the direction that most closely mirrored the location of Adventure Canyon.

Good enough for me, mouthed Zip. She walked forward along the path Techni had chosen, trying to keep her light on the endless tunnel of gloom before her.

The walls were soft, almost organic despite being carved through the hard stone of the asteroid's surface. *Are the webs getting thicker?* It was a thought she immediately regretted because as soon as it had crossed her mind, it would not leave. *Why aren't the bugs following us?* A second bad thought right on the heels of the first one. There were no such things as happy coincidences in life, at least, not in Zip's life.

At the edges of the tunnel, the webs had grown to thick white strands, constricting the small party towards its center. Filaments on the tunnel ceiling flittered on the wings of an invisible wind. Zip's whole body tensed. Ordinarily, she would have blamed it on PTSD, but a dark tunnel full of webs was worth every bad reaction in the book. Her skin was cold, and she felt a single drop of sweat roll down her back. Something bad was about to happen, and they were walking right into it.

Zip snapped around just in time to see a serrated tail slithering out of a hole in the ceiling. "Eyes up! It's in the roof!" She had time to let out a single controlled burst of fire before the tail whipped down, piercing Big's left arm and dragging him upward.

Big screamed, the sound primal and deep. He lifted his rifle with a single arm, pressed the barrel to the tail, and opened fire. Some of the bullets ricocheted, embedding in the cave walls, but a few found their mark. The tail recoiled and released him. He fell to the floor with a thud, his head snapping back into the diamond.

There was a silent moment where every rifle was trained on the hole the tail had come out of. A single dribble of blood ran out and dripped to the floor.

"Did I get it?" asked Big, the words thick and slow.

There was no time to answer. The tail whipped down again, this time aiming for Tiny. Big scrambled to his feet, but with the diamond on his back, he was too slow. A barb shot through Tiny's back and exploded out its front. Its red eyes went wide with terror, and it hissed a gurgling scream as it was pulled into the ceiling.

Big screamed again. "Get back down here! Bring back my friend!"

Zip looked up, waiting for a final burst of gunfire, or another sign Tiny was alive. There was only silence. "Run!"

She grabbed Tom, pushed him forward, and sprinted back the way they had come. Her heart pounded in her chest, but she heard every footfall like a gunshot. Awareness pumped through her, crashing into her fingertips with a painful tingle reminding her that every move counted. Her footsteps mixed with those of the team behind her, and then once more with a slither in the ceiling. An instinct told her to stop, and she followed it without question, yanking Tom back.

A second later, a black tail whipped out of a hole in the ceiling, twin barbs exposed on its end. Zip fired, a few shots hitting their mark before the bug retreated once more into the ceiling.

Lars ran up beside her, breathless. "I think there's more than one."

"They're bugs, there's always more than one." Zip broke into a run once more. "Techni, nearest exit!"

"Nothing leads back toward Adventure Canyon!"

"Just get us back under the park then! They'll need more than one entrance." Likely, there were holes all over the park and Adventure Canyon was simply the most noticeable.

Techni cursed, hissed, and did everything in between. “Take the next right.”

Simple enough. Zip tried to keep up her pace while also keeping her flashlight trained on the ceiling. It left her off balance, but it was the only way to stop herself from running headlong into the bug’s tail when it decided it wanted another crack at them. Fortunately, or unfortunately, she didn’t have to do so for long. The tunnel ahead split, the webs on the sides growing thinner, but before she could reach them, two hulking chitinous forms slid out of the walls and blocked the path.

The others skidded to a halt behind her. “Oh shit,” said Lars.

“Watch out for the third one behind us.” Zip sighted her rifle.

“The third one?” asked Techni.

9

The Third One

Tom barely had time to make a half-turn before the barb slammed into his back. Luckily, his natural armor-plating blocked what might have otherwise been a fatal blow. Still, it felt like he had been punched by a mantis shrimp. He was launched through the air and collided with the tunnel wall. What little light there was winked out as the air was knocked from his lungs. Reflexively, his appendages went out before him and the rifle sprang into them. The force of the wall against his back caused him to pull the trigger and the last thing he heard before blacking out was a sudden hail of bullets.

Tom blinked and the world was back in a mixture of flashing chaos. Gunfire rang through the tunnel with deafening regularity, illuminating the gloom in strobes. In the flashes, he watched as Zip fired up at the holes in the ceiling, her teeth bared in a warrior's grin. A tail flashed down and he tried to call out but could make no sounds beyond garbled static. His translator box which had somehow survived everything up until that point was smashed, sending painful shocks down his limbs with every attempted use.

Luckily, Zip didn't seem to need a reminder that they were in a fight. The tail reached out to strike her, but she was ready, wrapping an arm around it and yanking with all her might. The creature spilled from the ceiling, filling Tom with equal parts horror and fascination. Its shell was dark, camouflaged with the tunnels it inhabited. Where the other bugs had mandibles, this one had a maw filled with needle teeth that shook with every roaring exhalation. Its back was a series of segmented armor plates, beginning wide at its head and narrowing to a long tail ending in a sharp barb. It was a creature designed for death and designed well.

Zip seemed momentarily surprised by the bug's heft after pulling it down, but quickly moved for its head, firing as she went. When the rifle ran dry, she pulled a knife out of a thigh-mounted holster and drove it in just below the creature's mouth. It shrieked and thrashed, but she held firm, driving the knife deeper. Jets of orange blood squirted as Zip pounded the knife repeatedly, screaming with each thrust. The creature thrashed, jerked, and finally went still.

Tom rose to his feet, looking for a way to help. Instead, another barbed tail flung in front of him, missing by inches. It was at that moment he realized some of the gunfire was getting farther away. Jack and Big were making their way down the tunnel, the diamond still strapped to Big's back. Meanwhile, the creatures had been drawn to the sound of their fallen comrade. Two of the scorpion-like things advanced on Zip who immediately returned to a firing position. Techni moved beside her, submachine guns pointed out. Lars was a few feet away, grim determination on his face as he loaded another magazine.

The creatures were only ten feet away when Techni shouted, "Get down and cover your eyes!"

Without question, Tom curled into himself and pressed his eyes tight beneath the fold of his tail. Strictly speaking, it was not a flattering or well-defended position, but it was the only one where he could get his eyes mostly covered. A few seconds later there was a deafening concussion, like thunder, and a flash so bright that it illuminated the individual blood vessels in his carapace. The flash subsided, leaving strange tendril afterimages. He uncurled and tried to get his bearings.

The creatures shrieked as more bursts of gunfire filled the tunnel. Techni wasted no time. She ran and jumped onto the back of the larger bug, scrambling up towards its neck. Then, she pointed both of her guns at the creature's neck and fired. The force of the bullets rocked the creature's body and quickly cut through, severing the head neatly—well, as neatly as possible when the cutting implements were rapid-fire weaponry. The creature's limbs spasmed, kicking out in all directions, and slowly went still.

Meanwhile, Zip wrestled the tail of the other creature to the ground while Lars pumped rifle rounds into its stomach. It wasn't as effective, but in the end, it did the trick. The cacophony of the cave died to eventual silence as the three humanoids stood panting.

What little respite there was only lasted a moment. Zip sucked in a lungful of air, just enough to breathe, "Please tell me someone put a tracker on that asshole when he wasn't looking."

Tom turned his head down the tunnel in the direction Jack had run and shook his head. "Th—" His translator box shocked him and he fell silent.

Techni brought up the map again, the small movement taking mammoth effort. Paths spiraled away from their position with labyrinthian complexity. "I don't like our odds."

Zip shook her head. "He'll be easy to find."

"I don't see ho—"

"Jack might talk a big game, but he's a coward. Cowards are predictable. He's going to take the first path that leads him back toward the park and he's going to continue doing that until he sees daylight."

"You think that will work?"

"Either that, or we just follow the trail." Zip pointed at the floor. Big's footprints, as well as occasional scuff marks from the diamond hitting the ground, were clear as day.

"We can work with that," said Techni.

Lars still stood atop the scorpion-like creature, laughing to himself. "Can you believe this shit?"

"The story should get us a few drinks at least back on Prota," admitted Zip.

Lars laughed again. "Better be more than a few. Permission to get the hell out of this c—"

The tail whipped out of the ceiling with blinding speed. Lars's chest swelled and then burst as a ragged barb punched straight through it. He looked down. "Well imagine that." He coughed, wet and bloody. His eyes went wide in a sad, resolute stare. "Run." As the tail dragged him toward the ceiling, Tom watched Lars's hand drop to one of the many explosives he kept on his belt.

No, Tom thought, desperate for something, anything to prove this wasn't real. Zip's hand grabbed him by his vac suit as sound left the world and his limbs turned to lead. He felt hands on his carapace, yanking him into the darkness. The blank space where Lars had been seemed impossible. A few seconds later there was a rumble and a bang that shook the walls, but Tom barely heard it. Lars was gone. One moment he was there, and the next he wasn't. Pain bloomed in Tom's chest, followed swiftly by anger.

Against his better instincts, he tried to run back, to fight. Zip's arms were strong. No matter how hard he tried, she pulled him back. Muffled words came through the haze of the world but made no sense. Tom didn't understand. He didn't want to keep moving, he just wanted Lars back.

Time passed in a nonsensical blur. At some point, he

stopped fighting and followed Zip and Techni through the dark tunnels. His legs moved, but it felt like someone else was using them. Words needed to be said. Someone had to speak to the tragedy that had just happened. Even if his translator box had been working, Tom wasn't sure what he could have said. He clung to the broken machinery, his last vestige of home, but there was no comfort to be found in the cave.

Zip ran at the front, jaw set and pointing straight ahead. She paused occasionally, checking the direction of Big's trail, but said nothing.

Techni, no doubt sensing Tom's use as a rear guard had diminished, was doing double duty. If there was hurt behind her eyes or fear, Tom could not see it.

He's gone. The words stabbed at Tom even as thoughts. *He's gone because of a shiny rock.* Tom could feel his heart beating faster, pulsing at the edges of his vision. *The Manchesters are going to pay for this.*

They traveled in silence, constantly moving with a singular purpose: Get out alive. The consistent nature of the smooth walls made the passage of time impossible to determine. A distant pain told Tom his limbs were on the verge of exhaustion, but he pushed through it, sadness replaced by numb anger. When Zip finally held up a hand to stop, he skidded to an awkward halt, falling onto his side in the dirt.

He considered laying there and never getting up. It would certainly be easier.

Techni moved in front of him and offered her hand. "Nearly there, Tom." The words were gentle and crystal clear.

Tom grabbed Techni's hand with a few limbs and pulled himself to a stand. "Than—" A painful jolt of electricity coursed through his limbs as the translator box arced.

Techni looked at the device and held out a hand.

Tom looked at the box and then at Techni. With great reluctance, he unclasped the device and passed it over.

She took it, turned it, and shook her head. Looking at Zip, she asked, "Air still breathable?"

Zip nodded, taking a deep breath.

Techni set the box down and removed her helmet. Then, with ruthless efficiency, she stripped the comms system from it. She motioned to Tom, holding a bundle of loose wires and diodes.

Tom moved closer.

Techni stuck patches to the lower part of Tom's head and attached the wires to sections of his suit. Tiny flares erupted from her fingers, followed by the smell of burning metal. "I can't fix your box, but this should do until *you* can." She made a few adjustments and then stepped back. "Not my best, but it will work."

"Why are we stopped?" asked Tom, his voice as clear as it had been in the suit's helmet. Techni was a miracle worker.

Zip pointed ahead. The tunnel made a sharp bend, and in the new silence, Tom heard a distant din.

"Lights off," whispered Zip, and she crept forward.

Tom followed, turning his light off and pointing the rifle forward. The AI in the weapon seemed almost excited at the prospect, moving with stiff sweeping motions in front of him.

When he rounded the corner, he noticed a few things. The first was a gaping hole in a concrete wall. The second was the room beyond, filled with green foliage, and the terrifying visage of a *Tyrannosaurus rex*.

10
Journey to Old Earth

ZIP HAD READ ALL about dinosaurs as a child. To some extent, she still never believed the history that Old Earth had once been ruled by an entire species of giant lizards. The cold-blooded nature of it all felt supremely improbable. Still, as children had for eons, she obsessed over the creatures for the better part of her youth. Their power, their ferocity, and most of all, their teeth. As she crept toward the jungle room at the end of the tunnel, she was struck by just that: A gleaming set of white teeth on an animatronic *Tyrannosaurus rex*. The creature roared, stomping through the foliage before disappearing.

Zip was counting on Jack's old habits dying hard. Even on patrol, he had never been great at checking his six. His strategy was to always to ambush first so he didn't have to worry about someone else stabbing him in the back. With any luck, Jack already assumed they were dead, and they'd be able to walk right up behind him.

Judging by the massive animatronic dinosaur, they had stumbled right into the Journey to Old Earth ride. Further complicating matters, based on the dinosaur's movement, the ride was on.

Zip slipped up to the edge of a broken wall, feeling a warm, humid breeze blowing through the hole. It smelled sickly sweet, just like a real jungle. The tunnel had clearly been dug after construction. Remains of the concrete wall littered the floor, and metal struts poked out at odd angles.

The ride appeared to be in perfect working condition. An all-terrain vehicle with fifteen riderless seats careened around the corner with the faux screech of tires. It stopped at the edge of a small rise, lights flickering. A moment later, the Tyrannosaur crashed through the underbrush, letting out an earsplitting roar. The vehicle zoomed away with another screech of tires and zipped around a corner through a hidden track in the foliage. The dinosaur did an awkward moonwalk as the struts beneath it eased the animatronic back between its designated trees.

"This will make it more difficult for the bugs to find us," said Tom.

"How the hell is it still running?" As Zip asked it, another car came screeching around the corner, waiting for the inevitable roar of the dinosaur hiding just out of sight.

"I think I might have an answer to that." Techni tapped furiously at her wrist, filing through lines of code. "Remember when you asked me to turn on the coaster in Adventure Canyon?"

"I remember shooting the control box." Zip was still quite proud of that.

"Yes, you did. Well, something about that control box failing and the code I wrote to turn on the ride triggered a cascade of tests."

"Do I need to point out that we're short on time?"

"The park is on. All of it."

Zip would never admit it aloud, but her heart leaped. "All of it?"

Techni looked down at the terminal, still spooling through code. "I can't be sure without reading through this line by line, but yes, looks like all of it. I'm not sure how long these tests take, but my guess is the park is online for the rest of our stay."

"Think that's enough noise to cover our escape?" Zip asked.

"I think that's an optimistic way of viewing this situation. The bugs may not be able to hear us specifically, but all the noise is going to draw them out, at least if your reports were accurate. A lot of it seemed like conjecture."

Zip couldn't help herself, she smiled. "You read the reports."

"Of course I did. I don't want to die."

"Me neither."

Zip looked at the ride tracks. Big's blood trail might as well have been a neon arrow to Jack's position. She looked back at the tunnel they had come from—only death that way. "I guess we follow the blood."

She stepped onto the tracks and was almost immediately confronted by another screeching car. White lights blazed and she rolled out of the way. A moment later, the car zoomed past, its faux engine rumbling. "Right, this is going to be fun." She motioned to the others to follow.

Together, the three of them crossed the tracks and moved to the edge of the jungle. Despite fake foliage, Zip still found the effect was convincing. Each step reminded her of a war movie, but not the kind that portrayed accurate conflict—the kind meant for popcorn consumption. They moved steadily through the foliage just on the edge of the ride's track system. Ordinarily, the blaring noise would have put Zip on edge, but in that moment, it gave her small comfort. Hopefully, it would keep the bugs disoriented, at least long enough for them to get out.

As they continued, the foliage parted to reveal a car speeding out of a tunnel filled with flashing lights. A metal door shut with a snap-hiss as the car exited, blocking the tunnel from view. Zip looked at the ground and saw the blood trail leading in. "Well, if our friends can be quick, so can we."

Tom bent low. Despite his many limbs, Zip knew he wasn't fast, but Zip had to worry about her own speed. The door snapped open, and a car roared forward. Without hesitation, Zip sprinted, slid through the opening and into the tunnel. She turned to see Tom struggling. He stumbled and fell, his torso landing right on the pinch point between the two doors. His movement grew frantic as he tried to scramble across the dirt, but it was of no consequence.

"PLEASE REMAIN SEATED IN YOUR VEHICLE," came an automated voice over a loudspeaker. "OUR JOURNEY THROUGH TIME AND SPACE HAS BEEN MOMENTARILY PAUSED DUE TO A COSMIC DISRUPTION. YOUR ADVENTURE WILL CONTINUE MOMENTARILY."

A car pulled into the tunnel and sat with its lights on, idling.

It was Techni who helped Tom to his feet and pulled him in. "We didn't have to run. This is a theme park; you think they would build something that could kill the guests?"

Zip shrugged. "Corners have been cut before."

"The Manchesters didn't get rich by paying for lawsuits."

"Thank you," said Tom.

Techni merely nodded.

All at once, the tunnel blazed to life and the door snapped shut behind them. A voice from the car yelled, "This is it this time, I'm sure of it. Don't worry, we'll get you back to your proper timeline in no… time." The tunnel filled with lights meant to mimic electricity. Projectors embedded in the floor painted the walls with cosmic stars and spaghetti that felt uncomfortably similar to actual warp speed. At least someone had done their homework.

"Alright, exiting dimensional space in three, two—" The door behind Zip snapped open and the car roared out, heading to meet its eventual encounter with the toothy dinosaur. The three of them rushed out the other end of the tunnel and into a cobbled street flanked by animatronics in armor and tall stone buildings.

"This is just embarrassing," said Techni. "Old Earth never had cities like this."

"It is exciting," offered Zip.

"And you are the reason they build this shit." Techni stopped short and amended: "Captain."

Zip grinned. "We make it out of this, you can stop with the faux deference."

Techni did not retort and instead pointed a silent finger forward.

The ride's track gave way to a large square where some sort of medieval tournament was meant to be happening. Jack and Big were standing in the center, stock still. Jack's eyes were trained on the upper floor of one of the buildings, as was Big's rifle.

Before Zip could put her own sights on him, Jack spoke, quiet and calm. "Zip, trust me when I say you really don't want to do that."

A car sped by, blaring plunky medieval music. All the animatronic patrons in the square cheered. Jack and Big moved a few feet and then stopped still once more.

What the hell is he playing at? Following Jack's eyeline, Zip looked to the ceiling and saw them. What she had initially mistaken for artificial clouds of smoke to complete the scene of medieval debauchery, were much, much worse. Thick cocoon-like egg sacs hung from every inch of the attraction's ceiling. Their bulbous white fibers sagged down, and by the dim lights of the ride vehicles passing beneath them, Zip saw movement. Spindly legs scraped against the inside of the cocoons in various stages of growth.

"What are we looking at?" came Tom's newly amplified voice.

Zip wished he had a mouth for her to clamp a hand over but settled for a strong shushing motion instead. She looked back up at the eggs. Some stirred, but none were splitting open and bursting just yet. Dark shapes moved along the ceiling using long limbs to fuss with the edges of the cocoons. They were different than the bugs they had encountered below the surface. Their arms ended in clean hooks which they used to navigate the webwork without piercing the egg sacks. They also had a few extra limbs compared to their terrestrial brethren. These skinny appendages moved with lightning speed and light touches in what could almost pass for tenderness.

A car zoomed past. Zip didn't think. In the blur of sound and movement, she lunged toward Jack and Big, making a gain of a few strides.

"Now is not the time for a chase," hissed Jack, freezing in place again.

Zip followed suit and was relieved to see her companions doing the same. "I agree, so stop running, and we can all have a little chat. You love little chats."

"Ha. Ha." Jack's hand moved toward his pistol.

"Real classy, Jack. This is starting to feel like the end of the road for us." While Zip had fantasized about killing Jack on numerous occasions, the thought of actually doing it brought her pain. They had history, whatever that history was. Bad, good, it all blended into memory and made a person who they were.

"I don't sup—"

A vehicle zoomed by, catching Jack off guard.

Zip leaped several strides toward them but stopped short as Big calmly took out a knife and pointed it toward her. He shook his head, dark eyes never leaving hers.

Jack smiled. "You see, what Big understands is that guns are noisy. Now, I prefer the noise if it means a quick getaway, but he likes to get up close and personal. He just lost a friend, so I wouldn't push him too hard."

In response, Big bared yellow, cracking teeth, inviting Zip to do just that.

She looked down at the knife in his hands. How fast could he bring it to bear? Pretty fast she wagered. Sweat beaded on her forehead. It had been a long day to end all long days and she was tired of Jack's shit. She looked at the tracks the vehicles were running along. Not that much farther down the path was a door labeled 'Exit' in green.

Another car zoomed by and there was no time to think. Moving wildly, Zip sidestepped and leaped in front of Jack. It left her in the path of the next oncoming car but also put Jack in between her and Big.

Jack cursed. "You really want to do this right now? We'll both end up dead."

"I'm pretty attached to my team. Don't want to see them dead because some asshole stole their payday."

Jack's eyes flicked to her hands, likely judging how fast he could draw. "And here I am just hoping I can live to see another dollar. Maybe we aren't so different a—"

The car came. Zip lunged. Two guns went off.

She felt the impact of their bodies colliding. Pain, deep pain. Was the wind out of her? She looked down, no blood. She looked at Jack. His pristine outfit now bore a ragged hole in the midsection that went straight out the back. Blood dribbled down his still-grinning face. Why was he grinning?

The sound went out of the world as realization dawned on her. *He's grinning because he missed.*

11

Every Shot Counts

From Tom's perspective, the conversation turned deadly quicker than a blink. In one moment, Zip and Jack were playing a high stakes game of 'stop and go'—a popular game among Crustacean children... and some adults—the next, Jack had a hole through him. Tom knew Jack had missed Zip the second it happened; a big red splotch came out of him, but not from Zip. The implications of that miss took a few more seconds to sink in. It seemed that Jack fired mid-fall, sending his shot wide and up towards the ceiling. The bullet pierced one of the hundreds of egg sacks, and the reaction of the spindly creatures was immediate.

A piercing shriek rang through the attraction, drowning out even the rumbling vehicles as they passed. One by one, eggs began to wobble. Then, they dropped off the ceiling into unseen areas of the ride.

What Tom didn't see until it was almost too late was Big. Even with the diamond strapped to his back, he was fast. The man had a knife in each hand, and murder on the mind.

Zip was completely unaware of Big advancing, distracted by the shot that missed. Her eyes were turned up toward the ceiling with unflinching horror.

Tom looked for Techni but found she was doing the same. No one was looking at Big. No one but him. His heart did not pound, it stayed a calm and measured hundred beats per minute. Tom found his limbs moving on their own accord, swinging the rifle in front of him and bringing it to bear. The man was close to Zip, too close for error. Even the slightest miss could be catastrophic. More importantly, Tom's best friend was in danger, and for once, he could help.

He exhaled as Lars had taught him in their brief weapons

training. For once, the rifle held still. The barrel barked once, twice, and then fell silent. Two puffs of red mist exploded from Big's chest and neck. The man spun, wide eyes looking at Tom with a mixture of surprise and respect. Then they went dead as he fell to the ground, no longer human, but a hunk of ragged meat.

The acrid smell of gun smoke drifted up from the end of Tom's rifle. With the danger passing, the sounds of the world he didn't realize had been missing returned in a rush. The first thing he heard was the blare of a car horn—a few seconds too late.

Blazing white lights illuminated a very confused Zip in the middle of the track. She had enough time to flinch, bracing for the eventual impact, but it never came. Tom watched as the car screeched to a halt and a voice over the loudspeakers blared: "PLEASE DO NOT EXIT YOUR VEHICLES. WE ARE CURRENTLY EXPERIENCING A DISTURBANCE IN THE SPACE-TIME CONTINUUM. YOUR ADVENTURE WILL CONTINUE MOMENTARILY."

Tom stared at the car dumbfounded until Techni came up behind him and snapped her fingers.

"Same safety mechanism that saved your ass before. We need to move!"

"We're in trouble!" yelled Zip from afar.

Tom and Techni turned to see the spiderlike creatures emerging from the medieval town, scuttling across the cobblestones. It was an odd juxtaposition to the permanent party the animatronic characters were throwing around them. "Their evolution is remarkable." Such variation in cohabitating species was rare and reminded him of home.

"We can admire them later, right now we have one way out."

Tom looked toward the exit. Armored bugs, similar to what they had seen before, poured through the tiny doorway and filled the ride track. "Can you override the safety features?"

Techni nodded.

"Running out of time over here." Zip fired at the oncoming hoard, picking off a few bugs in an ultimately bloody, but futile gesture.

"Zip, we are going to go on another ride," said Tom. A knot tightened in his gut.

"WHAT?!" shouted Zip over the gunfire, still standing in the path of the car.

"Get in the car!" Techni fired her submachine guns and ran towards the vehicle.

Tom followed suit, letting out a few calculated bursts of his own. He didn't like killing, but the power of the rifle in his hands certainly illuminated the appeal. Where one bug fell, another immediately appeared in its wake. Tom tried not to focus on the futility of the action and instead scuttled as fast as his body would allow.

Automated announcements continued to blare from above. In the village scene, the animatronics celebrated, despite the tide of bugs swarming over them. Some of the machines fell and were trampled, sending off fits of sparks and garbled sound effects. Others simply continued their repetitive actions as if nothing had changed.

Tom was nearly to the vehicle when he remembered the diamond. In Big's death tumble, it had fallen to the ground. *If we go back without it, we die.* He didn't have to do the mental calculation, his limbs made it for him. Tom put on a burst of speed and slid across the ground. With a quick swipe, he severed the cables tying the stone to the now dead man's back, and began dragging it through the dirt.

Behind him, the sound of a thousand horrible terrible things fought with the cheering of the townspeople which in turn fought against Zip's steady gunfire.

He wasn't sure how he did it, but the next thing he knew, Tom was bumping up against the vehicle's back door. He hoisted the diamond, limbs shaking, and dumped it into the back row. Using what was left of his strength, he hobbled in behind it. A row of safety belts with bright yellow tags were all buckled in preparation for an exciting journey. Tom turned the diamond upright and used one of the belts to secure it. Remembering his last ride, he did not buckle himself in, instead opting to hold on as tight as he could. No sooner was he seated than Zip slid across the hood and hopped into the driver's seat. Techni was not far behind.

"Anyone know where the gas is on this thing?" asked Zip, slapping a fresh clip in her rifle.

"I think—" started Techni, but in the same instant the car roared to life.

"Middle Ages?! We've gone back too far!" shouted a voice from the console. "That idiot intern must have calculated the wrong jump points. This is going to be messy!" The car leaped forward just as the horde of bugs closed in behind them. They were gaining momentum when Tom looked forward and saw a hulking brown bug standing in the way.

"That is a problem." He leaned to the side and fired at the creature. The rifle did its best to find the creature's weak points, but with the angle, most of the rounds bounced off its armor with little effect.

"Everyone hang on," said Techni, tapping furiously at her wrist-mounted computer. "Safety controls are overridden, so this is going to get rough."

"Professor, the portal is open!" The voice was tinny and garbled coming through the loudspeakers implanted in the car's dashboard.

"Brilliant, my boy. Now everyone hold on tight!"

The car leaped forward, straight at the bug, and straight for the stone wall behind it.

"This is going to be close, just a little more speed!"

The bug let out a roar, spreading its arms as if preparing to catch the car.

The car sped forward, the faux rumble of its engine filling the world.

Tom spread his legs out in the vehicle, gripping wherever he could.

"Almost there!"

The car smashed into the bug with tremendous force, knocking it flat off its feet and towards the stone wall. At the same instant, a hidden door in the wall opened, revealing the time travel tunnel they were about to enter. The bug was catapulted inside, hitting the back wall with a crunch, but remained standing.

"Prepare for interdimensional travel!"

The tunnel illuminated in a cavalcade of light and sound, and then the doors closed, sealing them in.

12

Enjoy the Ride

ZIP HAD EXPERIENCED HER share of weird days in her time passing through the galaxy. Staring at a seven-foot-tall brown bug in a strobing tunnel while a fake professor droned on about time travel was near the top of the list. She was still processing the fact that Lars was dead, she had killed Jack, and had nearly been killed herself shortly after, but life had a way of getting in the way of intimate self-reflection. Sitting in the front seat, she had a clear view of the bug as it charged through the strobe lights, its movements appearing staccato—like it had come straight out of an old horror film. What she also saw was the cracked armor in its abdomen where the vehicle had struck.

"I've had enough of you and your brood's shit for one day!" Zip leaned forward over the hood of the vehicle, locking the butt end of her rifle against a foam safety bar. It was made to prevent tourists from getting concussions; as a brace, it would serve just fine. She took careful aim at the bug and held down the trigger. The initial bullets bounced, ricocheting into the tunnel walls and sending sparks flying from the lights they hit. Zip wondered how much damage they had caused and whether the Manchesters would have the gall to take it out of their payment.

The creature continued, but then the cracks in its armor widened. One by one, bullets started finding their mark, punching through the soft meat beneath the creature's outer shell. Zip could hear the clacks as they hit the armor plating in the back and then bounced around inside the creature's body. Orange goop poured from the opening, and the bug fell forward, skidding to a halt just in front of the vehicle.

"This is it, I'm sure of it. Don't worry, we'll get you back to your proper timeline in... no time!" shouted the voice from the car's loudspeakers.

Muted thuds sounded on the wall behind them. Zip did not turn around for fear that she would see a hundred pincers slowly prying the doors open. Screeching chittering squeals came through muffled. She turned to Tom and Techni. "You alright?"

Tom bobbed his head with the enthusiasm of a man on the gallows.

Techni said, "No. I need a soft bed and a whole lot of money."

Zip looked at the diamond in the back seat. "Well, if we're lucky, we might get both of those things. I suggest you cover your faces."

"Why?"

Zip leaned back in her seat and put her arms up.

"Exiting dimensional space in three, two, one..." The engine roared and they sped forward, smashing through the bloody corpse in front of them, leaving a smear across the hood.

The vehicle jostled back and forth as they careened through the jungle where they had entered. "D-Dinosaurs?! This isn't right either. That's it, I'm calling off the mission. Bring them home now!"

From off to the side, there was a deafening roar. Branches rustled as if something huge were moving between them. Zip hoped it was the animatronic dinosaur. The car jumped forward, bumping and rattling along before they could get a clear look at what was causing the disturbance.

Even though Zip had been there once, she was still surprised when the car rounded the corner to the grinning maw of the T-rex. The creature lumbered forward into their path and roared. Hot breath with a semi-realistic predator stink wafted into the vehicle. *Incredible.* Even amidst real danger, artificial danger still held its appeal.

"We've got problems down here, boy!" snapped the voice from the console. "Get us an exit, now!" The car jumped forward, careening down a steep incline and narrowly missing the dinosaur's feet. The timing couldn't have been better as the horde of pissed-off bugs exploded from the tunnel behind them at the same moment.

Right, real danger. Zip turned around and saw that Tom was already pointing his rifle out the back of the vehicle. The fact that he was leaning on a priceless diamond for stability injected the humor she needed to continue.

The jungle whipped by as the car sped onward, much to the angry roars of the T-rex. Trees rustled and shook at the edges of the track. It was a cheap trick to not show the beast again, but Zip supposed the Manchesters had to cut corners somewhere. Eventually, they came to a surging waterfall. "Dead end!" shouted the voice. "Please tell me you have something!"

"According to my readings, Professor, there is a cave system just beyond that waterfall."

Techni's eyes suddenly widened. "I don't like getting wet."

Zip glanced at the jumble of technology that was Techni's body and immediately understood why. She dug around in the compartments meant to hold personal belongings in the seats below. "There's got to be a poncho or something." There certainly wasn't, but sometimes the illusion of help being on the way was enough.

"A poncho?!" exclaimed Techni.

"We're going through the waterfall, folks!" shouted the professor's disembodied voice.

"Oh hell," said Techni.

Tom held his rifle over the back of the vehicle and said nothing.

Zip gripped the safety bar in front of her.

The car splashed through the pond at the base of the waterfall, heading right for the mass of sheeting water. Zip only felt a slight mist before the water parted, allowing them safe passage into the caves beyond. She looked over to Techni, sitting sullen and furious, curled into a position that protected as many of her orifices as possible.

"I don't know how many times I have to say it, but I never want to come back here," Techni said.

The car roared through the tunnel, picking up speed, headlamps bouncing off the walls before them. "Beware of cave spiders!" shouted the professor. Lining the walls were several boxes that Zip could see labeled 'Cave Spider Animatronic 001-01' and so forth. She said a silent thank you that they hadn't been installed yet. There were enough real spiderlike things for her liking to add fake ones to the mix.

"Alright, this time we've got it. This should get us back!"

Before Zip could register that the cave was ending, they were in another tunnel of bright flashing lights. Among them, a flashbulb went off, momentarily blinding them and leaving Zip with searing afterimages. Then, as quickly as it started, the lights stopped, and the car pulled slowly forward to the tune of triumphant music. They entered the ride's unloading station which looked halfway between a library and a laboratory. High bookshelves lined one wall and orange lights imitated a blazing fireplace.

Up in a glass control booth, overlooking several large monitors and complex gadgets, an animatronic professor, complete with crazy white hair, was clapping. "We did it! Well, you did it, but I like to think I helped a little. It might not have been the journey we planned for, but it was certainly Old Earth… Just maybe a little older than we expected. Please disembark your vehicles to the right and if you have any complaints, you may file them with the interdimensional transit board." This was followed by a guffawing laugh that indicated there was no such agency.

All at once, the seat belts in the vehicle released. Zip scrambled out onto the loading dock and took up a defensive posture. Tom unstrapped the diamond and Techni helped him heave it out.

"All this for a god damned rock." Zip thought about Lars. The memory ripped at her chest like a dull knife. She filed it away for another day, or realistically, never.

"But it's so sparkly." Techni spat on the stone.

"I do not like it either." Tom made to kick the diamond but thought better and glared at it instead.

Zip took a breath and summoned what little energy her body had left. Then she made for the exit. "Let's get the hell out of this place."

13

Trouble in Paradise

Journey to Old Earth's exit passageways were a series of cramped hallways packed with books, bubbling substances in scientific beakers, and framed photographs of the white-haired professor. The small walkways made moving the diamond with any efficiency cumbersome and awkward. Despite the humanoid's penchant for murder, Tom found that he briefly missed Big. Adding to the annoyance, triumphant music played on a never-ending loop. It was punctuated with exclamations from the professor of "You did it!" or "I can't believe you aren't dead!" blaring from loudspeakers. Ordinarily, Tom liked encouragement in any form, but at that moment, he wanted nothing more than to be as far away from Kedasi as possible.

Before exiting the ride, they came to a bank of monitors displaying rows of images of empty cars. As they walked by, a picture of the three of them appeared. Zip's arms were in the air with a triumphant grin, Techni was curled in the back seat, and Tom's head was turned. Even still, he wished he could get a copy. The moment of happiness quickly died as the next set of pictures came through showing hordes of bugs tearing the autonomous vehicles apart. Tom quickened his step.

They exited into the stark daylight of Kedasi's dawn. They were on the cobbled streets of idyllic Old Earth once again. To their left, the entrance to Journey to Old Earth was in smoldering ruins. It was only by sheer chance that Jack's team had missed the exit when they sealed the attraction off. In the distance, Tom saw the towering red rocks of Adventure Canyon. They were so close to being free, and yet so far away. Tom's limbs wobbled with exhaustion, and loss clung to him like a shroud, but he continued to push forward. *One step at a time, all the way back to The Hog.*

Zip's voice broke through his stupor. "Our best course is back the way we came. Straight past Adventure Canyon and right through the main gate."

"Or—" started Techni, but Tom didn't hear the rest.

The ground beneath their feet trembled. At first, it was light enough that only he noticed, but it quickly grew. Both he and Techni let go of the diamond. It made a loud thunk as it fell onto the cobblestones.

"Oh dear," said Tom, raising his hands. The rifle jumped into them.

Zip's shoulders slumped. "How many?"

"A lot."

There was no way of knowing for sure, but based on the strength of the tremors, they were about to witness the full strength of an infestation directed onto one spot.

"I'm going to do something, but you have to promise you won't be mad," said Techni to Zip.

"Is it going to save us?"

"Maybe."

Zip threw up her arms. "Why ask permission then?"

A stream of armored bugs pressed their way out of the exit of the Journey to Old Earth ride. They formed a wall around them, blocking off the path back toward the midway.

Zip raised her rifle, a gesture that looked more than a little futile. "Whatever you're going to do Techni, you might want to do it fast."

"I'm working on it. The technology wasn't built for this."

"Everyone back-to-back!" Zip didn't wait for a response and faced the wall of bugs behind them. Techni pressed her back against Zip's without a word.

Tom followed and felt a wash of color go over the world as if he were seeing it clearly for the first time. Everything was vibrant and detailed. He could see each armor plate on the hundreds of bugs before him. The street was beautiful, hand-painted, and full of life. He gave a sudden repeated intake of air, and it took him a moment to recognize what might have been his first genuine laugh. He wasn't sure why, but the absurdity of the situation called for it.

"Tom, don't stroke out on me," said Zip.

"I am laughing."

Zip grimaced. "Happy for you, pal, but that sound is horrifying."

"Noted." If they survived, Tom would find a way to translate the guttering wheezes into something more palatable to human sensibilities.

"What are they waiting for?" Zip's body was tense against Tom's back, but she didn't fire.

The bugs were fanned out in a circle, surrounding them. Horrible smells hit them in waves, stinging Tom's eyes. He allowed his attention to drift between the various horrors in the circle. They were waiting, coordinating, just like in Adventure Canyon. The attack would be sudden, but what were they waiting for? It was then that he noticed the ground hadn't stopped shaking. Despite the stillness of the bugs before him, Kedasi's crust rumbled. "I have a bad feeling about this."

"Just one?" asked Techni.

"Alright, I have several bad feelings about this."

"Me too, Tom."

A cobblestone popped out of the road and sailed into the air before shattering on the ground.

"Oh, that's not good," said Zip. "ETA on that miracle, Techni?"

"Depends, do you like our friend Tom?"

Tom nearly jumped at the happiness of having a new friend. "I am your friend?"

"Enough that I don't want to deep fry you."

Tom recoiled. "That's an option?"

"Techni, don't deep fry Tom!"

Another cobble exploded upward, followed by another, and another. They shot into the sky, raining back down on the street below, mixing with the chaotic rage of the bugs. Zip, Tom, and Techni backed away, but not so far that they would come into contact with the creatures behind them. Tom caught a glimpse of the earth beneath the cobblestones and saw that the dirt was churning. "It is the creatures from the caves."

"I thought we killed those," said Techni.

"There's always a bigger bug," answered Zip.

The ground burst as a hulking form snaked its way out of the ruined street, rising high into the sky and shaking off layers of grey-brown dirt. The scorpion-like creatures below had been large, this creature was huge. Limbs extended off each segment like a millipede, and the head was a convergence of six mandibles, all vibrating in tandem like a horrifying anthropomorphic meat grinder. It twisted into the air before finally finding its footing and looking down at the three intruders.

"Is it the queen?" asked Zip, unable to see the creature behind her.

"Doesn't look like a queen," answered Techni.

"How do you know?" asked Tom.

"Queens don't go into battle. This is something worse."

"Nothing is worse than the queen," said Zip.

"This is."

"How bad are we talking?"

"Bad."

"How big?"

"Very big."

"And your plan?"

"Just hit execute. We might want to hit the deck in a minute."

Tom looked over the edge of the giant creature and saw a faint glimmer of light on the horizon. "What is that?"

There was no time to answer. The large creature roared, and the bugs all charged at once. Zip's rifle erupted with fire, and she screamed.

Techni raised her own guns and fired at the crowd.

Tom did the same. To say it was ineffectual would have been an understatement worthy of comedy. His shots found their marks, cutting through the front row of the creatures, but as they fell, more were there to take their place. Puddles of orange gunk made the ground slick as the circle closed in around them. Gun smoke drifted skyward in a grey haze. The vibrating mandibles mixed with rattling gunfire drowned out everything else in the world, planting Tom in his singular, terrifying reality.

Time slowed to a crawl. He controlled his fire, watching the small sensor on the top of his gun as it went from green to orange. Soon, it would overheat and there would be nothing left to do but wait. He glanced up at the behemoth rising behind the hoard. To say it was terrifying would have been an insult to the world. The creature was world-ending—his world at least. The fight was futile, he knew that, but Tom also knew that Zip would never stop fighting, and he wouldn't either.

Zip screamed and Tom's peripheral saw her throw an empty magazine at the bugs in front of her. "I'm out!" The words were barely audible, muffled as if spoken underwater.

Tom couldn't hear the rattle of Techni's submachine guns, but he felt the impact of their recoil on his back.

Despite everything, he was thankful. It wasn't easy to be thankful looking into a wall of impending death, but he was. They were going to die, but at least he was facing that final moment with two friends. There were worse ways to go. The sensor on the top of his gun turned red and displayed: 'Overheat'.

The wall of bugs closed less than ten feet away.

A light glittered on the horizon. Tom squinted, trying to

make out the figure against the rising sun. "It can't be." He had read about hallucinations in near-death experiences, but it felt so real. *Nana's Hog* was flying straight towards them. Even through the cavalcade of noise and destruction, Tom heard the omnipresent hum of the antimatter guns as they buzzed to life. There was a split second where he wondered about the pinpoint accuracy of such weaponry, but then the world erupted into chaos.

Tom had only seen the antimatter guns fired from a distance. Being in the thick of their barrage was a singularly terrifying experience. All around him, pieces of bugs flew off, disassembling midair into component parts so small they resembled cubes of dust. The gigantic creature roared in pain as parts of its midsection were carved away, briefly making holes of light where Tom could see clean through to the other side. A moment later, the rest of the body caught up to what was happening and sprayed blood and viscera through the holes in a macabre imitation of one of Kedasi's many fountains.

Tom curled into a tight ball, waiting for the stinging feeling of an antimatter round hitting his shell. The pain never came. Sound, light, blood, and heat were all he felt. *The Hog's* engines hummed low over them, kicking out waves of wind and debris. The antimatter guns continued their rage uninterrupted.

Tom looked up from his position on the ground at the chaos surrounding him. The bugs were still attempting a charge, but many had started to hold back. With each advancement, they died by the hundreds. An antimatter round would pierce the front row only to spray the back row with the same material. It was a never-ending cycle of sudden disassemblage not seen on such a scale since one of the many mass extinctions. All in one moment, Tom understood why the guns were illegal and truly questioned Zip's reason for owning them. He was glad they were there.

A screeching squeal went up from the crowd around them and Tom felt the earth rumble. Over the myriad of corpses, he could just see the tail ends of the bugs as they returned to their hive deep below Kedasi's surface.

He let out an exhale, closed his eyes, and passed out.

14

Don't Touch My Ship

Zip rose from the dust of *The Hog's* antimatter guns, trying not to think too hard about the slime and viscera spread out in a circle around them. She wished she had more rounds to fire at the retreating bugs but settled for a howl that was a mixture of elation and pain.

Somehow, Techni's miracle had kept them clean, but all the same, Zip checked herself several times for orange gunk. When she was finally satisfied that she wasn't in immediate danger, her mind clicked over to what Techni had done. "Techni, what the hell did you do to my ship?"

"You said you wouldn't be mad."

Zip took a pensive breath and looked at *The Hog*. It had landed just outside the ring of corpses and almost looked pleased with itself in the morning light. "I'm not mad."

Techni brushed the dust off herself. "You seem mad."

Zip was mad, but she was trying her best not to be. "Automated, I assume?" She didn't want to admit the swell of hope she had felt when she saw *The Hog* flying over the horizon toward them. In that minute, there was the faintest glimmer that Lars had somehow survived and managed to find his way back.

"Automated is reductive. It's a complex neural—"

Zip stopped listening. For the first time, she felt the impact of Lars's loss, not so much for herself, but for Tom. There weren't that many people who were kind to Tom, and that alone meant the old mercenary had some good in him.

Tom! Zip spun around, suddenly realizing she hadn't heard his voice after the shooting. Her heart raced as she looked through the debris and piles of corpses. "Tell me you programmed the ship to recognize Tom!" Tom looked like a bug; it would have been tricky. One spare shot from the antimatter cannons and he was done for.

Techni laughed, the sound like a computer doing heavy processing. She pointed at the ground.

Zip spun and found Tom curled into a ball, rifle firmly plastered to his back, carapace moving up and down slowly. "Is he?"

"Yes, I just checked his vitals. He's asleep." Techni projected a pulsating green line as proof.

Zip let out a breath. "Well, what do you want to carry, shrimp or diamond?"

***

Zip placed Tom in his makeshift tank. The shrimp had stirred a few times in his sleep, but shock and exertion had knocked him out cold. She set the tank to clean, using the easy interface Tom had programmed. He really was a genius, even if he looked like a five-foot-tall walking monster. Water gurgled from above, splashing down, and Zip left the room. Tom might be confused when he woke up, but at least he'd be clean.

When she made her way to the cockpit, *The Hog* was already warmed from its last-minute charge. She made a cursory check of all the systems, but with Techni in the co-pilot's chair, it was a redundant exercise. Everything was ready.

"Let's get out of here before the bugs change their mind." Zip spooled through munitions counters. The antimatter guns were nearly half empty. Being illegal, replacing the rounds would be both costly and dangerous. Another adventure for another day.

"Course is set for Prota. Time to see if the Manchesters are a family of their word."

"They're not, but I've got a backup plan."

Zip didn't share, but instead stared out the window as *The Hog* began its automatic ascent procedures. The circle of corpses steamed in the sun, a blemish on Kedasi's perfect façade of life. She watched in the distance as Adventure Canyon's coaster crested the red rock hills before plunging back into the depths. Far off in the grey desert of the asteroid, The Opus gleamed triumphant in the morning sun.

"Everything checks out, we're good to go."

Zip took the controls in her hands. Somewhere down there, the bodies of Jack, Lars, the Cheri, Tiny, and Big were decomposing, all for the greed of a mega-corporation. She eased the controls forward and the landscape bled away.

The Hog rocketed through Kedasi's thin pocket of atmosphere with a single jolt. Then, there was just space, void on one side and a magnificent gas giant on the other. Somehow, against all odds, they had been to an infested bug asteroid and lived to tell the tale.

The warp speed button lit up green. Zip took a last look at the fading asteroid behind them, now nothing more than a black dot. Her hand hesitated. "Techni, how familiar are you with the programming behind UCP distress calls?"

Techni's eyebrows raised a fraction of an inch. "Intricately. They are near impossible to forge, but only need a bank account to function."

"How hard would it be to rig a distress beacon for a ship we're not on?"

Techni scoffed. "Trivial, so long as it has a bank account hooked up to it."

Zip smiled and passed Jack's ship access codes to the main screen. "Dead men tell no tales."

Techni whistled. "So, Jack is going to pay, and—"

"Suddenly Kedasi becomes a blinking red target for any passerby."

"But that would put any passing ship in danger..."

"You're telling me you didn't record footage while we were down there?"

"The Manchesters explicitly forbade..."

"Techni, you have god damned cameras for eyes."

She flinched. "I may have recorded a little."

"Cut together footage that doesn't have any of us in it, put it in the distress beacon, and give it a plucky voiceover."

"I don't have a plucky voice."

"So, pick something from the ship's archives, I don't care. The Manchesters can have their diamond back, but they're going to drown in the legal fees."

"They have the money."

"Of course they do, but that doesn't mean it won't hurt a little."

"It'll hurt more than a little."

"Good. Get it rigged and let's get the hell out of here. *The Hog* is known for making on-time deliveries."

Epilogue

1

An Interlude with Captain Tanskyrock

"**KEDASI IS A PLANET** unlike any other—Well, because it's not a planet, it's an asteroid, and boy oh boy is it infested." A clip played showing a creature with more legs than necessary, and a gaping maw with more teeth than were strictly necessary for any living thing. "Once a glittering monument to times long passed, this theme park asteroid is now home to an unknown species of bug. While we haven't had any time to research, we can tell you they're hostile, bear a corrosive substance that is a death sentence, and are generally unpleasant."

Captain Tanskyrock pushed pause on the recording. "Not very typical of a distress recording, is it?"

His first mate, Clement, looked at the frozen video screen with puzzlement. It had paused on an image of a hundred beetle-like creatures staring down an old-timey street. "Usually, it just plays the UCP fanfare and tells us to respond."

Tanskyrock nodded. "Well, I don't want to go to a bug planet."

"Asteroid," corrected Clement.

"Even worse. Who's the lad on board familiar with legal proceedings?"

"Reede, sir. Studied law on one of the outer worlds."

"Yes, bring Reede in."

A half-hour later, after a lengthy explanation about the rights of the universal working person and basic safety precautions, Tanskyrock knew they had a case. "So, what you're telling me is that this asteroid violates just about every code there is in terms of construction and worker safety?"

Reede, a skinny man with an undercurrent of chaos to his movements, squirmed. "I can't say for sure without going down there myself, but even the lack of a sign to warn outsiders of the infestation would be grounds for investigation."

Tanskyrock clapped his hands together. "Good enough for me. Clement, get us on a call with the UCP and the leader of the Asteroid Construction Union."

"We're not going to stop?"

"Oh, we're going to wait right here. I don't want to get my ship taken from me by UCP goons. But first, we're going to kick off legal proceedings that will make sure no one visits this rock ever again."

2

A Drink and Distant Vengeance

ZIP SAT IN THE same corner booth at Marvin's where she had always sat. It had been three days since their return to Prota, and with every swing of the door, her hand dropped to the pistol at her side. So far, the news feeds were empty about their little stunt, but a leak had just gone live that the Manchesters were in deep shit. That meant every patron coming through the door could be a potential assassin.

"You know I'm good at what I do, right?" asked Techni, guzzling down a drink so black it looked suspiciously like motor oil.

"I know."

"That video had Jack's prints all over it."

"I know."

It was at that moment that Tom returned from the bar carrying a large glass filled with colored liquid and several small squirming things swimming inside. "Is Zip still worried about assassins?"

"Yes," answered Techni.

"I am also worried about assassins."

"Ye of little faith, the both of you."

At that moment, an alert came over the tablet Zip had set in the middle of the table. She had set it to ping when any news of the Manchesters made it to the top five channels. She clicked and a full screen of a news reporter appeared. "While reports are unconfirmed, Captain Tanskyrock of the ship, *Fury*, stated that the Manchesters violated nearly a hundred labor laws. In addition, records have uncovered efforts by the Manchesters to recoup investments by putting recovery teams in extreme danger."

The screen changed to show a distressed man in white

robes with a greasy brown man bun. "The Manchester Corporation will of course be investigating these serious claims. We are an organization that values worker safety above all else. Over the—"

Zip turned the screen off. "Close enough. I'll drink to that."

"It'll never stick," said Techni.

"You're probably right, but I'll still drink to it. This thing just became so public that any attempt to have us killed is going to look a whole lot worse for the Manchesters."

Techni lifted her glass. "Alright, but you're buying. Paying off that charge for the antimatter guns wasn't cheap."

"Restocking them won't be either, but just this once, I'll get it. To Lars." Zip lifted her glass.

Tom wrapped several appendages around his oversized drink and raised it. "To a friend."

"To a stubborn bastard," said Techni.

Zip smiled and drank.

It hurt, but they were safe. For one moment, in one day, there was just a little bit of justice in the galaxy.

The Crew of *Nana's Hog* Will Return…

A Note from the Author

Kedasi is in many ways a story I've been waiting to write for a long time. When I was a kid, I loved theme parks, but specifically those with immersive theming. I would spend hours trying to recreate them in games or reading anything with a remotely adjacent setting. I remember finding one book about children being chased by some sort of murderer through an abandoned theme park, and I think I read it ten times.

As I grew older, my relationship with these places grew complicated. I still love the immersive theming of Disneyland and the like but have grown disdainful for the corporations that run them. *Kedasi* is my way of showing love and reverence for the individuals who built such incredible places while also expressing my frustration with a society run by the rich for the rich.

I hope you enjoyed reading *One Night at Kedasi* as much as I enjoyed writing it. I have plenty of adventures planned for *The Hog's* crew, and with any luck, you'll be able to read more of them soon.

Ashton Macaulay is a fiction writer living in West Seattle with his wife, scruffy terrier, and fancy cat. His other works include *The Nick Ventner Adventures*, tales of a drunken monster hunter traveling the world to confront creatures that aren't supposed to exist, and several short stories published across the literary spectrum.